STARLIGHT

STARLIGHT

and Other Stories

Edward M. George

~

TNSB
Montgomery

TNSB
105 S. Court Street
Montgomery, AL 36104

The painting on the cover is *Girl Watchers* by Donna Pate of Deatsville, Alabama.

Cataloging-in-Publication Data

ISBN 978-1-961938-01-4

Design by Randall Williams

Printed in the United States of America

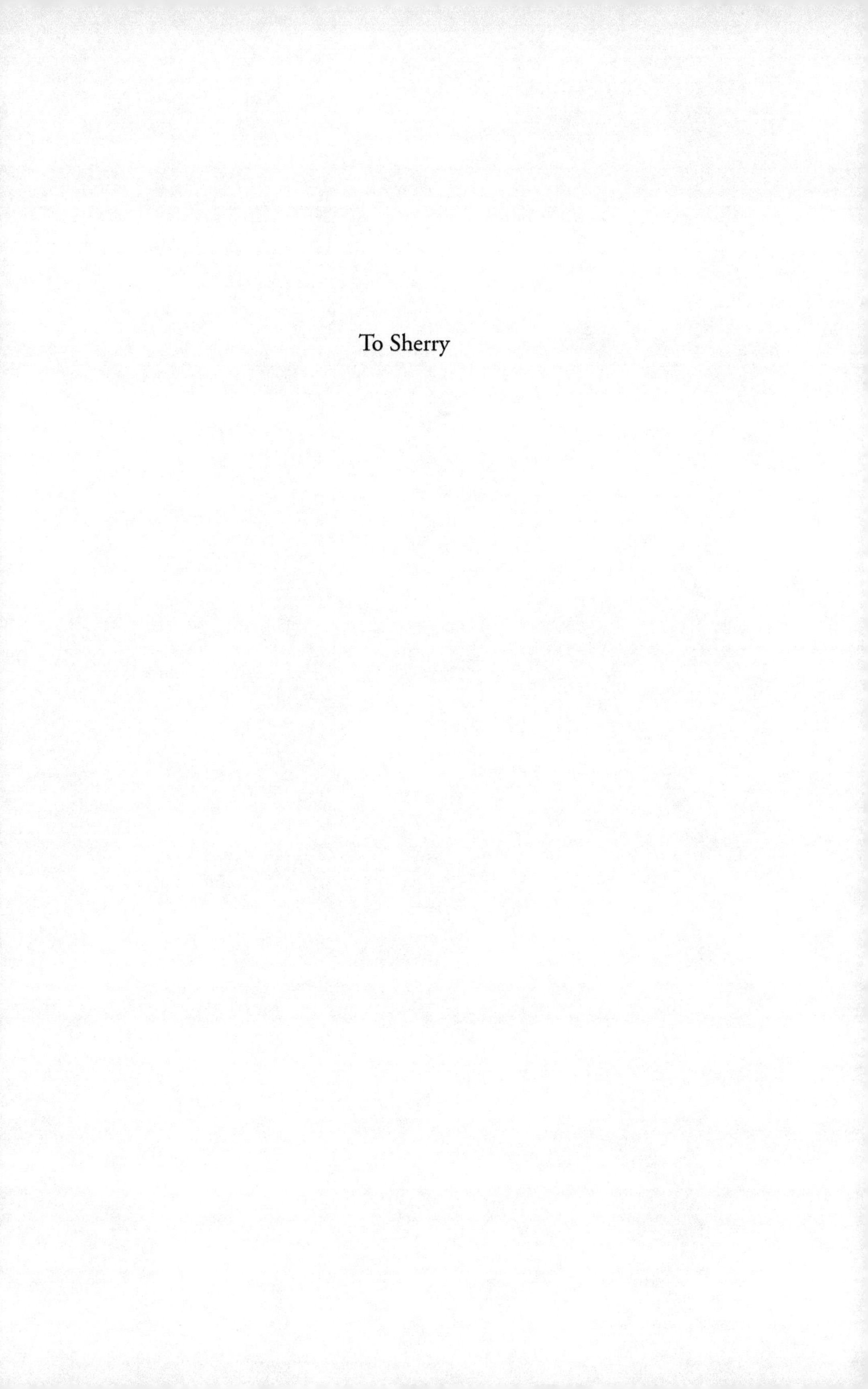

To Sherry

Contents

I

Starlight

A Novella

Chapter One

Ronnie slowly pulled into the parking lot of Global Music Services in the red Toyota Highlander that he had rented at Austin-Bergstrum Airport. He was still trying to decide exactly what he was going to say to Jack Burnham about what he'd found out the day before.

He parked the SUV in an open spot, and reclined his seat. He tuned the radio to KASE and listened half-heartedly to what they were calling "New Country." After about five minutes of being bored by the mundane music, Ronnie took a deep breath, got out of the Highlander, and tried to stretch away the stiffness that he had from the early morning flight from Atlanta to Austin. As he was massaging the back of his neck, he felt a trace of sweat and noticed that it was a lot hotter than he had expected.

Ronnie walked across the parking lot and saw that there was a new set of tinted glass double doors at the entrance to the Global Music studios and headquarters. The company had been housed for the past twelve years in the four-story red brick building that was built in the 1950s on the outskirts of Austin for a meatpacking company. On the right side of the building there were still the faint remnants of "Lone Star Meats" in what had once been bright blue paint.

When Ronnie reached the entry doors, he saw that each of them had the new turquoise and gold GMS logo painted in its top glass panel. He opened the right side door and walked into the spacious lobby, also decorated in turquoise and gold, and got the same tingle of excitement that he always got when he came in there. He heard a band tuning up in one of the recording studios on the second floor. He could barely make out the sounds, but he could tell that the drummer and bass player were warming up. The sounds seemed to be coming from Studio 2C, which was the one that Jack would rent out to bands who weren't under contract with Global Music.

There were three recording studios and a rehearsal room on the second floor. Ronnie had recorded his first tracks in Studio 2B, but since then he had always recorded in Studio 2A, which was the one that Jack used for his star acts. 2A was the largest studio and had the best equipment. It was also the most comfortable of the three studios.

Ronnie looked across the lobby toward the mahogany reception desk and saw Charlene, the company's office manager, standing in front of the desk and waving to him. Charlene was a chubby, middle-aged widow who wore her gray hair in a bun and almost always dressed in some shade of blue. She was a mother figure for all the company's employees, and always seemed to be in a good mood in spite of the raucous arguments about "artistic differences" that seemed to constantly spring up among the musicians, technicians, and producers.

"Well, Ronnie Roush, mister big-time rock-and-roll star. What brings you to Austin?"

After Ronnie gave Charlene a hug and a peck on her cheek, he said, "Why, I came to see you, of course. But while I'm here I'd like to see Jack, if he's not tied up. I called his office yesterday to make an appointment, but Renee said that she wasn't sure what time he'd be in today. Then I tried to reach him on his cell phone last night and this morning, but never got an answer. So, I decided to just come on by."

Charlene picked up her phone and rang Renee, Jack's secretary. Charlene spoke with Renee for a moment and then told Ronnie, "He's meeting with Pete Butler right now, but Renee wants you to come on up."

Ronnie thanked Charlene then walked over to the elevator and pushed the up button. Charlene watched him walk away and smiled to herself at how the skinny teenager who first came into their studio about eight years ago had grown into such a tall, good looking man, even if he did look a little tired today.

She knew from their company accountant that Ronnie's net worth was now over ten million dollars. She only wished that he didn't lead the wild life that she kept reading about on the internet and in the gossip magazines that she bought at the grocery store.

When Ronnie got off the elevator on the third floor, Renee was waiting at the open door of the executive suite with her arms outstretched. Renee was a redhead, much younger and more glamourous than Charlene. She was wearing a low-cut yellow summer dress that showed off the figure she had developed as a Las Vegas showgirl.

After they hugged, Renee took Ronnie's hand and told him that Jack was almost finished with Pete and would be right with him. She led Ronnie to an oversized turquoise leather sofa situated next to the door of Jack's private office. Ronnie sat down and listened to a loud discussion coming from Jack's office that seemed to be about a band called "Grey Flannel," Global's newest recording group.

Renee offered Ronnie a cup of coffee, which he politely declined and then almost immediately wished that he hadn't.

Just as Ronnie was getting settled into the plush sofa and about to tell Renee that he'd changed his mind about the coffee, Jack came out of his office with his left hand on Pete's shoulder and his right hand outstretched toward Ronnie. Ronnie nodded to Pete as he rose to shake Jack's hand and said, "I heard you two in there yelling at each other. Did y'all get whatever it was worked out?"

Pete was a short, stocky middle-aged man who always wore a rumpled blue-and-white-striped seersucker suit, except when he stopped by on his way to go fishing at Lake Austin. Pete pointed at Jack and said, "You know how he is. He thinks his artists should work for peanuts."

Ronnie winked at Jack and said to Pete, "He's always treated me fair."

As Pete walked away mumbling to himself and running his hand through his thin blonde hair, Jack motioned for Ronnie to come into his office. As usual, Jack was the essence of cool in his tailored jeans and black t-shirt. He was tall, fit, and tanned, with his graying black hair combed straight back.

Ronnie sat down in a Chippendale side chair next to the long mahogany table that Jack used for meetings. Jack pulled off his gray-tinted aviator-style glasses and set them on his desk. Then he smiled and said, "You know, I'm gonna give Pete what he wants. But, he's such a pain in the ass that I always have to make him sweat for a little while."

Jack hesitated a moment then walked over to the conference table, sat in a chair across from Ronnie, and said, "I think that I know what this is about. I heard from Fred, you know him, our company attorney, this morning."

"How did Fred find out?"

Well, according to what Renee tells me, a private investigator from Montgomery called yesterday afternoon and said that he needed to talk to me about a family matter. When we get that kind of call—you know, one that may possibly involve a paternity claim—I never take the call. Renee refers them to Fred so that he can check it out first. I wasn't here, anyway. I was at my personal attorney's office."

"Jesus, how many of those calls do you get? By the way, I've tried to call you on your cell phone for two days and you never answered. What's up with that?"

"I'm sorry, Ronnie, I should have told you. Carol and I are still in the middle of trying to negotiate a divorce settlement, and she was worrying the crap out me, calling at least every hour day and night. My cell phone was on her account, so I turned it off and got another cell phone from a different company and haven't given that new number to anyone but a handful of people. I'll give it to you now. I should have already done that."

Jack wrote his new cell phone number on a sheet of paper from the memo pad on the conference table and handed the number to Ronnie. Then he leaned over the table and said, "Now, as to your other question, we don't get too many potential paternity inquiries. It's pretty rare. But it only takes one to really screw things up, especially if you're married, or worse, in the middle of a divorce dispute like I am right now. That's what happened to one of our singers last year. You know him, Buster LaMaster."

"Yeah, I know Buster well. We used to run together. I see what you mean. His girlfriend's pregnancy created a mess for him, particularly since he was still married to Grace at the time. But this call we're talking about today has to be the weirdest call like that you ever got."

"Weird ain't the word for it. By the way, how'd *you* find out?"

"Let me start at the beginning. You know my last gig on the Starlight tour was on a Saturday night in Atlanta about six weeks age. Remember, we scheduled it that way so that I could go right from the concert to my townhouse."

"Yeah, I remember."

"Well, I was completely exhausted from that tour. I mean, we were flat partied out. That last set, we were playing on fumes, and still wound up doing four encores. So, right after we finished, I grabbed my stuff and got one of the security guys to sneak me out the back door and give me a ride home.

"When I got home, I opened the front door, slid the mail aside with my foot, and dumped my suitcase and travel bag on the living room floor. Then I went to the bedroom, took off my jeans and shoes and laid on the bed.

"I fell asleep in my clothes right on top of the bedspread. Then, for some reason, as tired as I was, I woke up in the middle of the night just *knowing*, I mean absolutely *positive*, that I needed to straighten my life out—you know, cut out the drinking and drugs and all the screwing around and acting like a spoiled brat.

"And then, right after I realized that I had to get my act together, I got this really strong feeling that I needed to find out who my birth parents were. I thought that it was maybe because I'd been having those bad mood swings since I lost Mom and Dad in that car accident last year.

"Well, anyway, the Monday after that Saturday night, I went to Montgomery to see this private detective there, because I knew that I was born in Columbus, Georgia, which is right across the Alabama line, and I knew that my adoption took place somewhere in Alabama. Besides, I didn't want to use anyone in Atlanta, because too many people there talk too much, and I wanted to do this quietly.

"I picked this particular guy, Dan Friese, because he was a friend of my Dad, and I had met him before. I also knew that he was former CIA, and I could trust him to do the investigation without the media picking up on it."

Ronnie went on, "Well, Mister Friese assigned his chief investigator, Mister Ellman, to do the investigation for me. Mister Ellman found out what hospital I was born was in, and, sure enough, it was in Columbus, Georgia. He also confirmed that I was put up for adoption in Phenix City, Alabama; and, well, as we both know now, he also found out that you're my birth father, and an artist in St. Louis named Muriel Gable was my mother, but she had recently died from lupus."

Jack got up and slowly walked around the table. He put his right hand on Ronnie's shoulder. He said, "Did the detective tell you that I had no idea about this? I mean, first of all, I hadn't heard about Muriel's passing. That was sad to hear. She was so young and such a decent person.

"And, talk about a bigger shock, I mean I'm proud to be your father, Ronnie, damn proud because we've always been so close anyway. But, really, I had no clue."

Jack lightly squeezed Ronnie's shoulder, then smiled wryly and said, "I'm glad that my divorce from Carol is almost final. She never liked you. Thinks you're too reckless and undisciplined. Damn sure wouldn't want to be your step-mother."

Ronnie smiled and said, "Yeah. I hadn't even thought about Carol. I'm glad I won't have to deal with her craziness. But, as for what I found out from Mister Friese, he told me that after his investigator found that Miss Gable was my birth mother, he tracked her to St. Louis.

"When Mister Ellman got to St. Louis, he found out that she had been sick for a long time and had recently passed away, but that just before she died, she told some of her friends that when she was seventeen, she traveled with your Jack Flash Band in Arizona when y'all were on tour back in the summer of 1993. She said that you gave her a job on the crew and that y'all had a fling that summer, and she got pregnant, but then never told you.

"She told her friends that when she left Arizona, she went back home to her foster parents in Phenix City, and then had a baby boy about seven months later in a hospital in Columbus. She told them that she gave up the baby for adoption right after he was born, but apparently didn't tell them that the boy was me. So, I still don't know if Miss Gable knew that I was her son, *am* her son.

"According to what Mister Ellman could figure out from talking to her friends in Missouri, Miss Gable . . . "

Jack interrupted, "You know you can call her your mother. That's who she was."

"Well, anyway, it seems that my mother was abandoned as a baby and became a ward of the State of Alabama and had grown up in several different foster homes, and, from what he could find out, didn't have a good childhood and was pretty rebellious when she was a teenager."

Jack interrupted again, "I'm familiar with that type."

Ronnie ignored that comment and continued, "Anyhow, that's how she wound up in Arizona. When she was on summer break from high school in Phenix City, she stole a couple of hundred dollars from her foster parents and took off without telling them. I don't know whether she intended to stay away or come back to Phenix City, but I guess when she found out she was pregnant, she panicked and went back to her foster parents because she had nobody else to turn to.

"It's kind of unclear, but it seems that her foster parents helped her get through the pregnancy, but really didn't want to have anything else to do with her after that; and they damn sure didn't want to have to take care of her baby. That's why she gave me up for adoption. I'm sure she didn't think that she had any other option.

"Anyhow, by then she was eighteen and had gotten her GED. So, not too long after the adoption, she left Alabama to go to an art school in Missouri that she had somehow heard about, and I guess that's how she wound up living in St. Louis. We don't know exactly how she got to Missouri or paid for art school."

Jack said, "Ronnie, Muriel was a pretty resourceful and tough young woman. I guess that came from how she grew up. But you should have seen her back then. She was really something, real tan in cut-off jeans and white t-shirt. God, she was pretty . . . She had dark brown hair like yours, but it was streaked from the sun. And she was really smart and confident about everything she did.

"But, man, I never had any idea that she got pregnant, and certainly didn't think that she was just seventeen. She told us she was a college student on summer break."

Jack walked over to the large picture window behind his desk and stared out. Then he went on, "Like I said, this is all new to me. And she had plenty of time to tell me about it, because she got back in touch with me about three years ago when we were finishing up your Moonglow album."

"She did?"

"Yeah, one day out of the blue I got a call from her. She asked me if I remembered her and told me that she was a commercial artist in St. Louis. She said she'd heard that we had a new Ronnie Roush album coming out and that she was a big fan of yours. She wanted to know if we could use her to do the artwork for the album cover. She said that she could use the money if we'd let her do the cover."

"Did she do that cover?"

"Oh, yeah. We could have used our regular people to do it, but she sounded like she really wanted it badly and, besides, I guess I wanted to see her again. She was a cool girl. Anyway, she came down here for a couple of days. She talked to Ben in our publicity office, and went over some of our other artwork to get a feel for what we wanted." Jack pointed upward, "She spent the night in one of the studio apartments on the fourth floor."

Jack took a deep breath. "It was real good to see her again. And it gave us a chance to catch up on things. But, by some of the questions she asked me, I got the impression that she had been following my career all along, and it appears now that she somehow found out that you were her son.

"She was still pretty. I noticed that she looked tired, but I figured that was from her trip down here. I didn't know that she was sick. Anyhow, after she was sure that she knew what we needed, she went back to St. Louis and did the artwork for the cover. She did such a good job that we also used her for your Starlight album. As a matter of fact, that's how we got the title for that album. I called her 'Starlight' back in ninety-three. I gave her that name because she was so, uh . . . sparkly.

"Funny thing, I knew that her real first name was Muriel, but didn't know her last name until she called me about the Moonglow job."

Ronnie walked over to the window and stood next to Jack. "Wow . . . my mother did both the Moonglow and Starlight covers. I love those covers, but I assumed that they were done in-house. I had Charlene send me framed prints of both those covers, and they're hanging on my living room wall in Atlanta. They're the first things I see when I come in.

"And I did an album named after my mother. How 'bout that."

Ronnie paused for a moment, and then he said, "I wish I could have known her. But, you know, I'm gonna have some free time once I take care of some things in Atlanta. I'll also have Mister Friese's written report by then. So, I'm going to take a trip to St. Louis as soon as I can.

"Mister Friese told me that the report would include the names and contact info on the three friends of hers that Mister Ellman talked to. Maybe her friends will have some photos or journals, or something. Or at least some memories they can tell me about. Mister Friese emailed me one picture of her, from about five years ago, but I don't know yet if he's got any others.

"I hope that I can visit with her friends in St. Louis without causing any kind of commotion. But, I guess if any media get a hold of it, I could just say that I was in the area, so I stopped by to pay tribute to the artist who did my favorite album covers.

"I know I can't visit her grave, because she was cremated, and her ashes were scattered at some lake where she and her friends used to hang out. But, maybe I can see some more of her art. Maybe buy some of it to bring back with me."

Jack turned to Ronnie and said, "I'll see if we have any of our acts playing up that way, so you can fly up with them in the company jet."

"I appreciate the offer, but I'm gonna try to keep it on the down-low. If I fly up with any of the bands, there's a good chance that somebody in the media might see me and make it hard for me to keep things quiet. Besides that, the drive up will give me some time to myself, which I could really use right now."

Ronnie took a breath, bowed his head, and wiped his eyes with the back of his right hand. He asked Jack, "How did y'all get together in the first place?"

"She showed up one day when the band was in some small town in New Mexico and said that she was on summer vacation from college in Alabama and needed to make some money so she could spend the summer out west. We hired her as part of our road crew for the New Mexico and Arizona gigs, and she turned out to be a really good worker as well as my steady girl friend.

"As far as I knew, things were going great. But, then one day I woke up in our hotel room in a little town just outside of Phoenix, and she was gone. I had no idea of where she went or why she left. And, like I said, I didn't even know her last name, or at least if she ever told me her last name, I didn't remember it. So I had no way to get in touch with her to find out what was up."

"How'd you pay her without knowing her full name? Y'all always pay by check."

Jack chuckled softly, "Man, this was the old days. It was different then.

When our band first started touring, we hired roadies wherever we could find them and paid in cash . . . or sometimes weed or coke, or t-shirts, or whatever. But, we always paid Muriel in cash, because she wouldn't take anything else."

Ronnie nodded and said, "Yeah, I've seen some pictures of y'all from those early days. It looked like fun. Not so serious as the business is now."

Then Ronnie asked, "When she came down here to do the Moonglow cover, did you ask her why she left?"

"I did, but she was very vague. Said she had to get back home for a family emergency. She apologized for the way that she left without telling me. So I just let it go at that. I figured that if she wanted me to know more, she would have told me. And I didn't want to make her uncomfortable."

Ronnie asked, "By the way, do you have any pictures of my mother from back then? Like I said, the photo that Mister Friese sent me was from probably five years ago, but I'd like to see how she looked back in the day."

"I used to have one of her and me standing next to our old funky tour bus, but right after we got married, Carol went through my photos and tore up every one of them that had a girl in it. She even tore up pictures of Darlene, my first wife. Even our wedding picture. You know, that should have told me something about Carol right then."

Jack shook his head, and stared out the window for a moment. Then he turned to Ronnie and said, "Speaking of business, you and I have a lot to talk about. I'm gonna have to start familiarizing you with the management end of things and, once my divorce is final, we can work out some sort of ownership share for you in the company. Because when you feel ready I want you to help me run this place. You've got a great head for the music business. There's a vacant office across the hall that I could renovate for you."

Ronnie nodded. "Sounds good. But let's wait until after you and Carol get through fighting over the divorce settlement. You've got enough on your mind right now. We'll talk about that stuff when the time is right. But, I'm willing to do anything I can for the company, you know that. Even now if you need me. We're a good team, and you signed me when nobody else would give me a chance. Remember, my band was playing at that joint just down the road from here, and you and Roscoe happened to be in there celebrating something."

Jack said, "Yeah, we were celebrating our first top-ten single, Jake Baker's "Redneck Love Affair." But, it wasn't a coincidence that we were there. Roscoe had heard about you from a friend of his in Birmingham, so we decided to go check you out. Obviously, I'm glad we did. It's been a good ride for us."

Jack again put his hand on Ronnie's shoulder. He said, "You know Darlene and I have a little girl, Karen. She's eleven now. She's a big fan of yours. So you've got a little sister who's already crazy about you. You've also got a new grandmother. You remember my mother. You met her at one of our company Christmas parties."

"Yeah. Cool lady. Have I ever met your daughter?"

"No, I don't think so. She and Darlene live in Little Rock with Darlene's second husband. I guess we'll make the introductions in due time, after we sort everything out."

"Yeah, it's gonna take me a while to wrap my brain around all this. By the way, I need a place to sleep tonight. Can I stay in one of the studio apartments upstairs?"

"Why don't you stay with me in the big apartment up there? It's got two bedrooms. I'm staying there for a while, because we're gonna have to sell our house as part of the divorce settlement, and in the meantime Carol's got the house."

"I appreciate the offer, but which apartment did my mother sleep in? I kinda want to stay there tonight, if it's available."

Jack pondered for a moment, then said, "Funny thing, I remember that. She slept in number 4, which is the worst one. It's the smallest, and doesn't have a shower. I remember that because she wanted a window with a view, and that's the only apartment with a window low enough to see out of. I tried to talk her into taking another one, but she insisted that she wanted the one with a window."

Jack turned around and reached into one of the drawers in his desk. He pulled out two keys and handed them to Ronnie. He said, "The silver key is for number 4, and the brass key is for the apartment where I'm staying.

You can come by my apartment in the morning and take a shower. You can eat breakfast there, too."

Ronnie nodded and put the keys in the right front pocket of his jeans. Then he looked out the office window again and saw two small boys playing with a puppy in the field below. The boys were throwing a football back and forth, and the puppy was jumping up at the ball each time it passed over.

Ronnie looked at Jack, who was now sitting in the chair that Ronnie had first sat in, and softly said, "You know what I keep thinking about. Mister Friese told me that my mother died at around three a.m. on June twenty-third. That was the same night that we finished the Starlight tour in Atlanta, and about the same time that I woke up that night."

Jack furrowed his brow and said nothing, but Ronnie could tell that he was processing that information.

Jack and Ronnie spent the rest of the afternoon with Roscoe Blake, the company's A&R man and sometimes producer, and Blanche Ward, the GMS head of publicity, discussing Ronnie's next album, which would be called "Sundown." They decided on that title because of the success of Moonglow and Starlight, and because the highlight songs on the new album would be three slow love songs co-written by Ronnie and Cliff Davis, the lead guitarist in his touring band.

Roscoe told them that he had taken care of licensing the album's other nine songs, so they were ready to go. Jack and Roscoe told Ronnie who they wanted as the arranger, producer, and musicians for the album, and Ronnie agreed with their choices, even though they denied his request that they use Cliff on lead guitar, because Jack thought, with some justification, that the road band members just weren't as good, or as dependable, as his studio musicians.

Ronnie knew that Jack was right, so he was going to have to figure out some other way to make Cliff happy.

The team decided that they should start recording the Sundown album in about three months. Roscoe said that he would nail down the date and have the musicians and the crew ready.

Then they talked with Blanche about her plans for packaging, promoting, and publicizing the album, and, as usual, she had some good ideas that none of the others had thought of. Even though Blanche, a long, tall bleached blonde in her early sixties, had come to GMS a few years before from being a singer on the honky-tonk circuit, she had a natural gift for promotion and was largely responsible for the success that GMS had in the pop music market.

After the meeting with Blanche and Roscoe broke up, Jack and Ronnie went up to Jack's apartment where Jack fixed them scrambled eggs with cheese for dinner. They watched a Rangers game on TV and talked about what the future might bring. During the game, Jack turned to Ronnie and asked, "So, how are your life changes coming along? Been able to clean up any?"

"Yeah, believe it or not. At first, I was having a tough time of it, but I found this lady psychiatrist, Dr. Cunningham, and she's been a big help. She's not only a psychiatrist, she used to run a drug treatment center, so she knew what I was going through and kinda led me through the rough spots.

"She's got this technique she calls 'segmenting' where she gets you to concentrate on one thing at a time instead of trying to change everything at once. On the back of her business card, it says 'You can eat an elephant if you do it one bite at a time.'"

Jack said, "Have you eaten the elephant yet?"

"Well, it took a while but I've got to where I don't have a strong craving for alcohol or drugs anymore. It's been about two weeks since I've had either one. Of course, I'm drinking the hell out of coffee." Ronnie chuckled, and said, "Dr. Cunningham told me that back when she used to run her drug treatment clinic the coffee bill was huge."

Jack said, "Same thing happened to me. When I had to stay clean after my hard core rock-and-roll years were over, and I started GMS, I was a coffee-drinking fool." Then he asked, "Think you can stay sober when you get back on tour?"

"Don't know yet, but I'm gonna give it my best shot. I'm kinda nervous about that 'cause you know how it is, there'll be booze and drugs all over the place. And half-naked women trying to get me to get high with 'em."

"Well, you look better than I've seen you look in a long time, and I'm proud of what you're trying to do. I hope you can keep it up. Especially now that you're gonna be my business partner, Son. So, be sure to let me know if there is anything, and I mean *anything*, that I can do to help."

Ronnie smiled and said, "Thanks, Pop, I will."

"Please. Let's keep it Jack."

After the Rangers game was over, Ronnie went to the end of the hall to apartment number 4. It was as sparse as Jack had described. But Ronnie slept peacefully in there until he was awakened the next morning by sunlight coming through the window.

Chapter Two

Two weeks after he had returned to Atlanta and taken care of some pending music commitments, Ronnie drove over to Montgomery on a Friday morning to meet with Dan Friese and pick up copies of the investigation documents that Mr. Friese had prepared for him. Ronnie had been told that, among the other info, the investigation file included the names, phone numbers, and email addresses of his mother's three friends in Missouri whom Mr. Ellman had interviewed.

Ronnie's plan was to meet with Mr. Friese, spend the night in Montgomery, and then leave for St. Louis on Saturday morning. To make his trip, Ronnie rented a white Ford Explorer from an Avis rental center in Atlanta, where Sally, the rental agent, recognized him and sheepishly asked him if he would give her an autograph for her daughter Brandy, who she said was his "biggest fan."

Ronnie said, "Sure," and signed the back of a blank Avis receipt form "For Brandy, my biggest fan, Ronnie Roush."

Sally said, "She's gonna love this."

Ronnie's reasons for using a rental car were, first, that he wanted to be as inconspicuous as possible, which excluded driving his custom candy apple red Corvette, and, second, to have room in his vehicle to carry back any of his mother's paintings that he might be able to purchase.

The Friday meeting took place at Dan Friese's office, which was on the sixth floor of an ancient office building in downtown Montgomery. At a few minutes before nine, Ronnie knocked on the heavy oak door on which there was a small embossed brass sign reading "Friese Investigations." When he heard Mr. Friese invite him in, Ronnie opened the door and nodded to Mr. Friese, who was a well-built, middle-aged man with light brown hair cut military style, wearing gold rim glasses. He was sitting behind a large walnut desk in a padded brown leather swivel chair, wearing a white dress shirt with no tie.

As he had noticed on his first meeting with Mr. Friese, the office looked like a set from a 1940s black-and-white detective movie. The room was about fifteen by twenty feet, and very dimly lit. Behind where Mr. Friese was sitting was a small window with tightly drawn white metal Venetian blinds. Facing the front of Mr. Friese's desk were two wooden arm chairs. Not far away was a small round conference table with four side chairs, and along a side wall was a row of old-fashioned tan metal file cabinets. Next to the file cabinets, Ronnie saw an open door to what looked like a smaller office.

"Have a seat over here, Ronnie," said Mr. Friese, as he walked around the desk and pointed to the conference table where a tall, sallow, gray-haired man was already seated. He was smoking a cigarette and organizing some papers on the table. Mr. Friese pointed at the man and said, "This is David Ellman, my chief investigator that I told you about. He's going to go through the file with us. Please feel free to ask him or me any questions that you may have."

Without standing or smiling, Mr. Ellman reached across the table with his open right hand and nodded toward Ronnie. Ronnie shook the hand, noticing how powerful the grip was and thinking *this guy is nobody to mess with*. Ronnie thanked him for finding his mother. Mr. Ellman nodded again.

Mr. Friese sat in one of the other side chairs and handed Ronnie a large brown folder that had a flap closed over its top. He said, "This is your copy of the file to take with you. You can just put it down for now." He pointed to the stacks of documents laid out on the table and said, "David and I are going to go over our copies of everything that's in your file, and, as I said, please let us know if you have questions about anything."

The meeting started at shortly after nine and lasted about an hour. Mr. Ellman went over each document in detail, and when their discussion was over, Ronnie was amazed at how, in such a short period of time, he was given a virtual biography of his mother, including a photo of where she had lived in St. Louis and three photos of her, including the photo of her that he had already been sent. One of the pictures was of a smiling Muriel and four other people standing next to a lake. Mr. Ellman said that he thought that photo was about four years old.

Mr. Ellman pointed out one of the two men in the photo and said, "This is Earl Cohlen. He's married to Adrienne Cohlen, who's right here. He pointed again. They're a couple of artists who own an art gallery. She's in her forties, and he's probably ten years older. They seem like good folks . . . if you like old hippies."

Ronnie smiled.

Mr. Ellman pointed to another woman in the photo, and said, "This is Mildred Jordan. She lived in the apartment across the hall from your mother. She's around the same age as your mother was. She's friendly enough, too. I don't think that you'll have any trouble talking with any of those three. They were all real fond of Muriel. Just don't get pushy. Keep it low-key."

Mr. Ellman discussed in detail each of his interviews with Muriel's three friends, and he gave Ronnie some more advice on how to go about asking for any information that he wanted from them. Then he told Ronnie that even though they were friendly enough when he interviewed them, he could tell that they were keeping something from him.

Mr. Ellman said that whatever it was that they weren't telling him didn't have any impact on his finding out what Ronnie had asked them to investigate, so he didn't spend any time on it. Then he leaned over the table and peered into Ronnie's eyes. "But I'm still curious. So if you find out what they were hiding, let me know."

Ronnie nodded and assured him that he would certainly do that.

Among the documents in the file were copies of Ronnie's birth certificate and his adoption papers, as well as a copy of his mother's death certificate. He noticed that the birth certificate didn't name any "Father."

He read the death certificate, and saw that it said Muriel had died from "Complications from Lupus."

Ronnie held up his birth certificate and said, "This is the first time that I've seen a copy of my original birth certificate. It says my mother's name was 'Muriel Ann Campbell,' not 'Gabel.' And I was born 'Ronald Sims Campbell.' What's with that?"

Mr. Ellman said, "Her correct last name was Campbell, but when she was a kid, she sometimes used the name Gable. And when she was twenty-three, she had her name legally changed to Gable. There was no clear explanation of why she changed it in the paperwork I saw. Maybe she was just trying not to be found by anyone from her past."

Mr. Friese added, "Or maybe she was trying to start a new chapter of her life, and the name change was part of that. We don't know. Maybe you can find out when you go to St. Louis."

Ronnie replied, "I'll see if I can. Did that name change make her harder to find?"

Mr. Ellman said, "A little, but we have our ways of dealing with that kind of thing, because it happens more than you would think."

The documents also included a copy of Muriel's diploma from St. Louis Community College, which indicated that she had majored in art, as well as a number of certificates from other art training that she had received.

Ronnie felt melancholy as he studied the items in the file, realizing that they were the only connections that he had so far to the mother whom he had never known, and that even though he had been given more information on his mother than he had ever expected, there were still many questions that had not been answered, and maybe never would be answered.

Mr. Friese asked, "When are you planning on going to St. Louis?"

"I was planning on spending the night here and leaving in the morning."

"That's a bad plan. It you do that, you won't sleep worth a damn. All you'll be thinking about is the trip up there and what you'll be doing when you get there.

"It's only a little after ten. What is it, David, about eight and half hours to St. Louis?" Mr. Ellman nodded. Mr. Friese continued, "If you leave now, you could be in St. Louis by seven o'clock. You could spend the night there and get an early start tomorrow."

Ronnie thought for a moment, then said, "That makes sense. I'll just go on up today. By the way, I really appreciate what y'all have done for me. It's refreshing to deal with people who know what the hell they're doing and how to get things done." Ronnie chuckled and said, "In the music business, you can't be sure that anybody's gonna do what they say . . . including me."

As he walked out the door, Ronnie looked back and envisioned Humphrey Bogart leaning over the round conference table, smoking a cigarette and talking in low tones with Mr. Friese and Mr. Ellman.

Ronnie knew from their discussion that his mother's friends all lived in the Tower Grove neighborhood, so when got to his car he used his iphone to find a bed-and-breakfast that appeared to be in the vicinity of where they lived.

Then he called the B&B and made a reservation for Friday and Saturday nights.

Chapter Three

The trip to St. Louis was relatively uneventful. Ronnie was wearing blue jeans and a black Rolling Stones t-shirt, and he put on sunglasses and a Cardinals baseball cap each time he stopped somewhere. He was only recognized, or at least only approached by someone who recognized him, twice during the trip. The first time was when he stopped for gas just north of Nashville, and the second was when he stopped to eat at a Burger King about thirty miles outside of St. Louis. Each time he was awkwardly approached by a teenage girl, and on each of those occasions, he gave the girl an autograph and a hug, and posed for a photo.

Ronnie enjoyed the drive to St. Louis. The Explorer was more comfortable than his Corvette, and the trip gave him a chance to think about the changes that he was going to make to his career and his life in general. He noticed that, even though he was getting a little tired from the trip, he felt better physically than he had in years. He hadn't had a drink or any kind of drug in about a month, and he had been sleeping and eating on a regular basis for the first time since he had gotten into the music business. He might have even gained a few pounds.

While he was at the Burger King, Ronnie made notes on what he needed to ask his mother's friends. He had learned a great deal about Muriel's history during his meeting at Mr. Friese's office, but he still didn't know enough about her as a person. He wondered: *Did she have a sense of humor? Did she sing or play music? What kind of friend was she? How much did she suffer during her illness?* As Ronnie thought of those and other questions he had about his mother, he tried to remember what Mr. Ellman had told him about how to ask questions in a way that wouldn't make his mother's friends uncomfortable.

It was twilight when he reached St. Louis, but Ronnie didn't have any trouble finding the bed-and-breakfast. It was a two-story brownstone that looked to be in pretty good shape. He parked the Explorer in the fenced parking area just behind the house. Then he got out, stretched his back, massaged his neck, and retrieved his suitcase from the rear of the SUV.

Ronnie walked to the front of the house and up the brick steps to the front door. He set his suitcase down, and rang the doorbell. In a few moments, he was greeted by a portly middle-aged man who looked at him as though he seemed to know Ronnie from somewhere, but couldn't remember where.

The man opened the door wide, and Ronnie could see the foyer behind him. It was decorated with a burgundy and gold Persian rug and antique furniture. The house looked comfortable.

The man held out his right hand and said, "Hello. I'm Doug Middaugh. You must be Mister Roush. Come on in. You look like you could use a cup of coffee."

Ronnie shook the extended hand, which felt like the hand of a working man, and said, "Yes sir, that's sounds good, if you have any decaf."

"Sure do. Just put your suitcase over there by the reception desk and follow me."

Ronnie placed his suitcase in front of the reception desk and followed Mr. Middaugh through the living room and into a large dining room with a long dining table, and then into a kitchen that looked like one from the fifties, except for the commercial stove and microwave oven, and the large double-door refrigerator.

Ronnie said, "Mister Middaugh, I like your kitchen. It's really homey."

"Call me Doug. Yeah, it better look good. My wife spent a fortune on it. We had to un-modernize it from what the previous owners had done. But I've gotta admit, I like it, too."

Doug handed Ronnie a large steaming white mug of coffee and a spoon. He said, "The cream is in the refrigerator, on the left side, and there's some sugar on the counter right behind you."

Ronnie opened the refrigerator door and saw a can of Carnation. He poured a little in his coffee, and then walked over to spoon some sugar from the bowl on the counter.

As Ronnie was stirring his coffee, Doug said, "We just finished eating dinner a little while before you got here, so if you're hungry, the food's still fresh. We got some grilled catfish and coleslaw left."

"Thanks, but I ate about forty-five minutes ago. I wish that I'd waited now. Grilled catfish sounds a lot better than a Burger King cheeseburger."

"Well, if you want a snack later, let me know. I saw from your reservation that you're from Atlanta. Are you an Atlanta native?"

"No, I'm from Prattville, Alabama, just outside Montgomery, but I've been in Atlanta for close to seven years now."

"I get to Atlanta once in a while. I hate the traffic."

Ronnie smiled. "Everybody does."

"What do you do for a living in Atlanta?"

"I'm in the music business."

"I thought you looked familiar. You're a singer, right? I think I might have seen you on *Entertainment Tonight*."

"Coulda been. I've been on *ET* a couple of times."

Doug nodded and said, "Yeah, I'm sure that's where I've seen you. You must be famous."

Ronnie never knew how to respond to comments like that, but he said, "I have a small following, mostly young girls."

Doug pondered that for a moment, then said, "That might be good. You could be like Elvis. He got older, and his fans got older with him and kept coming to see him."

"Well, I'm no Elvis, but maybe I can keep some of my fans."

"How about next time you're on *Entertainment Tonight*, you put in a good word for St. Louis."

"Will do."

"By the way, your reservation is for tonight and tomorrow night. Do you think that'll be long enough? The reason I'm asking is that we're pretty much booked up, but we have Sunday night available for your room if you need it."

"Thank you, but I'm gonna have to be back in Atlanta on Sunday."

"Well, let me show you to your room. You can take that coffee with you. You don't need to check in. We got all your info when you made the reservation. We can run your credit card when you check out."

Doug led Ronnie back to the reception desk, where Ronnie picked up his suitcase. Ronnie followed him up a walnut staircase to the second floor, and then down the hall to the last door on the right.

Doug opened the door and said, "Here we are. You've got cable TV, but we'd appreciate it if you don't play it too loud."

"No problem."

As Doug walked away, he said, "Remember, if you want a snack or cup of coffee, you can ring me at the desk until about eleven. Just pick up the phone and hit zero."

Ronnie thanked him, then entered the room and looked around. He saw a queen-size mahogany bed with an old-fashioned floral quilt over a thick mattress. Then he looked into the bathroom and saw that it had a shower, but no bathtub.

The television set was similar to those Ronnie had seen in motels on the road. He picked up the remote control and pushed the power button. When the TV came on, he ran through the channels until he found ESPN. He looked at the baseball scores until he saw that the Braves were trailing the Mets 3-2 in the fourth inning. He scrolled through the other sports channels trying to find the Braves broadcast, but had no luck, so he tuned back to ESPN to keep up with the Braves score. He turned the sound down and opened his suitcase. He got out the underwear and t-shirt that he was going to wear on Saturday, and then got out a pair of sweatpants and a plain white t-shirt to sleep in.

After he showered and washed and combed his hair, he set the alarm clock for 6:30. Doug had told him that breakfast was served from seven to nine, so that sounded about right.

Ronnie was road weary, but not sleepy. He got out the notes that he had written at the Burger King and read through them twice before he folded them and stuck them back in the right rear pocket of his jeans. Then he stretched out on top of the quilt and turned the sound back up a little on the TV. The Braves were now behind 4-2 in the top of the sixth. Ronnie reminded himself that it was a home game, so they would have four more at-bats to catch up.

Between innings he tuned in to Fox News where a panel was discussing how China was stealing American technology. Ronnie said out loud, "Yeah, and they've been pirating my records, too." Then he tuned back to ESPN.

When he woke up at around ten p.m., he saw that the Braves had lost 4-3. Then he found a local channel and listened to the news for a few minutes before he nodded off again.

Chapter Four

The TV was still on when the alarm went off at 6:30. Ronnie went into the bathroom and washed his face, shaved, and combed his hair. As he got dressed, he watched a local morning show and saw that the weather looked good for the next few days. At around 7:15, he went down to the dining room.

Sitting at the long dining table were Doug, a young couple, and three men in dark business suits. Ronnie nodded to those sitting at the table and said, "Good morning, everybody." The young woman looked as though she might have recognized him, but she only nodded back to him and went on eating her scrambled eggs.

Doug looked up from his plate and said, "Good morning. Are scrambled eggs and ham okay with you?"

"That'd be great, Doug. Could I get a cup of coffee with it?"

Doug got up and walked to the kitchen door where he gave his wife Jeanette the "one more" sign, along with the "cup of coffee" sign.

There was very little talk at the table. Doug was reading a paper as he ate, and everyone else was eating quickly, as though they had somewhere else to go. That didn't bother Ronnie. He wasn't used to being up and around this early and probably wouldn't have been much of a conversationalist, anyway.

After he finished his meal, Ronnie went over to the kitchen door and told Mrs. Middaugh how good it was. She smiled and thanked him.

He then walked into the foyer where he dialed the cell phone number for Adrienne Cohlen. He had called Adrienne from Montgomery the day before and told her who he was and that he was going to be in St. Louis on Saturday. When he called on Friday, Ronnie told Adrienne that Muriel Gabel had done the artwork for two of his albums and that he'd heard she had passed away. He said that that he was a big fan of Muriel's work and wanted to see some of her paintings, if that was possible.

Adrienne told Ronnie that she was familiar with the album covers that Muriel had done, and that she and her husband had a gallery where several of Muriel's paintings were on display. She seemed glad to hear from Ronnie, and told him she was looking forward to meeting him.

When Adrienne answered his call on Saturday morning, Ronnie could tell that she hadn't been awake very long. He apologized for calling so early and asked when and where they could meet. He said that it didn't have to be right then, but whenever was convenient for Adrienne.

Adrienne asked where he was, and Ronnie gave her the address for the B & B. She told him that her gallery was on the next street behind there and about six blocks away. She said that they could meet at the gallery at nine o'clock, if that was okay with him.

Ronnie wrote down the address that Adrienne gave him, and said that he would be there at nine. Then he put the address in his back pocket with his notes.

After the call, Ronnie looked at his watch and saw that it was already ten past nine, then remembered that his watch was on Eastern Time. He shook his head and went to the kitchen for another cup of coffee.

Chapter Five

It was right at nine when Ronnie got to the address that Adrienne had given him. On the way, he had enjoyed looking at the old buildings, some of which were offices, some homes, and some small stores. The address he was looking for turned out to be a two-story brown brick building the bottom floor of which was an art gallery.

From the design of the building, Ronnie thought that the first floor might have at one time been a store, or maybe a café. It had two large picture windows in the front, and the door to the gallery was on the right side of the building inside a small alcove. The tall wooden door had the gallery's address in brass numbers at its very top. Painted in white in the middle of its upper panel was "Cohlen Gallery."

Ronnie tried the brass door knob and found that the door was locked. He peered through one of the plate glass windows, but didn't see anyone, so he rang the doorbell next to the door. Right after he heard the doorbell ring, he heard another door open about eight feet to the right of where he was standing. Exiting that doorway was a thin, gray-haired woman in maybe her late forties. She was wearing blue jeans and a green medical smock. Ronnie recognized her as Adrienne Cohlen.

Adrienne smiled at him, and said, "You're Ronnie Roush, aren't you? I looked you up on the internet after you called. I'm Adrienne."

Ronnie held out his right hand to shake hers and said, "Adrienne, please don't believe whatever you've read about me on the internet. I'm actually pretty sane."

"Too bad. Some of my best friends are crazy."

Ronnie laughed. "Mine, too."

Adrienne walked back to the door that she had come out from and motioned for Ronnie to follow her inside. When Ronnie went through the door, he saw that she was walking up a flight of stairs. When they got to the second floor, Adrienne led him into the living room of a residence up there.

Ronnie liked what he saw. It reminded him of some of the loft apartments that he had seen in Atlanta. The living room was furnished with well-worn furniture, and on one wall there was a large bookcase that was filled with hardbacks. On another wall was a Kimball upright piano.

An antique chandelier hung from the ceiling, and a stereo was softly playing a James Taylor album.

There were large windows on the wall opposite the front door, and that made the apartment very bright. Above each window was a valence made of what appeared to be old flour sacks.

Ronnie said to Adrienne, "Those are cool valences."

"Thanks, Ronnie. They were made by the Jamison sisters in Gee's Bend, Alabama. Earl and I took a trip down there several years ago. I know you've heard of the Gee's Bend quilters."

"Yes, ma'am."

Adrienne motioned to Ronnie and said, "Ronnie, come in here. I want you to meet someone."

Ronnie followed Adrienne into a bedroom and saw a tall, skinny man asleep on a messy wrought iron double bed. Ronnie assumed from the photo he had seen that it was Earl Cohlen.

Adrienne shouted, "Wake up, Earl. You've got company.

The man grunted, groaned, and rolled over. Rubbing his eyes, he looked at Ronnie and asked, "And who's this stranger in my bedroom?"

"This is Ronnie. Remember I said that someone from Atlanta called me yesterday and said he was coming up today."

"Oh, yeah. Ronnie. Hey, Ronnie. I'm Earl. You and Adrienne go have a seat in the living room, and I'll be in there in a bit."

Adrienne led Ronnie back into the living room and invited him to have a seat in a green corduroy recliner. Ronnie sat down and sank into the padding of the chair. Adrienne sat on a nearby brown burlap sofa.

Ronnie asked, "Is this where you live?"

"Yeah. Earl's my husband, and we live up here and run the gallery downstairs. By the way, you mentioned that you were a fan of Muriel's work. When Earl gets fully awake, we can go downstairs to the gallery, and I'll show you the paintings of hers that are on display in there."

"That'd be great. I told you that Muriel did the artwork for two of my albums, but I never had a chance to meet her. I wish I had. She must have been really talented. Maybe you can tell me about her."

Just then Earl walked noisily into the room. He was about six-foot-three and wiry. He had long reddish-gray hair that was pulled into a pony-tail. He was wearing faded gray sweat pants, a paint-smeared long sleeve white t-shirt, and untied combat boots. As he walked in, he bumped into a chair and then almost knocked over a standing lamp. He caught the lamp as it teetered and said, "Oops. Sorry, I'm not awake yet. I worked late last night."

Ronnie said, "It's my fault, not Adrienne's. I called her early this morning and asked to meet with her. I guess that she thought you should meet with us, too."

"Now, who'd you say you were?"

"Ronnie Roush."

"Ronnie Roush the singer?"

"Afraid so."

"I'll be damned. We knew your mother."

Startled, Ronnie looked at Adrienne, who blushed and said, "I guess the cat's out of the bag now."

Ronnie thought for a moment and then asked, "Who else knows?"

Adrienne said, "Just us two and Mildred Jordan."

"Mildred Jordan?" That was the third name that Ronnie had gotten from Mr. Ellman.

"Yeah, she's on her way over here. She wants to meet you."

Ronnie pondered what he had just found out about their knowing about him and decided that maybe it was for the best. Now he wouldn't have to pretend that he was there for some reason other than to get to know more about his mother.

He said, "Actually, I guess I'm glad y'all know. I can be open about why I'm here."

Adrienne reached over and placed her hand on Ronnie's arm. "Your secret's safe with us."

"Apparently so. Y'all didn't tell Mister Ellman, you remember, the investigator, that you knew. You just told him that you knew that Muriel had a son when she was a teenager, but, according to him, you didn't let on that you knew who the son was."

Earl spoke up, "Yeah. Mister Ellman told us that his client was a family member whose name he couldn't disclose yet. But, a few years ago, when Muriel found out that she didn't have much time left, she started trying to find out what happened to her son, and when she did finally find out, she told us about you, but asked us to keep it a secret. So, we figured it was you who sent the investigator. But we weren't going to violate her trust in us."

"I appreciate y'all keeping it a secret. Most folks wouldn't have been able to. When did she find out about me?"

Earl said, "It was right before she went to Austin to do that first album cover. What was it, Moonshine?"

"Moonglow. But Moonshine might have been better. It might have got me some country music fans."

Earl said, "That's right, Moonglow. That trip was about a month after she found out who her son was."

"Why in the world didn't she tell me?"

Adrienne spoke up, "She didn't say. But, knowing Muriel, my guess is that she didn't want to burden you with a dying mother. That's how she was."

Just then a doorbell rang, and Adrienne said, "That must be Mildred. I'll go let her in."

A few moments later, Adrienne came back with a woman whom Ronnie recognized as Mildred Jordan. Mildred appeared to be a little younger than Adrienne, maybe around the same age as his mother was, as Mr. Ellman had said.

Mildred had long dark hair parted in the middle and looked as though she might have Middle Eastern roots. She was dressed in a long-sleeved flowing white cotton dress. She was wearing very little, if any, makeup.

Adrienne introduced Ronnie to Mildred, and then told Mildred that Ronnie was there to talk with them about Muriel.

Ronnie stood up to shake hands with Mildred. She grabbed him in a bear hug and said, in a soft voice, "We all loved Muriel so much. She was better than us. She was our saint. We were better people when she was around us."

Earl said, "That's right, a saint." Adrienne nodded in agreement.

The four of them spent the rest of the morning talking about Muriel. Adrienne showed Ronnie several photos of Muriel that had been taken over the years. In almost every photo, Muriel was smiling. She was very pretty, with long dark hair. She looked very healthy and had the figure of an athlete, or maybe a dancer.

Ronnie found out that Earl had for many years been an adjunct art instructor at St. Louis Community College, and that he was one of Muriel's first instructors when she went to school there.

Earl said to Ronnie, "I could tell right away that Muriel's talent was something special that first semester that she was in my class. She didn't have great technique, but she had an unbelievable eye for composition and color."

Smiling, Adrienne said, "I was one of Earl's students, too, but he has never said that about me."

"Yeah, but I gave you my body."

"And smooth talked me into marrying you."

"Hey, what can I say. You were a hot chick. I mean *are* a hot chick."

Ronnie turned to Mildred, "Where do you fit into this scenario?"

"I moved here not too long after Muriel did. I didn't go to St. Louis CC, but I went to one of their student art shows, and that's where I met her. I was knocked out by her work. Like Earl said, the technique wasn't fully mature yet, but her sense of color and light were way beyond mine, and I had studied art since I was ten years old.

"We got to talking, and then went to a coffee shop near campus and talked some more. We hit it off from the beginning. I could tell she was special. I wanted to be her friend, and, fortunately, she seemed to like me, too. I was still living with my mother at that time, but a few years later when I started working full-time, I moved into an apartment right across the hall from Muriel, and we lived across from each other from then on."

"Where was that?"

"A few blocks from here. I'll show you, if you like."

"Thanks. I'd like that."

Adrienne added, "About the same time that Mildred and Muriel first became friends, Muriel had asked me to help her find a new place to live. She knew me from my being with Earl, and knew that I was a St. Louis native.

"When I brought her home with me one day, she said that she liked this neighborhood. So, I helped her find the apartment that Mildred was talking about."

"How long have you and Earl been together?"

"Close to twenty-five years. When we met, Earl was living in a rundown house not too far from here, and I talked him into moving here. When we first moved here, we were renters. We didn't have the space where the gallery is now. It was a deli.

"Mister Casmus, who owned the building and ran the deli downstairs, let us use one of his storage rooms in the back of the building for our studio. He even sealed off the inside door and let us use the back door as our entrance, so that we could come and go as we pleased. There's some back stairs off our kitchen, so it was a great arrangement for us.

"About ten years after we moved here, Earl got an inheritance when his father passed, and it was his idea to buy this building and turn the first floor into a gallery, and to use the other two storage rooms as studios for Muriel and Mildred.

"Mister Casmus had told us before then that he was ready to retire, but needed to sell the building in order to do so. When he told us that, he said that he was really sorry that we might have to move when he sold the building, because he had grown to think of us as his children.

"So, when Earl got his inheritance, he went up to Mister Casmus and made an offer to buy the building. Even though our offer was about twenty thousand dollars less than what Mister Casmus was asking, he agreed to sell us the building if we would let him sell off the deli furniture and equipment and appliances, and keep what he got from that.

"We signed the papers that same week, and closed the sale a few weeks later. Then we spent all of our spare cash and spare time for about the next three years remodeling the downstairs into the gallery and studios."

Mildred said, "They never charged Muriel or me any rent for the two studios that they built for us, or any fees to hang our art in their gallery."

Earl said, "Yeah, but we made up for it in commissions on the paintings that we sold for you two."

Ronnie said, "Sounds like everybody came out ahead in the arrangement."

Adrienne said, "The best part was that we got to hang around together all those years."

When Ronnie asked if they had always made a living as artists, they all laughed.

Adrienne said, "We must have had every kind of low-wage job there is. We were waitresses, sales clerks, bartenders, housepainters, maids, janitors, and I can't even remember what else. Earl always had his part-time job at the college, but until the gallery started making some decent money, he always had another job along with that one."

Mildred added, "Muriel worked for several years in a big fancy gallery downtown before she got a better-paying job with an advertising firm. I eventually got a job as a graphic artist because I was good with computer technology, and that's what I'm still doing."

Earl said, "When Muriel started working at the gallery downtown, she would make notes about how it operated and then come by and tell me what she had learned, because she knew that it was my goal to have my own gallery someday. And after we bought this building, she helped me design and lay out our gallery. She even explained to me how her gallery did their ordering and billing and advertising, and made me copies of some of their contracts. I don't think that our gallery could have made it if Muriel hadn't helped me figure out how to organize it."

He paused. "I still have her notes somewhere. There're really good because along with the notes she would give me sketches and photos of how their gallery was laid out for shows. I mean, I had set up a lot of student art shows, but I had no idea how to set up a commercial gallery." He looked at his watch and said, "Speaking of galleries, it's almost time to open ours for the day. I need to go shower and change clothes."

As Earl headed back toward the bedroom, Ronnie turned to Adrienne and said, "I can't believe how much I've learned about my mother today. How many of her paintings are on display downstairs?"

"I think fifteen pieces. You know, Ronnie, it's our position that they're all yours now, because you're Muriel's next of kin, but we'd really appreciate it if we could keep a few of them."

Ronnie said, "I'm sure we can work something out. Let's see what you have."

They went downstairs, and Adrienne unlocked the front door to the gallery. As they went in, Adrienne turned on the lights, and Ronnie looked around the gallery. He saw that there were probably around sixty paintings on display. As he walked through the gallery, looking at the paintings, he saw that they included several by Earl and Adrienne and one by Mildred. He didn't have to look at the tags to know which of the other paintings were by his mother. He felt an immediate connection to her style, which was impressionistic with a lot of light greens, light blues, shades of coral and pink, pale yellows, and shades of white. Three of her paintings were abstracts. The rest were landscapes, seascapes, still lifes, and garden scenes.

Ronnie noticed that she signed her paintings "Muriel" and dotted the "i" with a little star with lines coming off the star, symbolizing light rays. He turned to Adrienne and asked, "Do you know why Muriel dotted her i's with a star?"

"No. Why do you ask?"

Ronnie said, "Just curious" and smiled at the secret between his mother and him.

As Ronnie was studying Muriel's paintings, he looked at the prices for each. The prices ranged from $2,000 to $3,500.

He asked Adrienne, "Which ones do y'all want to keep?"

She said, "No, Ronnie. As I said, the paintings are yours. You make the call."

"How about this. I'll pick out the ten that I like the best and pay the listed price on each one. Then I'll leave y'all the rest under the condition that you leave them on display and don't sell them."

"Ronnie, you don't understand. They're already yours. You'd be buying them from yourself. And even if we sold them to someone else, all we'd be due is the commission, and you'd be due the rest."

Ronnie said, "I get that. But I want to do something in return for all that y'all did for my mother when she was so sick. And besides, without Earl and you, there might not have been any of my mother's paintings for me to buy at *any* price. She may not have even been an artist without y'all."

"I don't know about that. But, you're still being too generous."

Earl walked in at that time. He was wearing blue jeans and a Grateful

Dead t-shirt. He waved to a couple who had come in and were discussing one of the paintings on display on a far wall.

Adrienne told him what Ronnie was proposing, and Earl agreed with Adrienne. He said, "No, Ronnie. We want you to have the paintings. They're yours. We just want you to leave us a few to remember Muriel by, if that's okay with you."

Ronnie walked up to Earl and softly but decisively said, "Earl, I'm going to pick out ten paintings and pay you the list price for each one, with the only condition being that y'all keep the rest of them on display for as long as this gallery is open."

Earl looked at Adrienne and said, "Mama, this boy is just as hardheaded as his mother was. We might as well give him what he wants." Earl turned to Ronnie and asked, "Ronnie, how do you want us to get your paintings to Atlanta for you?"

Ronnie asked, "Can you package them in such a way that they'd be safe to carry in the back of the Explorer that I've rented?"

"Yeah, I can do that. Just tell me which ten you want, and I'll box them up for you and label each one."

Ronnie already knew that he wanted the three abstracts and two of the landscapes, so he walked through the gallery and carefully studied each of Muriel's other paintings to pick his other five. In about twenty minutes, he went back to Earl and gave him a list of which paintings he had selected. Then Ronnie told Earl that he would go for a walk with Mildred to the apartment house where his mother used to live while Earl was packing the paintings.

It only took about fifteen minutes for Ronnie and Mildred to reach the apartment house. Ronnie recognized it from a photo that Mr. Ellman had shown him. It was a two-story, brownish brick house of a design similar to several others in the neighborhood. It had limestone trim and a large front porch with round white columns.

Mildred told Ronnie that there were two apartments on each floor. She said that she would have shown him his mother's apartment, but it had already been emptied and repainted, and she had given her key to the apartment manager.

Mildred told him that Muriel had asked that her furniture, appliances, dishes, and clothes all be donated to a local domestic violence shelter, but that she had three boxes of Muriel's papers and other odds and ends.

Ronnie thought about that for a moment, then asked, "Did she have a boyfriend?"

"Not after she got so sick, but before that she had a few serious boyfriends and all kinds of other guys trying to get together with her. She was even proposed to a number of times, but always said no. She told me that she loved her independence too much for any kind of long-term serious commitment. That was Muriel. Freedom was everything to her."

Ronnie nodded. He said, "I've got a feeling that she was disappointed by a lot of people before she came up here."

"She used to hint at something like that, but she never came right out and said anything specific. It was almost like she didn't want to think of anything bad from the past."

Ronnie asked, "Did you know that she changed her last name from Campbell to Gabel when she was twenty-three?"

"Yeah, we talked about that. She said that Gabel was her 'getaway' name. Told me Gabel was the name she used every time she ran away from one of her foster homes. Said that when she was a teenager, she even had a fake ID with Gabel as her last name.

"She told me that this was her last and final getaway, and that she had decided to make it official by changing her last name to Gabel. But, I had a suspicion when we talked about the name change that maybe she was also trying to put a barrier between her and somebody or something from her past. I mean, I don't know that for sure, but it was a feeling that I had at the time."

Ronnie looked up toward the apartment where Muriel had lived and again wished that he had been able to talk with his mother just once before she died.

They were still standing in front of the apartment house when Mildred turned to Ronnie and said, "Ronnie, there's something else. When Muriel decided to try to find you, she also decided to try to find her mother. I'm sure the detective told you that Muriel was taken away from her mother by the State of Alabama when she was a baby, and lived in foster homes until she left for here."

"Yeah, that's what I found out."

"Well, a couple of months before she died, she told us that she finally found her mother. I don't know if I should be telling you this, because I don't know if Muriel would have wanted you to know, but she found out that her mother was in a nursing home somewhere in the Birmingham area."

"Wow. I drove through Birmingham yesterday on the way up here. Do you know what nursing home, or what her mother's name is?"

"No. Muriel never told us any details. That's one of the reasons we haven't mentioned it to you. You already have enough on your mind. But it occurred to me just now that whatever she found out may be in one of the boxes that I have of hers. So, how about if I go through those boxes in the next few days, and let you know if I find anything in there about her mother."

"I'd really appreciate that," Ronnie said. He pulled his wallet from his left back pocket and found one of his business cards. He handed the card to Mildred and said, "This has all my contact info on it. If you find anything, you can call me anytime, day or night."

"I will, but even if I don't find anything about Muriel's mother, I'll send you anything else that I find that looks like something you should have. And I'll also make you copies of the photos that we looked at today."

Ronnie said, "Thanks. That would mean a lot to me."

When they got back to the gallery, Earl had already packed six of the paintings. He said, "It's almost two. You three go upstairs and eat some lunch and bring me back a turkey and swiss sandwich. I'm getting hungry, but I need to stay down here and keep the gallery open. So, I'll finish boxing these paintings while you eat."

Mildred, Adrienne, and Ronnie went upstairs, where they sat in the living room and ate turkey chili that Adrienne had made the night before. While they were eating, Mildred pointed at the Kimball upright and asked Ronnie, "Do you play piano?"

"Yeah. I've got a Yamaha electric that I use for songwriting. Why do you ask?"

"Muriel gave that piano to Earl and Adrienne not long before she passed.

She was a really good piano player. Liked to play the oldies. Sinatra songs, especially."

"I'm glad you told me that. I'd never heard that before."

After they finished eating, Mildred and Ronnie helped Adrienne clean up, and then they returned to the gallery and found that Earl had all ten of the paintings boxed, labeled, and lined up next to the door.

Adrienne gave Earl his sandwich and said, "That was quick work."

Ronnie thanked Earl for getting finished so soon, then pulled a folded blank check from his wallet, and a pen from his pocket, and asked, "Who do I make this check out to?"

Earl said, "Cohlen Gallery, LLC."

In a few moments, Ronnie handed Earl a check in the amount of $28,450.

Earl said, "I still don't feel right about this."

Ronnie said, "I'll go get my SUV and be back in a little while. If you can help me load these paintings, I'd sure appreciate it."

Earl said, "Sure, just park out front and we'll load them up."

Later, as they were placing the boxed paintings into the Explorer, Ronnie said, "Y'all have no idea how much today has meant to me. I mean because of y'all I feel like I know my mother now."

He could see that Adrienne and Mildred were crying, and that Earl was doing all he could to hold back his tears.

Ronnie didn't mention what Mildred had told him about his grandmother.

Adrienne walked up to Ronnie and hugged him. She held him closely and said, "Please don't let this be the last time we see you."

"It won't be."

Chapter Six

On his way back to the B&B, Ronnie decided that he was not going to spend the night. It was only about three-thirty, and he didn't have anything else that he needed to do that day.

Doug was at the reception desk when Ronnie got back. He saw Ronnie come in and asked, "How's it going, Ronnie? Want something to eat?"

"No, but I would like a cup of coffee, if you don't mind."

"Decaf?"

"No, regular this time. I've decided that I'm gonna hit the road this afternoon."

"I hope nothing bad happened."

"No, just the opposite. Everything went great. I was able to finish up early."

"Well, why don't you go upstairs and pack while I make a fresh pot of coffee, and then we can check you out while you drink your coffee. You need to get away before the traffic gets too heavy."

It was a little after four when Ronnie got back on the road. The traffic was heavy, but it wasn't too long until he was on I-55 headed south. As he drove, he tried to mentally reconstruct everything that he had learned that day and put it all in some kind of order.

In particular, he began to contemplate what he had learned about his grandmother. He wondered: *How old would she be? If she's in a nursing home, does that mean she's not doing well? What if Mildred doesn't find anything, should I ask Mister Friese to try to find her?*

He decided that it would be best to just wait and see what Mildred found out before he did anything about finding his grandmother.

As with the trip up to St. Louis, the drive home was relatively uneventful. Ronnie made three stops, each time wearing his sunglasses and baseball cap, this time a Georgia Tech cap, but only once did anyone approach him to ask if he was Ronnie Roush. It happened at a gas station near Nashville.

A cute young blonde was at the pump next to Ronnie's, gassing up a black Corvette convertible. She was dressed in tight black jeans, a white t-shirt, and an orange University of Tennessee baseball cap. She looked at him at least three times before she finally asked, "I hate to bother you, but are you Ronnie Roush?"

Ronnie looked up from pumping his gas and said, "Yes, ma'am."

"I thought that was you. Don't you have a red Corvette? What are you doing in that boring Ford?"

"It's a rental. I'm using it to haul some stuff."

"Still got the Vette?

"Oh, Yeah."

She said, "That's good. Well, have a good trip in your boring Ford," and then she laughed and put the gas nozzle back in place and waved goodbye to Ronnie.

Ronnie thought: *Well, actually, I kinda like this Ford. I might buy me one.* Then he topped off his tank and went into the station to get a Starbucks bottled frappuccino.

Ronnie got to his Atlanta townhouse at around midnight. He parked in his driveway and took the paintings, two at a time, into the house and placed them in his guest bedroom, and then he brought up his luggage and the folder that he had gotten from Mr. Friese. After he got everything into the house, he came back out and drove the Explorer to the garage in back and parked it next to his Corvette.

After he parked the SUV, Ronnie came through the back door into his kitchen. He fixed himself a slice of peanut butter toast and a cup of decaf and took them into the living room, where he turned on the TV and tuned to ESPN.

Ronnie had checked his email and phone messages, and answered a few of them, when he stopped in Tennessee, so the rest of the night was his.

He sat down in his favorite leather recliner to eat his toast, drink his coffee, and watch Sports Center.

Twenty minutes later he was sound asleep.

Chapter Seven

Three days after Ronnie returned to Atlanta, he received an email from Mildred. She wrote him that she had found some notes in one of Muriel's boxes that included the name of her mother, "Louisa Campbell," and the name of the nursing home where she was staying, "Oak Forest."

Mildred wrote that she had mailed him those notes, along with copies of the photos that he had seen when he was in St. Louis, as well as copies of a few other photos that she found among Muriel's things.

Mildred went on to tell Ronnie that everything was going well with the Cohlens and her. She wrote that the Cohlens were going to spend the money from his purchase on improving the gallery. They were going to refinish the floor, repaint the walls, and get new track lighting installed. They were also going to build two new display panels.

Ronnie wrote his response, thanking Mildred for sending the package and asking her to send him a photo of the gallery after all the improvements were made.

It was 4 p.m. when he got Mildred's email, so after he read it and sent his reply, Ronnie decided to look up the number of Oak Forest nursing home and give them a call.

A pleasant female voice answered his call, "Good afternoon. Oak Forest. This is Miss Howell. How can I help you?"

"Miss Howell, I'd like to be connected with one of your residents, Miss Louisa Campbell, if she's available."

"Oh, I'm so sorry, sir. That's not possible."

"Well, can I leave a message for her?"

"Are you a relative?"

"Yes ma'am. I'm her grandson."

"Are you Mister Roush?"

Ronnie didn't immediately know how to answer that question, but decided to just say, "Yes, ma'am. But, how did you know my name?"

"I'm very sorry, Mister Roush. But I have sad news. Miss Campbell has passed away. But before she passed, she told us that if we ever got a call from you to please contact her immediately, so I just assumed that you were a relative. And we also had a package that she left for us to give to you. She gave us the package a few weeks before she passed away, and told us to get it to you if she passed."

When he heard that his grandmother had died, Ronnie's chest tightened to the point where he had trouble breathing. He regained his composure as best he could and asked, "When did she pass away?"

"Wednesday night two weeks ago around eleven. She died peacefully in her sleep."

"Has the funeral been held?"

"Yes, sir. We held the service in our chapel on the Sunday afternoon after she died. She had been cremated, and after the service the ashes were scattered over our lake, like she requested."

"Were any of her family there?"

"No. As far as we know, there is no other family."

It pained Ronnie to realize that, if he had known, he could have at least attended her funeral. He asked, "What did she die of?"

"A heart attack. She'd been dealing with circulatory issues for years. That's what brought her to us in the first place. She'd had two strokes in the last few years, and a previous mild heart attack.

"But she never let it break her spirit, and she almost never complained. She was one of the most positive people I ever met. When she was able, she would play the piano in our residents lounge and sing to the other residents."

"I didn't know she was a musician."

"Oh, she was great. She used to be a professional."

Ronnie thought about that for a moment, then asked, "Can I come pick up the package that you mentioned?"

"We already mailed to you, I think last Friday."

"I haven't received any package. What address did you have?"

"We didn't have your address, but Louisa had a note attached to the package telling us that in the event of her death to mail it to you in care of

Global Music Services. So that's where we mailed it, Global Music Services in Austin, Texas."

"That'll be fine. They'll get it to me."

Ronnie talked with Miss Howell a few more minutes and thanked her for talking to him and for sending the package. When he finally got around to awkwardly asking her if she knew he was, she said that when she looked up Global Music to send the package, she found out that he was a singer on their label.

Ronnie asked her if could please not tell anyone for a while about what she found out about his grandmother's relationship to him. He told her that he wanted to release the information in the right way at the right time. As he was asking, Ronnie could tell that she had no idea what he was getting at, but Miss Howell assured him that she wouldn't tell anyone without his consent.

Ronnie made a mental note to himself to do something nice for Miss Howell.

Right after Ronnie ended his call to Oak Forest, he phoned Charlene to find out if GMS had gotten the package he'd just found out about. Charlene said that they got the package that afternoon, and that she had it ready to go out in the next day's mail. Ronnie asked if she had opened the package, and she said no, she just put in a box and addressed it to his Atlanta home.

Ronnie asked, "Charlene, can you do me a big favor? Can you get that package overnighted to me? There's something in there that I need to get as soon as possible."

"Sure, I'll do that. No problem."

"You're a sweetheart, Charlene."

"That's what they tell me."

Late the next afternoon, Ronnie received the package at his townhouse.

Chapter Eight

When Ronnie got the box from Charlene, he was so anxious to open it that his hands were trembling. He took the box to his kitchen and placed it on a counter next to his knife rack. He pulled a small knife from the rack, and carefully cut open the box. Inside the box was a smaller box, which he also cut open. Inside the smaller box was a large manila envelope that was sealed with postage tape. Ronnie sliced open the top of the envelope and took it into his dining room. He carefully pulled out the contents and spread them out on the dining table.

Among the contents were a long letter, a few photographs, some documents, and a CD with a red "Jazz Kings" label. Ronnie picked up the CD and saw that it was music by the Gary Folsom Quartet. Ronnie recognized several of the songs on the CD as old standards that might be played by a jazz band in a nightclub setting.

He picked up one of the photos and saw that it was creased and worn across the middle where it had apparently been folded for a long time. It was a black-and-white wallet-size picture of a baby girl with dark curly hair. When Ronnie turned the photo over, he saw, in faded blue ink: "Muriel, 9 mos." Ronnie turned the photo back over and studied the face of the baby girl for several minutes before he laid it on the table and smoothed it out as best he could.

He took the photo to his computer and scanned it, then emailed it to Blanche Ward with the message: "Blanche, could you please do your magic on the old baby picture that I've attached. It's a family photo that I'd like to frame if you could clean it up for me and enlarge it to 5 x 7 and mail it to me. If you can do that, I'll owe you one. Love, Ronnie."

Ronnie went back to the table and sat down in one of the side chairs. He picked up the letter. It was neatly handwritten in blue ink on high grade white stationery. He noticed that the date was June 23, the day that his mother died. The letter read:

Dear Ronnie:

If you have gotten this letter, it must mean that I have had the misfortune to have died without ever having met you. Let me introduce myself. I am the mother of Muriel Gable, whom you may or may not know by now was your birth mother. A while back, I received a phone call from Muriel, whom I had not seen or heard from in well over forty years until that call. In her call, she told me that in the summer of 1993, when she was 17, she hooked up with a young musician named Jack Burnham in Arizona and wound up getting pregnant by him, and having his baby in Columbus, Georgia, without ever having told him. She went on to tell me that she gave up the baby boy, you, the week after you were born, and had only within the last few years found out your name and where you were.

She said that at the same time that she was looking for you, she was also looking for me, and went on to say that the reason for her searching for us was that she was very ill and did not expect to live much longer. She said that she had checked on you and found out that you were doing wonderfully, but she had not contacted you because she did not want you to feel obligated to take care of her.

She told me that the reason she called me was to find out how I was doing and invite me to come see her before she passed on. She started crying and said that she never wanted to talk to me before, because I had abandoned her as a baby and left her to be cared for by strangers. Then she said that she had grown weary of carrying that hatred around and wanted to call and tell me, before it was too late, that she had forgiven me.

I told her I wished that I could come see her, but that I was not doing well at all and may not have long to live myself. I also told her that I had tried several times to find her, but had no luck. She said that was by design—that she didn't want to be found.

We both lamented about how ironic it was that now that we had found each other and wanted to get together, we were both too ill and weak to travel to see one other. But I also thanked her for forgiving me for what I had done to her and told her that knowing that she had forgiven me would make whatever days I had left easier to bear.

I sent her a photo of me (from a few years ago when I didn't look so awful) and asked her to send me one of her. Unfortunately, I never got a photo of her, but she did send me an article about you that included a photo of you. You are such a handsome young man! I was proud to hear that you are a singer. I was also a musician, a pianist. You'll see that I'm including with this letter an album that I recorded with the Gary Folsom Quartet back when I was playing piano professionally.

I'm writing this letter at this time because I called Muriel's number earlier today, and the person who answered the phone told me that she had passed away during the night. I have always heard that the most painful thing that can happen to a mother is to lose a child, and now I know that is true, even though in my case I have now lost Muriel twice.

I can only hope that you somehow got to meet Muriel before she died, but my fear is that you did not since she never told me in any of our phone conversations that she had changed her mind about contacting you. In case you're wondering, the reason that I never contacted you was that, even though I want very much to meet with you and talk to you, I share your mother's position on not wanting you to feel any obligation to take care of me.

I know that you're curious about who and what I was, so I'll tell you my story as best I can. I wish that I could tell you that I've led a wonderful life and was a grandmother that you could be proud of, but that wouldn't be true. Until I was thirty-eight years old and hit rock bottom, I led a pathetic life and did some terrible things. And the reason that I'm going to tell you some of the many things that I regret is that Muriel told me she had some concerns about how you were living your life.

Obviously, I'm in no position to tell you how to live your life, since I did such a dreadful job of living mine, but I do hope that some of what I am about to tell you will give you some insight into how harmful certain misbehaviors can be. And, even though I'd never been a very religious person, I pray for you each night.

As for me, I was born in Mobile, Alabama in 1949. I was a "miracle" baby. My mother was almost forty when I was born, and my father was in his mid-fifties. They had been married for about a year when I was born. They had both been married before in what I heard were bad marriages, but their marriage was loving, and I had a wonderful childhood.

My father worked for L&N Railroad in their Mobile office; and when I was ten, he was transferred to the Birmingham office. We moved to Trussville, which is just north of Birmingham. My mother never worked when I was a child, but she was an independent spirit and was always involved in some social or civic activity.

In Trussville, we had a neighbor, Miss Eugenia Kelly, who was a piano teacher; and my mother insisted that I take piano lessons, which I faithfully did three days a week. My mother bought me a nice upright piano so that I could practice at home.

When I was sixteen, Miss Kelly was hired by the then-new Alabama School of Fine Arts, and she encouraged me to apply to go there. I was a bright kid and had good grades, and was already a decent piano player, so I was accepted by the ASFA. When I was there I concentrated on classical piano and jazz piano, as well as composition and music theory. Miss Kelly was kind enough to let me ride back and forth to school with her on most days, and she became my idol. I thought that I might one day be a high school music teacher like her.

When I graduated from the ASFA, I got a partial music scholarship to the University of Alabama and started school there when I was eighteen. I only lasted one semester. That was my first experience away from home, and I handled it badly. I fell in love with a guy whom I met at one of the local college bars, and he introduced me to the proverbial "sex, drugs, and rock-and-roll." I managed to get through my first semester without flunking out or being expelled, but, at the end of that semester, I decided that I wanted to be in a rock band. My father hated the idea, but my mother convinced him that it would be a good experience for me. Their only requirement was that I come back home to live.

Through my boyfriend's connections in the music business, I managed to join a rock band in Birmingham, and we played a lot of the bars and clubs, and other venues, in the area. We were actually pretty good, but the more money we made, the deeper into drugs we got. Eventually, my boyfriend and I broke up because I didn't have time for him anymore. Shortly after that, the band broke up because everybody got just too hard to get along with. As you probably know from being in the music business, hard core drug use almost always changes your personality and makes you suspicious of everybody else.

When that first band broke up I had already turned twenty and wanted to be on my own. It broke my parents' hearts, but I joined a band in Atlanta, and we played nightclubs there as well as private parties, reunions, etc. It was while I was in that band that I used heroin for the first time and started down a long, dark road.

One of my band mates, Chuck, the lead vocalist, and I began a relationship, and when he got offered a recording contract in New York, I went with him. He was also doing heroin, and the first thing that we did when we got to New York was make our drug connection, a shady guy named Harold, whom everyone called "Snake." Harold was originally from Birmingham and had been a friend of Chuck's when Chuck lived in Birmingham before he moved to Atlanta. So, Chuck had called Harold when he decided to move to New York and made arrangements to see him.

As it turned out, Chuck's record label made him clean up at the threat of cancelling his contract, and he managed to get off heroin. After he got clean, I didn't want to be around him anymore, because in my mind he just wasn't any fun. So, I moved in with Harold in his dingy New York cold water flat. After a couple of weeks, Harold told me he was moving back to Birmingham and wanted me to go with him.

I agreed to go back to Alabama with him, and, as you can imagine, that turned out to be a huge mistake. But with Harold, I had all the drugs I wanted and only worked when I felt like it. And I didn't like New York anyway. When we got to Birmingham, Harold got back into the drug ring that he had started with, and we got a small apartment downtown. And I would even go and visit my parents once in a while in Trussville. They hated what was happening to me, but they knew they couldn't stop me. I guess they figured that they would have to let things run their course.

When the word got around that I was back in Birmingham, I got several offers to play music again, but I was only able to do that every once in a while, because Harold was jealous of the attention that I got when I was on stage.

Harold and I stayed together for several years, but those years are mostly a blur to me, because I was stoned almost all the time. When I was twenty-six, I got pregnant with your mother. I'd been pregnant twice before, but had a miscarriage each time. Somehow I got it into my mind that if I would clean myself up and have a healthy baby, then maybe Harold would also clean up and find an honest way to make a living, and we could live a normal life like my parents did. I even wondered if my father could get him a job with the railroad. I know now how dumb that sounds, but I was still young and idealistic and in my addled mind I could see Harold and me, and our baby, having Sunday dinners with my parents.

Somehow, I managed to stay clean all the way through the pregnancy and beautiful Muriel was born in 1976 when I was twenty-seven. (I've never told anyone this before, but the name "Muriel" came from the brand of cigar that Harold smoked. How dumb is that.)

Muriel was the best baby ever, but Harold hated being a father. He hated that we couldn't go out every night like we used to, and he hated that I was sober. So we argued all the time until one day I just couldn't take it anymore.

I wound up leaving him with no idea of where I was going. My father had died shortly before then, and my mother was living in Texas with her sister. And I had no close friends left in Birmingham or Trussville. The only person who offered me a place to stay was another drug dealer, Sammy, who was a competitor of Harold's and probably took Muriel and me in just to spite Harold. I didn't like Sammy very much. He was mean, arrogant, and not very bright. But in my young, stupid mind, I thought that it would be all right to stay with him until something better came along.

After a few months with Sammy, I felt so desperate and depressed that I let Sammy talk me into doing a hit of heroin. Looking back, I know that he was just trying to get me high so that he could get in my pants (I had resisted up to that point), but at that moment, the attraction to the needle was just more than I could resist.

Of course, after that first hit, I got right back into the habit, and Sammy and I got high together every night. Sometimes the nights were good, and sometimes we'd get into a fight and raise holy hell. On one of our holy hell nights, a neighbor in one of the apartments on our floor called the police. When the police got there, they banged on the door of our apartment, and Sammy, not knowing it was the police and being stoned out of his mind, opened the door and yelled, "What the hell's going on out here?"

That night was what led to Muriel's going into foster care. Both Sammy and I were charged with possession of narcotics with intent to sell, and the police called in the social services people to take care of Muriel while I was in jail. Sammy and I wound up pleading to misdemeanor possession and spending six months in jail. When I was in jail, social services naturally had to review my living circumstances, and it didn't take them long to figure out that I was an unmarried, unemployed, long-term heroin addict who was living with my drug dealer in a squalid apartment.

I was in such a state at that time that I didn't fight Muriel's being taken from me. I'm ashamed to say it, but I think at some level I was relieved not to have the responsibility for her anymore. I never saw Muriel again after that.

I went on leading that pathetic life for about another ten years. It was then that Sammy was shot and killed by an irate customer of his. For some reason, when Sammy got killed, I called my mother, even though I hadn't talked to her in years because I was so ashamed of what I had become.

My mother, being the person that she was, told me that she was moving back to Trussville to be with me. A few weeks later, she came back home and rented a nice three-bedroom house in the same neighborhood where we had lived when I was a child. She never mentioned my drug addiction, but I felt obligated to try to get clean again so that I could live a normal life. By that time, I was thirty-eight, and my mother was close to eighty, so I knew that I would have to sober up so that I could take care of her.

It was hard and painful, but I was able to get clean. And I started playing music again. I got a job with the house band in a jazz club and was able to make a decent living. My mother and I bonded like we had never been apart, but it only lasted one year before her health declined, and she had to go to a nursing home. As a matter of fact, she came to live in the same nursing home where I am as I write this letter.

My mother only lasted about six months after she came here, but I saw her every day, and every day she'd make me promise that I'd never do heroin again. It's been hard sometimes, but I'm proud to tell you that I've kept that promise.

After she died, I stayed in the house where we had lived and managed to continue to make a living for many years as a piano player and singer. I mainly played in clubs, but also played concerts and private parties, weddings, reunions, etc. Eventually, when I was close to sixty, I came back and played piano with the house band at the club where I had played when my mother and I were together. Of course, the band had totally different members by then, but we played a lot of the same music. In addition to playing piano at the club, I would sing a few songs each night and engage in banter with the audience. One night, during a band break, an older man whom I'd seen many times before in the club came up to me and said, "Miss Louisa, my name is Ron Barton, and I like you and want to get to know you better. I've been watching you for several months now, and there's something about you that makes me think we should be friends."

Ron went on to tell me that he was sixty-nine and had been widowed for about a year. He said that it was a few months after his wife died that he started coming to our club, because he couldn't stand to be home alone. He told me that he wasn't looking for a wife, or even a girlfriend, but wondered if I would consider coming to live with him and keep him company. I told him that I had heard a lot of pick-up lines in my life, but that had to be the worst. He laughed and said that he was out of practice, but was serious about what he was saying.

Just for the fun of it, I told him that I'd have to see his house first and maybe his bank statement. He asked for my address and phone number and told me that he'd pick me up the next afternoon and show me the house.

Sure enough, he called the next day and told me that he was on his way to my house. At first I was a little leery about going off with a stranger, but then told myself that this was far from the scariest situation that I'd ever been in.

Ron told me that he lived in Riverchase in Hoover, and I knew that was a really upscale neighborhood, so I got kind of curious. It turned out that he had a beautiful six-bedroom brick house with a small brick guest house not too far behind the main house.

He gave me a tour of the main house, and told me that I could have any bedroom that I wanted and that I wouldn't have to cook or clean, because he had a cook and maid service. He just wanted me to stay with him and keep him company.

He showed me a top-of-the-line Yamaha baby grand in what he called his music room and told me that his wife used to play for him before her arthritis got so bad. I told him that I wouldn't move in with him, but I would consider living in the guest house and visiting with him in the main house when it suited us both.

I told Ron that I wanted to continue my music career, because I wanted to maintain my independence. I also told him that I had just been offered an opportunity to cut an album with Gary Folsom, who was a good friend of mine and a great singer, and that I would not let that opportunity pass.

Ron thought about what I said for a few minutes and then took me by the arm and said, "Let me show you the guest house."

I gave my landlord notice that I was moving, and I moved into Ron's guest house at the end of the following month. Over time, Ron and I became best friends. He was the sweetest man I ever knew. He refused to let me pay anything for rent or food, and every once in a while he would bring me a small gift of some type.

Every Sunday afternoon, I'd play piano for him in his music room. He always teared up when I did that, and I know that was because it reminded him of his wife.

He even asked me on a couple of occasions if I would consider marrying him, and I politely declined each time. I found out later that he had told his two children that he was going to ask me to marry him, and they were adamantly against it.

(Ronnie, I realize that I'm running on and on, but you're my grandson, and I want you to know everything about me so that maybe you won't hate me for abandoning your mother.)

Anyhow, I did keep working at the club, and I did get to make the album with Gary. As I'm sure you saw, I've included the CD with this letter so that you can finally hear me play piano. I bought your Starlight CD the other day and listened to it twice. I am so proud of you. I wish we could have played together.

As for Ron, he passed away three years ago, which was about the same time that my cardiovascular system starting breaking down, no doubt due to my long-term heroin addiction.

Unbeknownst to me, and to the consternation of his children, Ron left me quite a sum of money when he passed, about a quarter million dollars, along with a lifetime right to stay in his guest house. But, sadly, I had to give up the guest house a while back and move into Oak Forest. I first moved into the assisted living facility here, but then moved into their nursing home because my health was getting progressively worse.

I've left a will with attorney Robert Atchison in Birmingham naming you as my Executor and my only heir. You may be hearing from him soon. The money in my checking and savings accounts will be my only assets of any value, because I sold my jewelry right after I moved in here and deposited that money into my savings account, and I donated my piano and my furniture to Oak Forest.

I know you don't need my money, but I want you to have what's left of it to do with as you please. I know that you'll put it to good use.

By the way, my parents (your great-grandparents) were Raymond and Barbara Campbell. They are buried next to each other in the Trussville Cemetery. I'm sure you're wondering what happened to Harold, your grandfather. He overdosed on heroin in January of 1979. His frozen body was found in an abandoned warehouse in downtown Birmingham. I never told Muriel what happened to her father. I only told her that he had passed away some years ago. I don't know where Harold was buried or even if he was buried. He may have been cremated.

Well, that's my story.

Please remember that, in spite of how bad things may have gotten in our lives, your mother always loved you, and I always loved her. And now I'll always love you, too.

Your Grandmother,

Louisa May Campbell

Ronnie wiped away the tears that had been flowing down his cheeks. Then he looked through the other items that Louisa had left him and found that one of them was his mother's birth certificate. She was born in Brookwood Hospital at 2:35 p.m. She weighed six pounds, four ounces.

Ronnie picked up another photo that had been in the package and saw that it was of his grandmother when she was probably in her thirties. She was sitting at an upright piano in some dark club. She was very thin, with light hair and a pretty face. But, in her eyes, Ronnie could see the faraway stare of a heroin addict. It made him sad.

Chapter Nine

The next day, Ronnie received the package that Mildred had sent him. Among the items inside were his mother's handwritten notes about his grandmother, copies of the photos that he'd seen in St. Louis, and some photos of his mother that he had not seen before. There was also the photo that his grandmother had sent Muriel from Oak Forest.

Among Muriel's photos was a 5x7 black-and-white picture of Jack and her standing next to the Jack Flash Band tour bus. Jack was right. Muriel was striking back then, and she looked older than seventeen.

Later that day, Ronnie made a call to David Ellman, Mr. Friese's chief investigator, and told him what he had found out about his mother and grandmother. He also told Mr. Ellman that Muriel's friends weren't being deceitful when they acted as if they didn't know that he was Muriel's son, they were merely keeping a promise. Mr. Ellman thanked Ronnie, said that he understood, and wished Ronnie luck.

"Mister Ellman, there's one more thing. If I give you the names of my great-grandparents, do you think you could do an investigation on them for me?"

"Sure, tell me what you know."

"Well, I know that my great-grandfather, Raymond Campbell, would have been born in the late 1800s, and my great-grandmother, Barbara Campbell, would have been born in the early 1900s. They lived in Mobile in the forties and then moved to Trussville in the fifties, and they are both buried in Trussville Cemetery."

Mr. Ellman took a few minutes to write down the information that Ronnie gave him, and then said, "That's a good start. I can get their dates of birth and death from their grave markers, and then I can look up their obituaries and go from there. You'd be surprised how much you can learn from an obituary."

"Thanks, Mister Ellman. I knew you could do it. There's no rush, but if you could fit it into your schedule, I sure would appreciate it."

"I'm wrapping up a couple of things this week, so, if nothing else comes up, there's a good chance I could start on your case next week."

Ronnie was surprised at how soon Mr. Ellman could get started on his request. He said, "Let me know if you need anything else from me."

After he finished the call to Mr. Ellman, Ronnie made a call to attorney David Atchison and arranged to meet him at three o'clock the following afternoon at his office in Birmingham. The next thing that Ronnie did after that was make himself a pot of coffee and put the Gary Folsom Quartet album in his CD player. When the coffee was ready, he poured a cup, started the CD, sat down in his recliner, and listened to his grandmother play. He was familiar with several of the songs including "Summer Wind," "Georgia on My Mind," "My Funny Valentine," "I Left My Heart in San Francisco," "Chances Are," and a few more. He was pleasantly surprised by how well she played, and decided right then how he wanted to spend the money that he would be inheriting from her.

After he had listened to the CD a second time, Ronnie called Mark Gordon, GMS's chief producer.

"Mark, this is Ronnie Roush. Are you busy? I've got a technical question for you."

"I've got a little time. What's your question?"

"I've got a CD that was made some years ago by a jazz quartet, and I'm wondering if there's a way that you can lift off just the piano from that CD and mix it into another recording."

"You mean have the piano parts singled out and transferred to music in a different recording?"

"Yeah."

"If the first recording is good enough, it could probably be done. It would take some work to eliminate all the other instruments, and just leave the piano. But, Charlie Groves has this new program that he's been using for that kind of thing.

"And then, once we got the piano isolated, the sound would have to be adjusted so that the tone and volume would fit in with the recording that you were inserting it into, and it would also have to be tweeked to be close to the same sound quality to sound right."

"So, what you're saying is that it can be done."

"Yeah, probably. Why don't you send me the CD and I'll see what I can do."

"I only have one, so I'll get it copied and mail it to you. I don't have a CD drive on my computer."

Mark said, "I've got a better idea. Do you still use that small studio across the street from your place where you and Cliff make the demos for the songs y'all write, the studio that Oscar runs?"

"Yeah."

"Well, go over there and ask Oscar to download the CD and send it to me electronically. That'll be just as good as sending the CD. If he can do that, I can listen it right away and let you know what I think."

Ronnie said, "I'll get it to him today if he's in. Thanks for your help."

Ronnie called Oscar and found out that he'd be available at around five.

At five o'clock, Ronnie left his townhouse and walked across the street to the Guild Building and took the elevator to the fifth floor. The door to Oscar's studio was standing open. Oscar was sitting at his control panel wearing headphones, listening to a recording that he'd just finished mastering.

Oscar was in his thirties, but looked older. He was a little pudgy with thinning brown hair that was cut short on the sides. He was dressed in faded blue jeans, cut off at the knees, and a white sweatshirt with ketchup stains on the right sleeve.

Ronnie tapped him on the shoulder and took a seat in the swivel chair next to Oscar's.

The studio was small, only about four hundred square feet, because Oscar's specialty was producing demos for songwriters. That meant that he usually used only a guitar or electronic keyboard, sometimes both, and an electronic rhythm section. The room had been soundproofed and had no windows. Oscar had told Ronnie that it used to be a storage room for a law firm.

Oscar took off his headphones and set them on the console. He said to Ronnie, "That's a godawful song I've been working on today, but I can't get the songwriter to listen to any of my suggestions." He shook his head and said, "Nobody's gonna record this song." Then he shrugged.

"Well, anyway, what you got there?"

"This is the CD I called you about. Mark wants you to download it and send to him today if you can."

"Hand it to me. I'll do it right now. It won't take long. I can copy it at high speed if you don't need to listen to it."

"I don't need to listen. Go ahead with high speed."

Oscar took the CD and slid it into a slot on his control panel. Then he started complaining again about the recording that he was mastering. It took just a few minutes to make the copy. Oscar handed the CD back to Ronnie and said, "I'll shoot this to Mark and then call him and make sure that it came through all right."

"Thanks, Oscar. I owe you one."

"You wish it was just one."

"Okay. I owe you a bunch. Put this one on my tab."

That night Ronnie got a text from Mark saying that he got the album from Oscar, that he would listen to it to see what they could do with it, and then call back the next day or the day after.

Chapter Ten

The next day, on his way back from his meeting with Mr. Atchison, where he found out that his inheritance from his grandmother was a little over two hundred thousand dollars, Ronnie got a call on his cell phone from Mark Gordon.

Ronnie pulled off the highway into a service station parking lot. He got out of his car and walked around while conversing with Mark.

Mark told him that he had downloaded the recording from Oscar and given it to Charlie Groves, his chief engineer, to see if the piano could be transferred to another recording.

Mark said, "Ronnie, there are ten tracks on the album, and Charlie tells me that we could probably use the piano on six of the tracks. The other four just don't cut it. Overall, this was not a high quality recording. It's not bad for that time, but not up to today's standards. But, even so, Charlie thinks we can use those six tracks. So, I told him to go ahead with isolating those six piano tracks and saving them for us. By the way, who's the pianist? He's really good."

"Louisa Campbell."

"A chick, huh. Anyway, she's good. Why don't you just get her to play live?"

"Too late. She's passed on."

"I see. Well, we'll get those tracks ready for you. But what are you gonna do with 'em? That's not your kind of music. It's old stuff. Elevator music."

"Tell you what. I'm planning on coming out there on Monday. We can talk about it then. Will you be available?"

"I will that afternoon. What time?"

"Don't know yet. I'll let you know."

Ronnie finished his call to Mark, and called Jack's office.

Renee answered, "Jack Burnham's office."

"Renee, it's Ronnie. How're you doing?"

"Not bad. What's up?"

"I need to make an appointment to meet with Jack, Mark, Charlie, and

Roscoe, and probably Blanche, on Monday afternoon. Can we do that?"

"I'll check and let you know. I can't do that right now because Jack's in court today, and I don't know when he'll be back."

"Is it part of the divorce business?"

"Yeah. It just never stops. I feel bad for Jack."

"Me, too. Just call me when you know something. I'm on my way home now."

At around 5:30, Ronnie was having a cup of coffee when his home phone rang. It was Jack.

"What's up, buddy? Why the meeting on Monday?"

"I've got an idea for an album, and I need for you experts to guide me on it. But, before we talk about that, how'd court go today?"

"Couldn't have been better. The judge didn't say so, but I could tell that he'd had enough of Carol and wanted to get us off his docket. He took us and our lawyers into his chambers and pretty much told us that we weren't leaving until we came to some sort of agreement. Then he walked out and left us there. I think he put the fear of God in the lawyers, because they quit arguing with each other about trivial crap and helped us work everything out.

"The good news for you and me is that in my grubby little hands I have a final divorce agreement that has been signed, sealed, and delivered. It's over except for the judge formally signing off on it, which I know he will."

"Glory hallelujah, Daddy."

"Whoa. It's still Jack."

Ronnie said, "Well, that news actually makes what I want to do easier. Here's the deal. I not only found out a lot about my mother, I also found out who my grandmother, my mother's mother, was and have a long letter that she wrote for me before she died. I found out that she was a jazz piano player, and she left me a CD that she had played on years ago."

"Is that the album that you sent to Mark? He told me about that and was wondering what the hell you were up to. I told him that I had no idea why you wanted to lift piano tracks off an old album, but now I'm beginning to see the light. You want to figure out some way that you can record with your dead grandmother."

"Jack, that's why you're the man. It's impossible to get anything past you."

"Cut the crap. Just tell me what you wanna do."

"What I want to do is make an album of those same ten songs with a jazz quartet with piano, drums, upright bass, and sax, but use my grandmother's piano on as many of tracks as I can.

"I know that this won't be a money maker, so I want to finance it myself, but still put it out on our label. So, what we could do is make the album using your usual process and then when everything is done, I'll reimburse the company for all the costs, including production, packaging, advertising, and everything else. That way it won't cost GMS anything."

"Let me think about it, Ronnie, because even if you reimburse GMS all the costs, that album might still take us away from another project that could make us some money."

"I know. I thought about that. That's why I want to talk to y'all. I mean, I could cut the album at another studio, but I don't want to do that. But on the other hand, I don't want to do anything that would hurt the label."

"Ronnie, we haven't even talked about the obvious. Can you even sing those songs? I mean, I know you can sing them, but can you do it up to your standard? I know how picky you are."

"I've learned all the songs and been practicing them ever since I got this idea. I'm no Sinatra, but I can do it.'

"Well, I guess if Rod Stewart and Willie Nelson can do it, why can't you."

"Yeah, and Hank Junior did 'Ain't Misbehavin'. That's one of the songs on the album."

"He did a pretty good job of that. But your voice is still just twenty-five years old. Those other guys all have a lot of smoke and whiskey in their voices."

"Jack. I can do it. Even if it's not Grammy material, I'm gonna do it. I just need for y'all to help me do it as well as possible."

"All right. Gotta go. See you at 3:30 on Monday. I'll have everybody there. We'll talk it out and see if there's a way to do what you want."

"Thanks, Jack. And congratulations again on the divorce."

"Yep. I'm about to go upstairs and open that bottle of champagne that I've been cooling for two months."

Chapter Eleven

At 3:15 on Monday, Ronnie walked into the GMS lobby. Charlene spotted him and waved. He walked over and met her in front of the reception desk. They hugged, and Ronnie smelled that reassuring fragrance that Charlene gave off. It reminded him of a flower garden.

"Ronnie, it's good to see you again. Are you still dating that actress, what's her name, Denise?"

"I see her sometimes when I'm in L.A., but it's nothing serious."

"That's not what the magazines say."

Ronnie laughed. "Are you still reading those gossip magazines?"

"Of course. They're very educational."

Ronnie shook his head as he walked toward the elevator.

When he got to Jack's office, Roscoe and Mark were already in there talking to Jack. Ronnie gave Renee a quick hug then walked into Jack's office and sat down at the conference table with them.

Jack asked, "Want some coffee, Ronnie?"

"Yes, thanks. I'll get it."

Ronnie began to rise from his chair, but Renee was already bringing his coffee.

"Thanks, Renee. You know me too well."

Charlie walked in and joined the group. Blanche was right behind him. Blanche walked over to Ronnie, and Ronnie rose to give her a hug. She said, "Good to see you again Ronnie. You're my favorite."

Ronnie smiled and said, "I bet you say that to all of us superstars."

Blanche sat down, placed her brown leather briefcase on the table and opened it. She reached into the briefcase and said, "Ronnie, before we start I've got something for you."

Ronnie looked at what she was handing to him and saw that it was a black-and-white photo in a brown walnut frame.

"Blanche, this is great. Thank you."

"Charlie asked, "What is it?"

"It's a baby picture of a relative. Blanche cleaned it up and enlarged it for me."

Charlie said, "Let me see."

That led to the photo being passed around the table and everyone commenting on what a cute baby she was. The last person to see the photo was Jack. He held the photo with two hands and stared at it. As Jack studied the picture, Ronnie could see his face soften.

Jack handed the photo to Ronnie. Then he tapped the table with his pen and began the discussion. "You all know why we're here. Ronnie has a project that he wants to do, and I want us to come up with a way to get it done."

Ronnie thought: *Man, that's certainly a change of heart from the other day*, but he said, "Thanks, Jack. I appreciate all of y'all being here, because I know what I want to do, but just don't know exactly how to do it."

Roscoe said, "Yeah, Ronnie, Jack met with us on Saturday and gave us the lowdown on what you want to do, and we've already decided that it's a go."

Ronnie said, "Wow. That's great."

Roscoe continued, "We can start your project three weeks from today and wrap it up by no later than two weeks after that. I've got the Frank Carter Quartet, a local jazz band, lined up, and I've got Studio 2A reserved, if that time period is good for you. If we do it then, it'll let you finish in time to start the Sundown album on schedule.

"The Carter Quartet already knows all of the songs that you want to record, and I gave them a copy of the album to go by, as far as the tempo, and the rhythm, and the keys. So, if you can sing the songs in the same keys and tempos that are on the CD, we can knock this out in no time. We need to copy the original arrangements as much as possible on six of the tracks, so that we can slide in those piano parts you want us to transfer. But, on the other four songs that have the piano parts that we can't use, you can do something different, if you want."

Ronnie thought for a moment and said, "Let's just do it as close as possible to the Folsom album. I've been practicing with the original CD, and I'd like to keep that same feel. I like what they did. Except, of course, the solo breaks don't have to match the originals. We can give the band some leeway there."

Roscoe nodded, then leaned back and said, "Well, all right, that's settled. This should be a smooth ride. Those guys will knock out these tracks in no time. They're old hands with a lot of studio time. The only hard part will be adding the old piano parts, but that might be fun.

"Like I said while ago, we've got the band lined up to start three weeks from today, and we've got Studio 2A reserved. Will that schedule work for you, Ronnie?"

"Absolutely. I'll come in the Sunday before so that we can start on Monday morning. Man, I can't believe how much y'all have already done."

Blanche said, "Now, before we leave, let's talk about packaging and promotion. What do you have in mind, Ronnie, in general?"

"Here's what I've got so far. I want the album to be called "For Louisa," and I've picked out a Muriel Gabel painting for the cover."

Jack spoke up, "Ronnie, I've already told them the whole story about your mother and me, and your grandmother, so you don't have to tiptoe around the Muriel and Louisa references."

Ronnie looked down toward the table, then raised his head and said, "Good. That'll make this quicker to explain. What I would like to include in the packaging is the story of my search for my mother and how that search led to me also finding out about my father, the lovely and talented Jack Burnham, and my grandmother, Louisa Campbell. Along with the story, I want to include some family photos that I've found, including one of Jack and Muriel standing next to the Jack Flash tour bus."

Jack sat up straight. "Where'd you find that?"

"Muriel had one, and a friend of hers sent it to me."

Jack said, "Unbelievable. Send me a copy."

Ronnie said, "No problem. I'll email it to Blanche, and she can print you a copy."

Blanche was beaming. She said, "This stuff is great. Ronnie, if you do this album, it will not only be a money-maker, it could be a sensation."

Ronnie asked, "How do you figure that?"

Blanche said, "Think about it. Famous pop star gets to record with the dead grandmother who he never met on an album with a cover done by the dead mother who he never met. And then you add that your father, who never even knew he had a son, is the head of the label that recorded the album.

"I'm telling you this story will sell the album to people who had never even heard of you before. I'll get you and Jack on some of morning talk shows and late night TV, where y'all could tell the story. Then maybe you could perform one of the songs off the album. We could even get Jack to sit in with the band.

"We might even be able to get y'all on *Dr. Oz* or *Dr. Phil.* And then there's *ET* and all the fan magazines and news shows. I'm telling you, this could be a big deal. Think about it."

All the men at the table looked at each other. Jack leaned back and looked up at the ceiling. Then he turned toward Blanche and said, "Blanche, you're a genius. I never even thought of the promotional strength of the back story."

Ronnie said, "That's all great, y'all, but let's please make sure this a first-rate album. I want it to be a musical tribute to my grandmother, not just a publicity stunt."

Roscoe said, "Don't worry, Ronnie. We got you covered."

Chapter Twelve

The For Louisa project went as smoothly as possible. The musicians in the Frank Carter Quartet were very talented and had no problem producing the sound that Ronnie wanted. The production crew was able to include Louisa's piano on six of the tracks on the album in such a manner that it couldn't have sounded more authentic. And Ronnie's voice was never better.

One reason that the project went so well was that Roscoe had tracked down Gary Folsom, who was living in a retirement community in Boca Raton, Florida, and hired him as a technical adviser for the album. Gary helped with the arrangements, and even though Gary told Ronnie that he didn't have the pipes anymore to demonstrate how to sing the songs, he was still able to coach Ronnie to the point where Ronnie sounded as if he was born to sing those standards.

After the first day's session, Ronnie took Gary to dinner and they spent a good part of the evening talking about Ronnie's grandmother. It turned out that she and Gary had been good friends, and he had come to visit her at Oak Forest the last time that he was in Alabama.

Soon after the album's release, Blanche was indeed able to get Jack and Ronnie on some of the network morning talk shows, as well as one of the late night talk shows, and *Dr. Oz* and *Entertainment Tonight*.

As a result of Blanche's shrewd marketing strategy, in the first six months after its release, sales of For Louisa brought in much more than enough to cover the costs of production, packaging, and promotion. So, Ronnie owed GMS nothing for the expense of making the album.

Since Ronnie did not need to spend his inheritance on the album, he donated the two hundred thousand dollars that he had set aside for the album to a Birmingham home for unwed mothers that was run by a non-profit religious organization. He asked that the donation be designated "In memory of Muriel Ann Gabel and Louisa May Campbell."

There were a number of other benefits from the album. The For Louisa publicity tour led to a spike in the sales of Ronnie's earlier albums and to a re-mastering and re-release of the original Gary Folsom album on the GMS label. It also led to a greater popularity in the Austin area of the Frank Carter Quartet. So much so that Roscoe and Charlie scheduled a GMS recording project for them.

And just as importantly to Ronnie, the success of the publicity campaign resulted in the Cohlen Gallery's being able to produce and sell prints of all of his mother's paintings, including those that Ronnie had purchased. To accommodate the demand that had arisen for prints of her paintings, Ronnie had licensed the Cohlen Gallery to photograph and make prints from the paintings in his personal collection, as well as those that were on display at the gallery, with the only condition being that the gallery frame and donate full sets of the Muriel prints to St. Louis Community College and to the Alabama School of Fine Arts.

Ronnie also had the gallery emboss prints of two of his mother's floral paintings onto porcelain urns, so that he could take a trip to Trussville and place the urns at the graves of Raymond and Barbara Campbell in Trussville Cemetery.

Ronnie had learned from Mr. Ellman's investigation of his great-grandparents that Raymond had come from a long line of Scottish warriors and had fought as an infantryman in the Argonne Forest in World War I. He was also told that his great-grandmother was from one of the founding families of Virginia.

On a Monday afternoon when he was on a break from touring, Ronnie drove to Trussville to visit his great-grandparents' gravesites. As he approached the entrance to the cemetery he saw a marker stating that he was at the site of the First Baptist Church of Trussville, founded in 1821.

Ronnie drove into the cemetery and parked near where he was told his great-grandparents' graves would be. He got out of his Corvette with the two embossed urns and walked along a gravel path reading the markers until he found the graves of Raymond and Barbara Campbell. In each of the urns were yellow daisies that he had bought at a flower shop in Atlanta.

When he got to the grave of his great-grandfather, he saw the following words beneath the name and dates on the headstone:

WWI
167TH INFANTRY REGIMENT
RAINBOW DIVISION

Ronnie kneeled down and placed an urn next to Raymond's headstone, then stood at attention and saluted.

Barbara's grave lay next to Raymond's. Her headstone showed that she was a Daughter of the American Revolution. Ronnie knelt and set an urn at her grave, then stood and placed his hand on top of the cool headstone. He stood there for several minutes, remembering many of the things that he had read in Louisa's letter and wondering what it would have been like to have known his grandmother and his great-grandparents.

As he walked back to his car, Ronnie thought to himself that it had been too long since he had paid tribute to his adoptive parents, who were interred at Prattville Memory Cemetery.

Even though his Mom and Dad had never shown Ronnie the same level of affection that they would likely have given a natural son, Ronnie knew how much they loved him. And he was always grateful for the way that they had taken him in and sacrificed so much to see that he never had to do without anything that he needed.

He couldn't wait to sit on the concrete bench next to their graves and tell them all that he had recently discovered, and thank them once again for saving him from what might have been.

He would also tell his Mom that he was finally getting his act together, as far as his personal behavior, the way that she had always asked him to do.

On his way to Trussville Cemetery, Ronnie had stopped by Oak Forest nursing home to give Miss Howell a framed print of one of his mother's landscapes. He also gave her an autographed copy of the For Louisa CD. She thanked him and said that she would hang the print in the lobby of the nursing home.

In spite of the busy promotion schedule for the For Louisa album, Ronnie had been able to get the Sundown album recorded on schedule, and once it was released, he went on tour with his road band. Ronnie made sure that Blanche added St. Louis to their tour schedule, and he had Blanche send backstage passes to his mother's friends.

The St. Louis concert was held at the performing arts center at the University of Missouri at St. Louis, and all three of Muriel's special friends made the show and visited with Ronnie backstage, before and after the performance.

Adrienne told Ronnie that, in honor of his visit, the gallery had put up a full display of framed prints of Muriel's paintings, and Earl told him that along with Muriel's prints, the gallery had on display a Gee's Bend quilt made by the Jamison sisters, entitled "For Louisa and Muriel."

Adrienne added, "Yeah, the quilt has on it a four-foot map of the State of Alabama made of flour sack pieces. And right where Birmingham is there's a star-shaped piece cut out of gold silk. You'd like it, Ronnie."

The band closed out their concert that night with "St. Louis Blues," which was one of the tracks on the For Louisa album. For that song, the band was accompanied by a piano instructor and saxophone student from the University's music department, and the enhanced band got a rousing response from the audience.

Before he sang that final number, Ronnie took off his black dress shirt to show the audience a t-shirt that Blanche had her PR crew make especially for him. It was a light gray shirt on the front of which was the black-and-white picture of Jack and Muriel standing next to the Jack Flash bus. A photo of Ronnie wearing that t-shirt later appeared in the entertainment section of the *St. Louis Post-Dispatch*, as well as in one of the more popular music magazines.

While Ronnie was still on tour, he got a call from Blanche telling him that the label had received so many requests from fans wanting to buy the Jack Flash t-shirt that she had to add it to the GMS merchandise catalog. She went on to tell Ronnie that he would get his standard royalty from the t-shirt sales.

Ronnie thanked her for coming up with the idea and for adding it to the catalog. Then he asked her to send three of the t-shirts to the Cohlen Gallery for Muriel's friends.

The night after he heard from Blanche, Ronnie received an email from Adrienne with an attached photo of the "For Louisa and Muriel" quilt. In her message, Adrienne told Ronnie that the quilt had been purchased for $3,000 by an agent for an anonymous buyer. She wrote, "I have no idea who the buyer was, but I'd like to think that maybe it was Oprah Winfrey."

Ronnie knew that the buyer was Jack Burnham, who had seen the quilt on the Cohlen Gallery website and decided to buy it to display in the Global Music Services lobby. It was meant to be a surprise for Ronnie, but Blanche had let it slip out when she called him. Blanche made Ronnie promise not to tell anyone that he knew about the quilt purchase.

A few days later, Ronnie got a call on his cellphone from Adrienne. She told him that the curator for the St. Louis Art Museum had approached her about buying one of Muriel's paintings that were on permanent display at the Cohlen Gallery. She said that the museum was offering twenty thousand dollars for the painting, but she had told the curator that the painting belonged to Ronnie, and she couldn't sell it without his permission.

Ronnie asked, "What do you think? Would that be good for my mother's memory?"

Adrienne answered, "Oh, yes. That's one of the best art museums in the country. It would definitely honor her memory."

Ronnie asked, "What would your gallery's commission be on a twenty thousand dollar sale?"

"Our arrangement with Muriel was a fifteen percent commission, so it would be three thousand dollars."

Ronnie thought for a moment. Then he said, "Tell you what. Tell the museum people that I'll donate the painting, if they'll pay the Cohlen Gallery a five thousand dollar commission and allow the gallery to retain the right to keep making prints of that painting."

Adrienne responded, "I don't know about retaining the license for making the prints. The museum has its own shop where they sell prints."

"Well, how about this. We've done this with some of our music. Tell them that your license will be a non-exclusive license. That way, they would own all the reproduction rights to the painting, but y'all could keep on making your prints. The museum could still make their own prints, or t-shirts, or whatever else they wanted with reproductions of the painting."

Adrienne said, "I think that they might go for that. I'll call the curator today and see what she has to say."

Just as he was getting dressed for his next show in Cincinnati, Ronnie received a text message from Adrienne saying that the curator thought that his offer was more than fair and she would begin the process to get the deal approved and, if it was approved, which she was sure it would be, the museum would prepare the paperwork and send it to him for his signature.

After Adrienne's earlier call, Ronnie had looked up the St. Louis Art Museum on his smart phone. As he read about the museum, he began to realize what it would mean for his mother's work to be on display there. He thought to himself: *Wow, this is a world class museum. My mother's painting being in there would put a crown on her career. She'd have been so proud of being recognized that way.*

That night, when he introduced himself and the band to the Cincinnati audience, he told the fans, "Tonight's show is dedicated to my guardian angels, my mother Muriel, the great artist, and my grandmother Louisa, the great piano player." Then he looked skyward and said, "I hope that they're up there listening together."

II

Stories

Kinfolks

The tall door is open. It's dark walnut with an upper panel of frosted glass on which is painted in bold black letters STANLEY E. EVERETT, MANAGING PARTNER. Foster enters the reception area for Mr. Everett's Office and nods at Executive Secretary Betsy Johnson, whom everyone at the firm calls "Miss Betsy." Miss Betsy is a short chubby sixty-year-old spinster who has been Mr. Everett's secretary for twenty years. Before that she was secretary for J. W. Everett, who was the son of James T. Everett, the founder of the firm of Everett and Everett, P.C. After J. W. retired twenty years ago, Stanley, his eldest son, became the firm's senior partner and inherited Miss Betsy.

Foster approaches Miss Betsy's desk and says, "Miss Betsy, how's everything? I got a message that Mr. Everett wants to see me this morning."

"Everything's good, Mr. Thornton. Just go on in. He's with Mr. Jake Kelly, the owner of Kelly Construction. They want to meet with you this morning."

Foster says, "Thank you, ma'am" and slowly opens the door to Mr. Everett's office. The office is about twenty-by-twenty feet with floor-to-ceiling walnut bookshelves on each side. On the wall behind Mr. Everett's wide desk, which is almost identical to the desk in the Oval Office of the White House, and hanging over the matching credenza, are several oil paintings from the collection of the Everett family. Two of the paintings are military-themed, reflective of the fact that both Stanley Everett and his father had served in the Marines and his grandfather James had served in the Army during World War I.

Mr. Everett rises from his seat at the Chippendale conference table in the middle of the room. He is a shorthaired, ruddy-faced man of average height in very good physical condition for a man of seventy years. As always, he's dressed in dark gray slacks and a navy blazer with a starched white shirt and striped tie. He says, "Come on in, Foster, and meet Mr. Jake Kelly."

Foster walks over to Mr. Kelly, who is also standing, and says, "Good to meet you, sir. I'm Foster Thornton." As they shake hands, Foster feels the strong, rough grip of a man who has done hard manual labor in his day. Mr. Kelly is slightly taller and heavier that Mr. Everett and appears to be a few years younger. He's very tan and has medium length gray hair. He's wearing designer blue jeans and a long sleeve khaki work shirt.

Mr. Kelly says, "Good to meet you, too, Foster. Nice suit. I've always liked pinstripes. Well, I've been sitting here for about thirty minutes listening to Stanley brag about you. If what he says is true, I think that maybe we can get something done today."

"Well, I hope that Mr. Everett didn't oversell me, but what are we meeting about?"

As Stanley is retaking his seat on the other side of the table from Foster, he says. "Have a seat Foster. We may have a new client in Mr. Kelly, if we can convince him that you can do what he needs."

Foster takes a chair directly across from Stanley and looks eye-to-eye at Mr. Kelly, who is sitting at the end of the table with a stack of documents and a yellow legal pad in front of him. Foster smiles and says, "I'm sure willing to answer any questions that you have, Mr. Kelly."

Mr. Kelly nods and says, "Well, here's the deal. My company, Kelly Construction, does a lot of business with government agencies—state, local, and Federal—and our in-house counsel is retiring this fall, about three months from now. Since I've been scaling our company down so that I can get into a position to retire myself when the time comes, I've decided that we don't need an in-house legal office anymore. But what I do need is an outside firm like this one to handle any legal matters that come up, such as contracts, leases, personnel issues, payment disputes, and so on. Stanley tells me that he thinks that you could be the man for the job."

Foster nods and says, "I'll be glad to do whatever Mr. Everett and you need, if y'all decide that I'm the one who can do it."

Mr. Kelly looks down at his notes for a moment. Then he picks up one of the documents in his stack and says, "I've been reviewing the resume that Stanley gave me and everything looks like a good fit, but I've been working with my present lawyer, Jim Lord, ever since I started my business, and our relationship is one where we can say anything to each other, and nobody's feelings get bruised.

"So, the main reason that I wanted to meet with you personally this morning is to find out what kind of man you are as a human being, and not just as a lawyer, because sometimes I can be hard to work with. I can even be a genuine pain the ass, because I'm such a perfectionist and want things done just so."

Both Stanley and Foster chuckle at Mr. Kelly's description of himself. Foster says, "Okay. Fire away. What do you need to know?"

"From what I can tell from your resume, you're in your mid-forties, you were a football player at Alabama State where you earned a bachelor's degree in business with an emphasis in accounting, and then you got your MBA there. Then you went to work for the State as an auditor and went to law school at night. Then after you finished law school, you got a job as an Assistant Attorney General and worked in their white collar crimes unit. Am I right so far?"

"Yes sir."

"And you've been with Everett and Everett for roughly eight years now."

"That's right."

"What position do you play at Bama State?"

"Outside linebacker"

"What are you, about six-three?"

"Yes sir, about that."

"About two-twenty?"

"Not quite, maybe two-fifteen, but I was around two-thirty when I played."

"Is that how you got the scar on your cheek, playing football?"

Foster runs his left hand over the scar on his cheek and says, "No sir. That's from a childhood accident."

"Well, I like it. It makes you look like a man of action. Maybe a soldier or a sword fighter."

Foster smiles and says, "Well, I've never been a soldier or a sword fighter. But thanks for the compliment."

Mr. Kelly looks down at his notes again, then says, "Stanley tells me that you grew up as a poor kid in a housing project. That so."

"That's right. Until I moved into a dorm at college, I lived with my mother in Trenholm Court. Do you remember Trenholm Court that used to be on Columbus Street?"

"Sure do. Where's your mother living now?"

"Actually, my mother passed away two years ago. She had a congenital heart ailment, and it finally got the best of her. She was living in a small townhouse in east Montgomery at the time she passed, not too far from where I live."

"So sorry to hear that. What about your father?"

"Don't know. I haven't seen my father in years. He and my mother divorced when I was seven, and I didn't see much of him after that."

Mr. Kelly looks at Stanley, then back at Foster. He says, "So, it was just you and your mother in the project together. How'd she make her living?"

"Well, she did what she could. She did housecleaning, waitressing, cooking. One time she worked at a laundry. She was a hotel maid at another time. Sometimes she worked two jobs. I wish that I had her gumption. She was a tough lady. Kept me straight."

"I'm assuming that you went to college on a scholarship."

"That's right. Then, after football, I got a job in the college business office while I went to graduate school."

"Sounds like you inherited some your mother's work habits."

"It's more like she pounded them into me. Made me do my homework before I could eat supper. Things like that."

Once again, Mr. Kelly looks at Stanley, then back at Foster. He says, "I think that I would have liked your mother… When you worked for the State as an examiner of public accounts, did you audit any construction projects?"

"Seems like it was hundreds. Most relating to construction or renovation on highways and at colleges, prisons, State buildings, and State parks, that sort of thing."

Mr. Kelly nods as he looks at his notes once more. "What about when you were at the AG's office. Did you investigate any shady construction projects?"

"Yeah, dozens of them."

"Ever have to put anybody in jail?"

"Afraid so."

"That's good. That means you'll know how to keep me *out* of jail."

Stanley and Foster smile at each other. Then Stanley says, "Don't pay any attention to that kind of talk, Foster. Jake's probably the most honest man I know."

Stanley looks to Mr. Kelly and says, "Well, Jake, are you convinced that Foster might be your man?"

"Getting close. One more thing, Foster. Sometimes we have to work odd hours or long hours, or on weekends. Would that be a problem? I mean, are you married, and would your wife have a problem with that?"

"Yes, I am married, but odd hours, long hours, and weekends are the norm around here, so that wouldn't be any problem."

"That's good. Got any kids?"

"One girl, Theresa. She's sixteen, and the spitting image of her mother, which is good. I first met Renee when she was a cheerleader at Bama State."

Mr. Kelly is writing some new notes on his legal pad as he says to Stanley, "Tell you what. If there's anybody who I think might be able to take over for Jim and do a good job for me, it's this young man. What I want us to do is have your firm draft a contract for legal services, which I will have Jim review, and then when we're all satisfied with the details, we'll sign the contract and have Foster and Jim work together on whatever projects come up over the next three months, and then, after that, we'll have your firm take over as our outside corporate counsel."

Stanley says, "That sounds good, but first, I want to let Foster know the general provisions before we start on the contract itself, and Jake, please correct me if I say anything that's not what you're looking for." He turns to Foster and says, "I'll give you the *Reader's Digest* version. Jake doesn't need for you to take over Jim's job, *per se*, because Jim is also over personnel and facilities. What Jake has done, because the company is being scaled down, is turn over personnel to his executive vice president and turn over facilities management to his business office. So what he will need you for is serve as an advisor and consultant on anything of a legal nature, excluding litigation or anything along that line. If there is any litigation, either our firm or another firm will handle that, but under a separate agreement.

"We figure that what he needs from us should take an average of eight to ten hours a week, so what I've agreed to is a two-year consultation contact that will make you available for no more five hundred hours a year and no more than twenty hours in any given week. There will also be a provision that if you're not available at a specific time, we will have the option of providing someone else from the firm in your place.

"Jake's company will pay us an hourly fee for your time, as well as all related travel expenses, so you'll file a separate Kelly Construction monthly timesheet with our business office, and they'll take care of the billing. Jake's company will supply you with a laptop that will be hooked into their computer network, so you can do a lot of the work here or at home, or even on the road if that turns out to be the best option on a particular matter.

"Is that about it, Jake? If so, Foster and I will draft a contract and have it to you one day next week."

Mr. Kelly says, "That sounded right to me. Just be sure to include under what conditions the contract can be terminated or amended if either party is dissatisfied with anything once we get underway."

Stanley says, "We always do that, and we also include language stating under what conditions the contract can be extended."

Mr. Kelly smiles and says, "Yeah, do that, just in case we need it, but I don't think extension is gonna be an issue, because on my seventieth birthday, which is two years from last Thursday, I'm putting the company on the market. That will be my birthday present to myself," Then he looks at his watch and says, "Gentlemen, it's been a pleasure, but I've got to get going. Gotta talk to a man about a football stadium."

They all stand up and shake hands once again. Then Mr. Kelly leaves, and Stanley and Foster sit back down. Stanley asks, "Well, what do you think, Foster?"

"Sounds like it's right up my alley. And I think that I like Mr. Kelly."

"Yeah, he's first rate. I've known him for over thirty years. He's a member of our church. He'll be more than fair with you, and the firm."

Foster says, "I know you're busy, so I'll head on back to my office." He begins to stand up when he sees that Stanley is signaling for him to sit back down.

"Not yet. There's something else that I need for you to do for me."

Foster sits down and asks, "What's that?"

"Well, I really hate to lay this on you right now cause I know you've got plenty to do, but our firm just got appointed by Judge Jackson to represent a defendant in a criminal case, and you're the only one here besides Henry with any criminal experience since Harvey left; and Henry's all tied up with the Amalgamated Aluminum fraud case."

"What kind of case is it?"

"Apparently one guy shot another guy during an argument over a drug deal."

"Not exactly my areas of expertise. Anybody die."

"No. And I don't think that it's gonna be too complicated. There were two witnesses to the shooting, including the victim, and the victim was unarmed. Probably gonna be a plea bargain. Do you still have contacts at the DA's office?"

"Yeah, a few. And they owe me some favors for helping them out with some fraud cases when I was with the AG's office."

"What about contacts at the Police Department?"

"Just one, a detective friend of mine."

"Well, maybe you can work something out without too much trouble. What do you say?"

"You're the boss. If you really want me to do it, I can probably work it in, if you can get me some help with the Langston merger."

"I'll get Larry to help you with that."

"Great, that'll work. He's already somewhat familiar with the situation. When and how do you want me to get started on the criminal case?"

"First thing is to meet with Scooter. He's got the file and has been doing some preliminary things on the case. If you can, get with him this afternoon."

"I'll do that. But, speaking of Scooter, I found out that he's somewhat of an expert in genealogy, and I've asked him if he could do some personal research for me on my ancestry. He said he would do it if it was okay with you."

"That's fine with me as long as it doesn't interfere with his firm duties, and as long as you pay his expenses and find some way to compensate him for his work on that. As a matter of fact, he did some personal research for me on my family and found some very interesting things that I had no clue about."

"Interesting. How'd you compensate him for that?"

"I had the firm buy him a new computer and laser printer/copier."

"Well, I don't know if I want to go that far."

"I'm sure y'all can work something out. But, in any case, it's all right with me."

"Thanks, boss."

At ten after two that afternoon, Foster completes a draft report that he is working on for the Langston merger and emails it to his legal assistant, Mary Jo Morton, to review before she sends it to Larry. Then he dials Scooter Riley's number.

Scooter answers, "Hello. Riley here."

"Scooter, it's Foster. I just got instructions from the boss to handle a criminal case you've been working on. Got time to meet on it?"

"Sure, Foster, come on down."

Foster says, "Be right there" and leaves his third floor office to take the stairs to the second floor office that Scooter shares with the firm's other investigator. Foster walks through the open door and sees Scooter at one of his computers. Scooter looks up and says, "Come on in, man. I'll tell what I know so far about that case."

Scooter, a short thin man in his mid-thirties with long reddish hair, gets up from his computer and walks over to a cluttered desk where he picks up two folders. He sits down in a chair at a small side table and signals for Foster to join him. Foster takes a chair then leans back and stretches his stiff neck. He says, "Okay. What do we have here? The boss says it should be something we can plea bargain."

"Here's what I've got from the PD so far. You've got a lowlife drug dealer named Billy Earl Butler from just outside Tallassee who's been accused of shooting another lowlife named Anson Parlor, apparently over some kind of drug dispute. Parlor was shot twice in the belly but somehow is pulling through. He's still in the hospital, but it looks like he's probably gonna make it. My guess is that Butler thought he was dead and wanted to get the hell out of there before anyone showed up. What he didn't know was that Parlor's girlfriend was peeking through a window from inside Parlor's trailer and saw the whole thing. She told the police that she couldn't hear exactly what they were saying but could hear them yelling at each other."

"Where'd it happen?"

"A country road just east of Montgomery but inside the city police jurisdiction."

"Who called the cops?"

"The girlfriend. Said she could tell that Parlor was still alive and she wanted to get an ambulance there as soon as possible."

Foster thought for a moment then asked, "Did she identify the shooter as Butler?"

"Yeah. Said she'd seen him there before."

"Did she see his vehicle?"

"Yeah. A red Ford pickup with an Elmore County tag."

Foster laughs and says, "Well, that certainly doesn't narrow it down a whole lot."

"It doesn't, but, according to a cop I talked to on the phone, she's certain it was Butler."

"Where's Butler now?"

"Right now, county jail. The judge set his bail at a half million dollars because of Butler's record and because he said that it wasn't certain that the victim would pull through. That was last week and it looks like Parlor will make it, so the judge may lower the bail now."

"What kind of record does Butler have?"

"Several juvenile arrests and two drug convictions as an adult. One when he was twenty-one for marijuana possession, pled down from possession with intent to sell, and the last one for dealing weed. They arrested him for dealing weed and coke, but dropped the coke charge for lack of evidence. Butler got a five-year sentence. Was released from Draper around three years ago after serving about three and a half years. He got off parole last year, and he's got a small body shop on some land out in the country next to where his house is. He makes a living doing that, but the Elmore County Sheriff's

Office told MPD that they wouldn't be surprised if he was still dealing. One of the Montgomery cops told me that they had suspected him for years before they finally caught him. I called his former parole office to see if he had any suspicions that Butler was back at it, and he said he had nothing solid but wouldn't be surprised either."

"So we may not have a first-class citizen for a client…How's your relationship with the city police right now?"

Scooter smiles and says, "Pretty good. I got them some help from an FBI friend of mine on rounding up an interstate car theft ring."

"Impressive. How about seeing if we can meet with the investigating officer before we interview Butler?"

"Will do. How's Thursday for you?"

"That'll work if we can make it after three."

"I'll set it up. By the way, what about that family research you asked about?"

"The boss says it's okay as long as it doesn't interfere with your firm work and as long as I pay your expenses and compensate you in some way."

Scooter rubs his chin with his right hand and says, "Compensate, you say… How about you draft a will for me."

"Sounds fair."

"Before you go, I'll need to get a DNA sample and some basic family information."

Scooter picks up a folder and retrieves a form with a list of questions for Foster to answer about his family. Foster looks at it and says, "I'll fill this out tonight and drop it by in the morning." Then Scooter hands him the package for the DNA sample.

At three-fifteen on Thursday, Foster and Scooter are met in the lobby of the Montgomery Police Department by Police Sergeant Fred Cook, a dark burly man with a closely trimmed curly black mustache who looks as though he might be around Scooter's age. Sgt. Cook says hello to Scooter and introduces himself to Foster. Then Foster and Scooter are led to a small conference room where Cook invites them to have a seat.

Cook says, "Counselor, I understand that you were appointed to this case by Judge Jackson and you don't usually handle criminal cases. So, if you have any questions, I'll do my best to answer them. But, first off, I have to say that, as far as we can tell, you've got a guilty career criminal on your hands."

"Well, Sergeant, as you know, my position has to be that my client is innocent until proven guilty, so I'll have to do my best to defend him."

Cook smiles and says, "I know. I'm just glad it's you and not me."

Scooter says, "Fred, is there anything new since I talked to you a couple of weeks ago?"

Cook says, "Yeah, but I'm gonna have to have Detective Thompson give you the details. He'll be here in a few minutes."

Foster asks, "Is that James Thompson?"

"Yeah, do you know him?"

"We worked a couple of fraud cases together back when I was an Assistant AG."

Sgt. Cook says, "That's good. You know Thompson, and Scooter knows me, so we can be straight with each other. None of that legal jibber-jabber."

Just then Det. Thompson walks in holding a letter-size manila envelope in his left hand. He's a tall man of about fifty with a receding blonde hairline. He's dressed in rumpled khaki pants and a wrinkled dark blue dress shirt. He appears surprised as he recognizes Foster and says, "Foster, what the hell are you doing here? You're in the big time now. You don't have to be down here in the gutter with us working folks."

Foster reaches over the conference table to shake James's hand and says, "Frankly, I don't know what the hell I'm doing here. But it's good to see you again. You're looking good. Looks like you've lost some weight."

"Had to. My blood pressure was about to blow the top of my head off. I'm down to one-eighty-four as of this morning."

"Well, I'm proud for you, James. Maybe we can start playing some basketball again. Now, what can you tell me about my innocent client, Mister Butler?"

"Well, the latest piece of evidence that I have on that white trash loser client of yours is probably not gonna make you happy. If Sergeant Cook will load this DVD on that TV over there, you'll see what I mean."

Det. Thompson hands Sgt. Cook the DVD that he has just retrieved from a manila envelope marked "Butler."

As Cook is turning on the DVD player and the TV, and loading the DVD, Thompson says to Foster and Scooter, "This is from a security camera at a gas station about a half mile from the crime scene about thirty minutes before the shooting. It shows Butler filling up his truck and driving away toward Parlor's trailer."

Cook turns to Thompson and asks, "You ready?"

"Yeah."

A grainy black and white video comes on the screen. It shows a tall, thin white man with long light hair under a light-colored cowboy hat putting gas into a dark 2009 Ford F-150 pickup. There is no clear shot of the face of the man, but it can be seen that he's wearing sunglasses.

Foster asks, "Is there a better picture of the face of the man?"

Det. Thompson says, "No, but the guy at the station identified him from the mugshot that we showed him."

Scooter asks, "Did he pay with a credit card at the pump?"

Sgt. Cook says, "No, he came inside and paid with cash, but the inside security camera was out of commission."

Foster asks Thompson, "Have you got the mugshot with you?"

Thompson reaches into his envelope and brings out two photos. He hands them to Foster. Foster sees that one photo is a mugshot and the other is a photo of the same man wearing a tan cowboy hat and dark glasses. The man in the photos looks as though he could be the man that Foster has just seen in the video. In the photos Foster can see that Butler is probably in his mid-to-late forties.

Thompson says, "We had him put on sunglasses similar to the ones in the video for that second shot. That's his cowboy hat. It was on a hat rack in his body shop when he got arrested."

Foster asks, "What about height and weight?"

Sgt. Cook says, "Butler is six foot and one fifty-eight."

Foster is becoming more and more convinced that he needs to start thinking along the lines of discussing a plea bargain with Butler, but his years of experience have taught him to never leave any stone unturned. He asks, "Do you have a photo of Butler's truck?" and Thompson reaches into his envelope and pulls out another photo that he hands to Foster.

Foster says, "Looks like it may be the same truck. Can I get a copy of that video and these photos to show to Butler?"

Det. Thompson says, "Those are your copies of the photos. We haven't made any copies of the DVD yet, but we'll be sure that you get one well before the trial date. By the way, we just impounded the truck. It's in the impound lot if you want to look at it. That's where we took this photo of it."

"You're sure that it's Butler's truck?"

"Yeah. It was towed directly from his body shop, and we checked the tag number and the VIN number. It's definitely his truck."

Det. Thompson pulls a document and two photographs from his envelope and hands them to Foster. He says, "There's a couple of more things you might need to see. This is the girlfriend's signed statement along with two photos of the crime scene."

Foster scans the statement and the photos and hands them to Scooter. Then he thinks for a moment and asks Thompson, "How about if I use my phone to take some shots of the video if you can pause it where I ask you to?"

"Sure, we can do that. Sergeant Cook, run it again in slow motion and stop it when Foster asks you to."

Cook picks up the remote and rewinds the DVD. Then he looks at Foster and nods. Foster pulls his chair up close to the TV and takes his cell phone from inside his coat pocket. He says, "Okay. Start it now and I'll tell you when to pause it."

While Foster is snapping photos of the video, there's a tap on the door, and another man walks in. It's Deputy District Attorney Harry Willis. Mr. Willis lays his hand on Det. Thompson's right shoulder and says, "I heard that you had the eminent J. Foster Thornton in here, but I didn't believe it."

When he hears Mr. Willis's voice, Foster turns and says, "Hey, Harry, what are you doing here?"

"Making sure that you don't mess up my ironclad case against Mr. Billy Earl Butler."

"Really, this is your case?"

"Yep. Ready to plea bargain yet?"

"Can't say. But I'm not sure I like what I've heard so far."

"Well, tell that lowlife Butler that as much as I'd like to take him to trial and let the judge throw the book at him, I might be amenable to giving him a break if he asks me real nicely."

Foster says, "I'll be sure to pass that on to him" then goes back to photographing scenes from the video.

Scooter, who has been quietly taking everything in, asks, "Have y'all recovered a weapon yet?"

Det. Thompson says, "We recovered a thirty-eight from Butler's house, which is the caliber used in the shooting; but we haven't done any ballistics on it yet. Butler's wife said the gun is hers, but that may be because she knows that as an ex-felon her husband can't own a gun."

Scooter asks, "Will you let us know when the ballistics results come in?"

Willis says, "Sure, no problem."

Scooter asks, "Does he have an alibi?"

Cook says, "Not really. Says he was home watching TV at the time of the shooting, but his wife was asleep. Said he was playing cards with his wife and two friends of his until ten o'clock, and then the two friends went home and his wife watched some of the news on TV then went to bed. The shooting took place at about 11:45 that night. We talked to the two friends that he named and they backed his story. But those two friends are fellow losers who would probably say anything he asked them to. Besides that, even if they were there till ten, Butler would have had time to get to Parlor's place by 11:45."

Foster turns to Thompson and asks, "What time was this service station video?"

"11:17 p.m. That's still not a problem as far as time to get there."

Foster asks Scooter to write down those times then goes back to taking photos of the video. Once he finishes, he stands up, thanks Sgt. Cook and says, "I think I've noticed a certain degree of disdain that you gentlemen seem to have toward Mr. Butler. Am I right about that?"

Cook looks at Willis and Thompson. Then he laughs and says, "Mr. Butler is what we in the law enforcement profession call a piece of, shall we say, excrement. He's been nothing but trouble since he was a little kid.

He was always getting into fights, vandalism, petty theft, and such as that when he was a boy, and he gradually got into bigger mischief. It's just that he's been very good at not getting caught at anything serious until we got him on that drug dealing conviction some years back and now on this latest caper. And, frankly, we wouldn't be surprised if he's also using his body shop as a chop shop, but Elmore County's out of our jurisdiction."

Foster says, "I see. It looks like our firm may have gotten a bad deal from Judge Jackson. Maybe I can get him to give it to some other lawyer."

Mr. Willis says, "No. Don't do that. We can be reasonable about this, as long as Butler understands that he doesn't have a snowball's chance in hell of getting off."

Foster nods and says, "I haven't met this fine young man yet, so I can't promise anything, except that I will promise that I'll always be as reasonable as circumstances will allow."

"Fair enough," says Willis. "But there are two things that we have to consider. One thing is exactly what charges the grand jury will come down with once we get all the evidence together. We've got him charged with attempted murder and ex-felon in possession of a firearm. They may indict him for attempted murder or it may be assault with a deadly weapon. And, as far as any drug charges, we're still evaluating that. We could add drug charges later if the evidence is there.

"The other thing is that it'll be a while before Mr. Parlor will be able to testify. We've been holding off on getting his statement because we want to wait until he's strong enough, and clearheaded enough, that there won't be any question about coercion. He's gotta have at least one more surgery, maybe more. So, we don't have any idea of a trial date yet. And there's also the possibility that he may not be clean of a drug crime himself, so we've still got work to do on that angle."

Foster gives that some thought then asks, "Are y'all always this cooperative with defense attorneys?"

Mr. Willis answers, "Only when we know we can't lose."

Foster says, "I see... By the way, how is it y'all know so much about this guy if he lives in Elmore County?"

Det. Thompson says, "He grew up in north Montgomery. My father says that he used to chase after him back when he was on the force. Arrested him twice when he was a juvie."

Everyone except Foster laughs at that. He just shakes his head and waves good bye. Then he motions to Scooter that it's time to leave. When they're in the lobby walking toward the front door, Foster says, "This doesn't look good, my man. But I still want to talk to Butler before I decide how to proceed. Can you set us up a meeting with him one day next week?"

WHEN THEY GET TO the county jail about eleven-thirty on Tuesday, Deputy DA Willis is waiting for them. He shakes hands with them and points toward a door down a hall from where they're standing. He says, "We've got Butler in that interview room where the deputy is standing. I told Butler that you're here to try to help and not to be his usual racist self."

Foster wrinkles his nose and says, "Wait a minute. You mean that we've got someone on our hands who doesn't like the idea of having a lawyer of the colored persuasion defend him."

"Yep, and he really hates the idea of having a black judge."

"I get the feeling that you're enjoying this."

Willis salutes Foster and says, "Drop by my office for a minute after you finish with him."

Foster nods yes, and he and Scooter walk toward the interview room.

The deputy greets them and asks to look inside the small tan briefcase that Scooter is carrying. After he examines the briefcase he opens the door for them.

Butler is sitting in a metal chair at a metal table with a plastic cup in front of him. He's wearing a short sleeve white jail shirt. He has a tan but slightly jaundiced complexion with pink veins showing in his cheeks. He has long stringy blonde hair that's turning gray. Foster saw from Scooter's file that Butler just turned forty-seven. His arms are thin but wiry, the type of arms often seen on a man who works with his hands. Tattooed on his left forearm is a Confederate flag. On his right arm is a pouncing tiger.

Butler takes a sip of water from his cup and stares at Foster, "You my lawyer?"

Foster holds out his open right hand and says, "That's right, Mr. Butler,

I'm Foster Thornton and this is my investigator Walter Riley."

Butler looks at Foster's hand but doesn't take it. Instead he takes another sip of water. He says, "This is a bum rap. I didn't shoot that guy. I hardly knew who he was. I knew his brother Tom years ago but didn't know him.

Foster and Scooter sit down at the table. Scooter takes a yellow legal pad and a pen from his briefcase.

Foster asks, "How'd you know Tom?"

"He was one of my customers back when I was dealing, but I never liked him. He was a weasel."

"What do you mean?"

"He was always trying to weasel some extra dope from me or else jew me down on price."

"When was the last time you saw him?"

"I'm not sure, but it would have been before I went to Draper. I hear he moved to Colorado."

"Did you ever meet Audrey Mitchell, Anson's girlfriend?"

"I don't know. It's possible. What's she look like?"

Scooter says, "Brown hair, average height, medium build, in her mid-thirties."

Butler chuckles and says, "That sounds like my wife. You're gonna have to get me a picture of this girl before I can say one way or the other."

Foster thinks for a moment then says, "Look we're gonna to be straight with you. Both Parlor and the girlfriend identified you as the shooter, and the police have a video of someone who looks just like you at a service station not too far from Parlor's trailer shortly before the time of the shooting."

Butler says, "Well, sure sounds like I did it. But I didn't. Can I see the video?"

Foster says, "We don't have it yet, but I took some photos of parts of the video that I'd like for you to see."

Scooter hands Butler six photos of the photos that Foster took of the video. Four show a man pumping gas and two show the truck driving away.

Butler studies each of the photos and says, "Damn that does look just like me, but it's not me."

Foster asks, "Who is it?"

"Beats me, but it's not me. And that's not my truck."

Foster asks Scooter for the police photo of Butler's truck and hands it to Butler. He says, "This truck, which the police have confirmed as yours, looks exactly like the truck in the video."

"No it don't. See, the side mirrors are different. My truck's got oversize mirrors. I put them on there because I use my truck to pull my car hauler." He hands the photo back to Foster who compares it to the photos of the truck in the video. Scooter, who's looking over Foster's shoulder, says, "Damn, those mirrors do look a little different."

Foster asks, "When did you put the oversized mirrors on?"

"When I bought my hauler, right after I opened my body shop."

"Do you know anyone who has a truck exactly like yours except for the mirrors?"

"Nah, can't think of anybody, but I've seen some others like it around."

Butler leans back in his chair and chuckles. He says, "I probably shouldn't have said nothing. Should have saved that for the trial. That would've made them look pretty stupid."

"Deputy DA Willis says that there doesn't have to be a trial, that he's willing to be reasonable on a plea bargain."

"Well, tell Deputy DA Willis to kiss my ass. I ain't pleading to nothing."

Butler picks up the photos again and looks at one in particular. He says, "Whoever this is in the picture is buying regular. My truck won't run on regular. It takes at least ninety-three octane."

Foster asks, "Why is that?"

"It's not a stock engine. It's a hot rod Cobra engine that I got in trade from one of my customers."

Foster tells Scooter to make a note to go to the impound lot and check the engine in Butler's truck.

Foster says, "The clerk at the service station also identified you from your mugshot."

"What's the clerk's name?"

Scooter looks at his notes and says, "A guy named Andy Norton."

"I don't know no Andy Norton. He's just dead wrong about that being me."

Foster says, "So you don't know anyone who looks a lot like you and drives a red 2009 F-150."

"If I did, I probably wouldn't rat him out."

Scooter looks at Butler a moment, studying his face. He asks, "Do you have any brothers?"

"Yeah, my older brother Joe Albert."

"Could that be him?"

"He's in the Federal pen in Tallahassee."

Foster asks, "What was he convicted of?"

"Robbing a bank in Panama City."

"You sure that he's still there."

"Oh, yeah. Unless he's escaped, which is possible. He escaped one time before, but he got caught about a half a mile from the prison. Dumb bastard."

Scooter makes a note to check on the whereabouts of Joe Albert Butler.

Foster looks at Butler and says, "It looks like you're enjoying this."

"Hell, yeah. For once I get arrested for something I didn't do. When are you gonna get me out of here?"

"Do you want me to try to arrange for a lower bail?"

"No, I want clean out. I'm not gonna waste money on bail."

"I'll do my best. But it sure would help if we could find out who this is in the video, if it's not you."

"It damn sure ain't me. I can tell you that."

Foster says, "Is it all right with you if I have Scooter talk to you wife about this?"

"Absolutely. Her name's Louise. She'll tell you I was home that night."

Scooter asks, "Do you own a thirty-eight caliber handgun?"

"No, but Louise does and she told me the cops confiscated it."

Foster says, "Yeah, they're gonna run ballistics tests on it."

"Fine with me, but they need to get it back to my wife when they're done. She needs it for protection."

"I'll see what I can do…By the way, I heard that you grew up in north Montgomery. So did I. I grew up in Trenholm Court."

"I'll be damned. You went from living in the projects to being a lawyer. That's pretty good. I lived not too far from there on Pollard Street when I was a little kid. We moved to the country when I was about eleven."

Foster is looking at Scooter's notes when he notices that Butler is staring at the scar on his left cheek. Foster says, "Wondering about the scar? It's from a childhood accident."

"How old were you?"

"Eight."

"Damn. That must've been tough. Had it all these years. How old are you now?"

"Forty-five."

"Just a couple of years younger than me."

Scooter asks, "Could we get a DNA sample from you just to have it available if the cops find DNA anywhere."

"Sure, so long as you keep it and don't give it to the cops so they can go smearing my DNA on something."

Foster says, "Well, Mr. Butler, unless Mr. Riley has some questions, I think that'll be it for today. But we'll be getting back to you after we check some things out."

Scooter says, "No questions. I'll come by sometime tomorrow for the DNA sample."

"Okay. But next time you see that sonofabitch Willis tell him that I didn't do it and I'm gonna sue his ass if he don't let me out."

Foster smiles and says, "I'll be sure to tell him that."

On their way to Willis's office, Scooter asks Foster, "What do you think? Is he telling the truth?"

"I get a feeling that he's holding something back, but I'm beginning to think that it might be possible it was someone else who did the shooting. The truck mirrors are definitely different, and we can check out the gasoline angle."

Scooter asks, "What if he changed the mirrors on the night of the shooting and deliberately got regular instead of high test just to throw the police off?"

"Well, unless he knew that the police would find the video and he knew that he was about to get into a dispute with Parlor and shoot him, that wouldn't make any sense. He'd have to be a world class evil genius to come up with something that devious."

Scooter says, "Yeah, I suppose you're right. But according to his prison record, he's a lot smarter than he lets on. He aced his GED and took some college courses at a correctional education center near Draper. His parole officer told me that he was always being suspected of some kind of some shady operation at Draper, but they never could pin anything on him. The parole officer also said that Butler enjoys the hell out of beating the system. Says it's a game to him."

Foster says, "Well, sooner or later we're gonna get to the bottom of this. Next thing I want you to do is check out every red 2009, or any year close to that, F-150 pickup in Elmore County and see if anybody who owns one of them meets Butler's general description."

They get to Mr. Willis's door just as he is arriving there from the other direction with a Chick-fil-A bag in his hand. Willis opens the door and says, "Come on in and tell me what you think of Billy Earl Butler. He's quite a prize, isn't he?"

As they're taking their seats at a small round table in Willis's office, Foster says, "What if that's not Butler at the service station?"

Willis asks, "What do you mean?"

The three of them have an intense discussion of what Foster and Scooter just heard from Butler.

After contemplating what Butler told Foster and looking at the truck photos and the photo showing that regular gas is being rung up, Willis says, "I wouldn't put it past him to set us up with this video. I mean, he's got a body shop. It wouldn't be any problem for him to swap the mirrors and then put them back. And it sure wouldn't be a problem for him to put some regular gas in just to throw us off."

Foster laughs and says, "That exactly what Scooter said. But that doesn't add up to me. I mean if he intended to kill Parlor and didn't know about the girlfriend being there, he would have thought that there'd be no witnesses, because Sergeant Cook told me that there aren't any neighbors close to Parlor's trailer. That means that unless he was positive that he would be blamed in spite of there being no witnesses, he wouldn't have any reason for a gas station charade. Nor would he have concocted any ruse if he went to Parlor's place expecting to make a drug deal with no confrontation.

"I think that we need to check out the mirrors and see if it looks like they've been swapped out and also check the engine in the truck. Have y'all tested the truck for any traces of drugs or gunpowder? And what about Butler's body shop and his house?"

Willis says, "Not yet, but we just got search warrants and that's gonna all get done as soon as possible. We want to get everything nailed down before the preliminary hearing."

Foster says, "How about this. Let's get back together after the drug test and the ballistics tests and examining the truck and the house, and whatever else y'all have warrants for, and see what we have. In the meantime, unless you have some objection, Scooter will interview Miss Mitchell and Mrs. Butler and the two friends who were at Butler's house that night."

Mr. Willis thinks for a moment then says, "That sounds fine, but promise me that if we'll stay straight with you, you'll continue to be straight with us. Because the last thing that I want to have is a bunch of loose ends hanging when this goes to trial, if it does. Is there anything else I need to know today?"

Foster smiles and says, "Yeah, there's one more thing. Butler asked us to make sure we tell that sonofabitch Willis that he didn't do it and that he's gonna sue his ass if he don't let him out."

Willis chuckles and says, "That sounds just like him."

ON FRIDAY MORNING, SCOOTER phones Foster, who is on the road, and tells him that he has interviewed Miss Mitchell, Mrs. Butler and the two friends who were at the Butler house on the night of the shooting. He tells Foster that Miss Mitchell was positive that it was Butler who did the shooting, but also admitted that she had only seen Butler once before and it was at night and at a distance. Scooter goes on to say that from the crime scene photos he could tell that Miss Mitchell would have been fifty feet or more from the shooting when it happened and that the shooting occurred under some overhanging trees at close to midnight, meaning that Parlor and Butler would have been in the dark.

Scooter tells Foster that Mrs. Butler and the two friends all agreed that their canasta game broke up around ten on the night of the shooting. They remembered that because Mrs. Butler wanted to watch the ten o'clock news on TV because she had heard that there had been a fatal accident on I-85.

Scooter goes on to say that he has compiled a list of every red F-150 that is registered in Elmore County that would come close to meeting the description of the vehicle in the gas station video. He says that there are fifteen potential similar trucks, but only two from year 2009. He tells Foster that he found one of the two 2009s, but was unable to locate the other because the owner, who lives in North Elmore, was apparently out of town. He says the one that he was able to locate belongs to a seventy-year-old retired navy veteran who bought him lunch at a local diner and told him that no one else had ever driven his truck but his wife who had recently passed away.

Foster asks Scooter to find out everything that he can about the owner of the other 2009 F-150 and let him know as soon as possible.

Scooter is out of the office when Foster gets back Friday afternoon, but just after Foster gets home he gets a call from Scooter, who is still in North Elmore. Scooter tells Foster that the name of the owner of the truck is Lewis Duncan who is single, thirty-nine years old, and lives with his mother. Scooter says that he talked to the mother and some neighbors, telling them that he needed to get in touch with Duncan about a legal matter. He says that neither the mother nor any of the neighbors knew where Duncan was. The mother said that he had packed up a suitcase and told her that he was going with his girlfriend on her vacation. She said that he'd been gone for about a week and a half and that she was worried because she hadn't heard from him.

Foster asks, "Did you get the girlfriend's name?"

"His mother didn't know it. She said all she knew was that it was some girl from Montgomery."

Foster asks, "What kind of job does Duncan have?"

"His mother said that he's a house painter but doesn't have a full-time job. Said that he just works when he needs some money. She actually seemed a little annoyed at him for running off with his girlfriend and not telling her where he was going. And I got the impression that she was holding something back, but I didn't press her on it. However, some of the neighbors hinted that the boy might be fond of chemical stimulation. One, a kind of rascally old man, came out and called him a coke head."

"Did you ask any of your law enforcement contacts about him?"

"Sure did. One of the Elmore County deputies that I know said that he has long suspected him of dope dealing, but never had any hard evidence of it. But here's the interesting part. According to the deputy, Duncan is a cousin of Billy Earl Butler."

"Interesting. Does he look like Butler?"

"Not really. His mother showed me his picture. Same general build, but with short dark brown hair."

"See if you can get a photo of him from his mother, as well as a photo of his pickup. Also, if you can, get the Sheriff's Office to be on the lookout for him and let you know if they see him."

"Already done. I snapped photos of a few of her pictures with my phone. I'm also wondering about whether or not I can get the mother to make a missing person report. But I don't want to upset her because he may just be out carousing somewhere."

"Yeah, hold off on that. By the way, when I got back I had a message that the Butler preliminary hearing is scheduled for about three weeks from now. Have you heard anything from Willis about their test results?"

"Not yet."

"Do me one more favor. Call your friend at the Elmore County Sherriff's Office and tell him to tell the other deputies that if they hear any rumors on the street about a shooting or a drug deal gone bad, or anything along that line, to let you know."

"Already done."

"And when you see Butler next week, don't tell him about this. I want to first see if there might be any connection here. Just let him know that we're still looking to establish that someone else may have been the shooter."

"Okay."

AT SEVEN-THIRTY ON MONDAY morning, Foster is coming out of the shower when he hears the phone ring. Renee comes to the bathroom door with the phone and calls out, "Phone call. It's Scooter."

Foster wraps a towel around his waist and takes the phone from Renee. "What's up Scooter?"

"Some potentially interesting stuff. It may be nothing, but it looks very intriguing…"

"Enough drama. I'm freezing here. What is it?"

"This morning the Elmore County Sheriff's Office got a phone call from a contractor who's building a house in North Elmore. He was sifting through the trash in the dumpster at his work site looking for piece of scrap lumber to use for a brace when he saw a gun barrel. That's when he called the Sheriff. When the deputy got there he took a photo then started moving the material from around the gun barrel…"

"Come on. You're driving me crazy with this buildup. What'd they find?"

"They found a thirty-eight handgun, a tan cowboy hat, and a long blonde wig."

"Where's that stuff now?"

"They turned it over to Montgomery PD, and they're gonna process it."

"When are we going to know if it has anything to do with our case?"

"Thompson told me that they're expediting it and that he'll get back to us in a few days."

"This is too damn coincidental. If Butler wasn't locked up, I might suspect that he planted that stuff to throw the police off."

Scooter says, "I don't think so. Whoever put it in the dumpster covered it up pretty well. I don't think they anticipated someone digging down that deep into the dumpster."

"Yeah, you're probably right. I'm beginning to sound like you and Willis about Butler's deviousness. Well, anyway, now we've got both Elmore County and Montgomery working on it, so maybe we can get some answers soon."

Scooter says, "One more thing. This afternoon will be a good time for me to get some more info from you for my research on your family.

"I could probably do it around three-thirty or four."

"Four would be a good time for me."

AT A FEW MINUTES after four Foster walks into Scooter's office and sees Scooter at one of his computers looking at some kind of list. Foster asks, "What's that?"

"This is my list of things to do for a background search. I'm gonna print this out for your file and then we can mark off what I've already got and see if there's anything else I need right now."

After the list comes out of the printer Scooter and Foster take seats at Scooter's work table. Scooter hands Foster a yellow legal pad, as well as a copy of the list that just printed out, and says, "Okay. I sent your DNA sample to Ancestry.com and two other resources that I use, and I'm waiting for info from them. But, in the meantime I can look at some census info and city directories and such using what you've already given me."

Foster writes a note on the back of the list saying that Scooter already has the name and last known residences of his mother, his father, and each of his grandparents. He tells Scooter, "Remember, my father left my mother when I was seven, and I have no idea where he lived after that, except that I seem to recall my mother telling me that he was living out of state. And I gave you what city my grandparents on both sides lived in but not their street addresses. And I gave you photos of my mother, my father, and my mother's parents."

Scooter says, "Okay. Let's go over the list again to see if you know anything that I don't already have."

"Let's see, I told you my mother's grandparents' names on her mother's side because they also lived in Montgomery, but I can't recall ever hearing anything about my father's grandparents. And I'm pretty sure that my father's parents are gone now, and so is my grandmother on my mother's side. But my mother's father, Frank Foster, is still alive. He's in a nursing home in Prattville. He's eighty-five now, but he's still pretty sharp. You might want to interview him when you get time. I visited him about a month ago and he was doing pretty well, so he may be able to help you. You know, I've never asked my grandfather anything about his family. I guess I need to do that next time I see him."

"So, what you're telling me is that you don't know anything about either side of your family beyond your grandparents and your mother's maternal grandparents."

"That's right."

"Okay. When you get a chance write down anything else about your grandparents and great-grandparents that you think might be helpful and, if you don't mind, I'd like to see any photos, documents, newspaper articles, obituaries, or anything else of that nature about any of them. By the way, when was the last time you saw your father's parents?"

"Not too long after my father left. I know that they were living in Montgomery at the time, but we never went to see them and they never came to see us, because my mother didn't really care for them. And, as I indicated in the info I gave you, I heard from my mother that they had both passed on somewhere in southern Georgia, it may have been Bainbridge." Scooter nods and writes a note on a form that he has printed out.

After Foster further studies the list that Scooter gave him, he looks at Scooter and says, "I get the feeling that I'm not being real helpful to you. There's so much I don't know."

Scooter holds up what he already has from Foster and says, "No. Believe it not, this is a pretty good start. I've done family histories starting from a lot less. But before we go any further, though, you've gotta tell me what created this sudden interest in your family background."

"Oh, it's not a sudden interest. It's something that I've been wondering about for as long as I can remember, because neither my mother nor her parents ever talked about the family beyond those who were still around."

"Is there anything in particular you're curious about?"

Foster smiles and says, "Scooter, you're very clever. You know exactly what I'm looking for. You can tell by looking at my facial features and those of my mother that somewhere along the along the line there had to be some Caucasian influence."

"You mean like a honky in the woodpile."

Foster laughs out loud. "Exactly. I've always been puzzled about that, because all of my grandparents and my father are dark skinned, but my mother is a good bit lighter. I'm darker than my mother but lighter than my father or any of my grandparents. And I've got this nose that is much more Caucasian-looking than anyone's other than my mother."

Scooter looks at Foster's face and says, "You're right. You've got kind of a Harry Belafonte look about you. And, of course, I kinda thought that was what this was about, but I don't blame you. I had a similar curiosity about my mother's family. She was born and raised in Mexico, and I only met her parents a couple of times because they were living in Mexico when I was growing up, and they still live in Mexico. And I don't speak much Spanish, so I couldn't ask them anything about that side of the family even when I did see them. But I was very curious about my Mexican heritage, and that's what got me started on doing family research."

"You damn sure don't look Mexican."

"No. I look just like my Irish father. He met my mother when he was in the Air Force at Lackland Air Force Base in Texas and she was working as a clerk at the BX. She was in America on a student visa going to college in Texas."

"How long was your father in the Air Force?"

"Twenty-four years. He was a jet mechanic, and we went all over the world when I was growing up. That's how I wound up in Montgomery. He was stationed at Maxwell. My mother and he are both retired now, living in Boca Raton."

"Well, what did you find out about your Mexican heritage? Are you related to Poncho Villa?"

Scooter shakes his head. "No, nothing that interesting, unfortunately. Mostly farmers, factory workers, and school teachers. That's what was my mother was, a high school teacher."

"I'll bet she taught Spanish."

"No. English."

They both chuckle at that, then Scooter says, "Well, we both have a lot to do, so I won't take any more of your time today. But I'll let you know if I find out anything interesting about your family."

"Like I'm related to George Washington."

"Yeah, I'll be sure to let you know right away if I find out that you're related to George Washington."

Ten days later, Foster arrives at his office after finally wrapping up the Langston merger. His secretary tells him that he had a call from Deputy DA Willis who left a number for him to call back. Foster lays down his briefcase on his desk. Then he takes off his coat and hangs it on the coat rack next to the door. He takes a couple of deep breaths and dials the number that

Willis left for him. The number rings three times before he hears, "Hello. Harry Willis here."

"Harry, it's Foster. I sure hope that you were calling with good news. I finally finished something that I had been working on for over three months, and I've got about one nerve left."

"Foster, I owe you one. You and Scooter led us right to the culprit in this Parlor shooting, and to my great chagrin, it wasn't Butler."

"Was it Duncan?"

"Everything points that way. Based on Duncan's being Butler's cousin and having suddenly taken off in a red pickup that matched the one from the shooting, we got warrants to test for DNA on the hat and wig that we got from Elmore County and to search Duncan's house and get a sample of his DNA. The DNA that we got from some items in Duncan's bedroom and bathroom matched the DNA inside the hat and on the wig, and the wig also had a trace of gunpowder residue. We also found what looked like a fingerprint of blood on the brim of the cowboy hat. We couldn't read the print, it was too smeared; but the blood was Anson Parlor's."

"Very interesting. What about the gun that was in the dumpster?"

"It was definitely the weapon used in the shooting. And just to be sure about whether or not anything pointed to Butler, we executed the warrants that we already had in Butler's case to search Butler's house, his truck, and his body shop. We found no traces of drugs or gunpowder in the truck, and we found nothing incriminating in the house or the body shop. We even looked at his emails, text messages, and phone records, and there was nothing there either. Nothing suspicious and nothing connecting him to Duncan.

"By the way, one of our mechanics confirmed that the big mirrors on Butler's truck had probably been on there for a long time. The mechanic said he saw one spot where a scratch on the truck had rusted into the mirror support. We even checked for the hot rod Cobra engine and, sure enough, that's what was in the truck. And by that time we had the ballistics results from the gun found in Butler's house, and there was no match. And just to be triply sure, I had one of our guys get videotaped at the gas station wearing the wig and cowboy hat found in the dumpster, and in that video they looked identical to the hair and hat in the evidence video."

"Man, if you're nothing else, you are thorough."

"Well, I had convinced myself that Butler was involved, so I had to make absolutely certain. If he was involved, he did a damn good job of covering his tracks. But, to be honest, I still can't rule him out. I've just got nothing to back that up. All I've got is my gut feeling."

Foster, who has been taking notes of everything that Willis is telling him, looks through his notes then says, "So, what I'm hearing from you is that everything points to Duncan and nothing points to Butler."

"Not quite. We've still got two eye witnesses who say it was Butler."

"Well, Harry, the way I see it is that they saw someone in a cowboy hat, sunglasses, and a wig who looked like Butler in the dark. And in the girlfriend's case, in the dark from fifty-three feet away looking between the blinds. I still think that a more likely scenario is that Duncan had been disguising himself as Butler in order to step in and rekindle Butler's old drug business after Butler was released from prison, because he knew that Butler himself would stay out of the business, at least for a while, knowing that the police would be watching him."

"That does sound plausible. We were thinking along that line, so we had one of our police artists take a photo of Duncan that we got from his bedroom and add the cowboy hat, blond wig, and sunglasses. And, sure enough, it looked exactly like Butler in his cowboy hat and sunglasses. Also, you have to take into account that Butler was away for about four years, counting his jail time and prison time, so his customers hadn't seen him for at least that long. That would have made it easier for Duncan to pull off that kind of scam."

Foster says, "That's true. Any leads on Duncan's whereabouts?"

"Just one. We found out that on the day he disappeared one of the neighbors saw him in his truck headed west. We've got a nationwide alert out on Duncan and the truck. We'll find him, no doubt. When we do bring him in, do you want to defend him, too?"

"Hell, no. I don't want anything else to do with that outlaw family."

Willis snickers. He says, "That's what I figured. With regard to Butler, As much as I hate to do it, I'm gonna move for dismissal, because we've got nothing to hold him on right now. But my gut still tells me that Butler was involved somehow."

"Man, you've gotta let go of Butler in this case. If he's the career criminal that y'all say he is, you'll catch him on something else sooner or later."

"You're only saying that to make me feel good."

SHORTLY AFTER FOSTER GETS off the phone call to Willis, he takes another deep breath and heads for Scooter's office. When he gets there, Scooter is sitting at his desk looking at several charts.

Scooter says, "I'm glad you're here Foster. I'm just now finishing up my charts on your family, and it has gotten really interesting, and not necessarily in a good way."

"That's great Scooter, but I've gotta tell you something first. Harry Willis and I just had a long talk, and it looks like your suspicion was correct. All the DNA and gun evidence points to Duncan, and they found nothing other than the two witnesses that points to Butler. And I convinced Harry that the witnesses' testimony would be very shaky and wouldn't hold up at trial."

"Does that mean we won?"

"Yeah it does. The DA's office and I are gonna file a joint motion for dismissal."

"That does sound like a win. Can I be the one to tell Butler?"

"If you want, but just make sure that he knows that it's not done until the judge grants our motion. And don't let on yet that you're the one who found Duncan. Let's wait and see what happens."

Scooter says, "Okay. I'll tell him tomorrow about the motion, but I'll tell him not to celebrate until the judge grants it. In the meantime, congratulations to us."

"You deserve all the credit, Scooter, for finding Duncan and getting Elmore County on his trail."

"Yes, I do, don't I. Yea me."

"Now what's this about my family?"

"That news about Butler is perfect timing, because there was an interesting finding in my research."

"What's that?"

"It appears that you and a certain Billy Earl Butler are related."

"Well, if that's true, I hope it's a very, very, very distant relationship."

"Nope, pretty close."

Foster, who has been standing all this time, takes a seat in front of Scooter's desk. He lets out a long sigh and says, "Go ahead. I'm ready. Tell me what you've got."

"Well, you've gotta listen carefully here because it's kinda complicated. It turns out that your grandfather Frank is not actually your mother's father."

"What? He was there when my mother was born. I've seen a picture of him holding my mother in the hospital the day that she was born."

"That may be so, but do you know that your grandfather and grandmother didn't get married until your grandmother was four months pregnant."

"No, I've never heard that before. That's a shocker. So, if Grandpa Frank is not my grandfather, who do you think is my grandfather?"

"A man named Erick Kelly."

"Erick Kelly. Are you saying that he's the honky in the woodpile?"

"Almost certainly. It started with a match that I got on your Ancestry dot com DNA. A woman named Patricia Armstrong. It turns out that she's a grandniece of Erick Kelly. Kelly is her grandmother's brother. She lives in Atlanta, but when she was a small child she lived in north Montgomery. She couldn't remember the street, but I did some research and found that it was Pollard Street.

"When I first contacted her I told her that I was doing some research for a possible relative of hers and asked if she would get in touch with me either by message or by phone. And she was nice enough to call me at the number I sent her and was very helpful. When I asked about any relatives other than her immediate family who ever lived in the Montgomery area, she gave me some names that included Erick Kelly, who it just so happens was living on Columbus Street right across from Trenholm Court the year that your mother was born. Once I found that out, I started putting the pieces together.

"I told Patricia that I couldn't yet disclose who my subject was, but she said that was all right. She only asked that in return I let her know of any information I came across that would be helpful to her in her ancestry research on some relatives in South Carolina. I told her that I was a professional investigator and had resources that she wouldn't have and that I would be glad to use my resources on her behalf if she could first help me with my research and then, after that, let me know what she needed to find out about her South Carolina ancestors.

"Are you telling me that she's related to Butler."

"His sister."

"Good Lord. That means that my biological grandfather Erick is also Butler's great uncle. Foster points at Scooter and says, "You've gotta give me your word that you won't ever tell anybody that... But how did my grandmother get hooked up with Erick Kelly in the first place?"

"Please bear in mind that I used up all my resources to figure out this puzzle. Here's how it goes. Erick Kelly lived on Columbus Street right across from where Trenholm Court was built in 1952. His wife was bedridden for a long time with some sort of serious illness. Your grandmother, who was a teenager at the time, moved into Trenholm Court with her family when it first opened, and she wound up being the Kellys' housekeeper and cook for a couple of years, and near the end of that time she got pregnant by Kelly. It was during that period that Mrs. Kelly had gotten in really bad shape, and your grandmother lived in their house for several months to take care of her."

Foster leans back and looks toward the ceiling. He says, "You know what, I have a vague memory of my grandmother and my mother talking to each other about a 'Mr. Erick.' It was right after my father left my mother, so I must have been about seven at the time. And I can't be sure of exactly what I heard, but it was something about my grandmother getting a loan from Mr. Erick to help my mother out financially. I must have assumed at the time that Mr. Erick was a family friend."

"Do you remember ever hearing anything else about that loan or Mr. Erick?"

"I remember my grandmother, the next day, bringing an envelope to my mother and saying, 'Don't worry about paying it back, it's okay', or something like that, and my mother hugging her mother. But that's the only time that I heard mention of Mr. Erick… No. Wait a minute. That's not true. I remember that my mother mentioned either that Christmas or the next that we got a card from Mr. Erick."

"It was probably the next Christmas. That would have been the year that Erick Kelly moved to Augusta, Georgia to work at Fort Gordon?"

"Was he in the military?"

"Not then. He was in his about sixty by that time. He had served in the Army Engineers right near the end of World War Two, but at the time that we're talking about he was a carpenter and house painter. He worked for a long time on a maintenance crew at Maxwell, but in early 1985, he was hired as supervisor of a maintenance crew at Fort Gordon and wound up retiring in Augusta. He died there and was buried there about a year after he retired. I made a copy of his obituary for you."

"Thanks. Next time I'm over that way I'll go visit his grave. What about his invalid wife? What happened to her?

"She died pretty young while he was still in Montgomery."

"You amaze me, Scooter. How in the world did you find all of this out?"

"Hey, this is what I do. But once everything started pointing toward Erick Kelly, I went to an impeccable source."

"Who was that?"

"Your grandfather Frank."

"What did he tell you?"

"He confirmed that what I had been surmising was correct and filled in some of the missing details. He asked me if I had told you yet, and I said no. He told me that it had been on his mind for a long time to let you know the truth before he died, but he was afraid of how you might take it. And, you know something, your grandfather Frank has to be one of the nicest people I've ever met. I wish that I had a grandfather that nice. He also told me that Erick Kelly never knew that your mother was his child. Your grandmother told Frank she had prayed on it, and God let her know that he would provide for her. Frank said that let him know that he would provide for her. Frank said that she always told him he was God's gift to her. He started tearing up when he told me that."

Foster says, "He's a jewel, and I'm ashamed to say I don't go to see him often enough. I'm gonna call him as soon as I get back to my office and thank him for everything that he ever did for us and tell him that no matter who my biological grandfather was, he's my true grandfather.

"You know, he worked all his adult life as a janitor for the county school system, but he was a proud man and always looked sharp and carried himself like a gentleman. I learned a lot from him, and I probably never told him how much he means to me. But did he tell you how he wound up married to my grandmother?"

Scooter says, "He said that he had loved her since he was a little boy living in the house next door to her, but she always acted like he was beneath her. Then when he was nineteen, he overheard his mother and your grandmother's mother talking to each other about the predicament that your grandmother was in. He said that without a second thought he went over to your grandmother's apartment and told her that he had always loved her and if she would marry him, he would always take care of her. He told her that he knew about her situation, but that it didn't matter to him. He would take care of that baby like it was his own."

"You know, that sounds just like him. And I never saw a couple who were happier with each other than they were. I just can't believe that this never got talked about among the family."

Scooter says, "People were different back then."

Foster says, "Yeah, I suppose so. Man, I can never thank you enough for all the work that you must have put into this. Drafting your will won't be enough. Just let me what else I can do for you. But first you've got to promise me something. You will never tell a soul that I am related to Billy Earl Butler. And I mean nobody."

"Okay, Foster. That'll be our little secret. But I'm gonna take you up right now on your offer to do something for me."

"You name it. It's yours."

"Tell me how you got that scar on your left cheek."

Foster takes a deep breath and says, "Okay, I'm a man of my word. Here's what happened. When I was eight years old, I was across Columbus Street from our Trenholm Court apartment when this little white kid with a blond crew cut who looked to be a couple of years older than me, but about the same height, because I was tall for my age, came up to me and said, "Hey, nigger, I hear your mama's a whore."

"Man, that's cold. What'd you do?"

"I hit him right between the eyes and knocked him on his ass. But just as I was turning to walk away he jumped up and hit me on the left side of my head across my ear and cheek with a piece of lumber that he found lying on the ground next to where he fell. He knocked the hell out of me then dropped the piece of wood and ran off. And I never saw him again.

"My ear was ringing like crazy and my left cheek was cut wide open. And I was barely able to keep from fainting from the pain. Fortunately, a neighbor lady saw me standing there bleeding, and she took me to her apartment and cleaned me up and put alcohol on the wound. Then she had me hold a rag tight down on it while she took me to her doctor."

"Where was your mother?"

"She was working."

"Anyhow, this doctor, an old black man, was probably a good doctor, but he was no cosmetic surgeon. He sewed me up with some ragged looking stitches and put a bandage on the wound. I told him about the ringing in my ear and was told not to worry, that it would go away. What he didn't know was that the impact of the blow had damaged my left ear drum, and I gradually lost almost all my hearing in that ear. When my mother found out about the attack, she almost went crazy, because I was her baby and all she had. But she took good care of my wound. She made sure that it was kept clean and didn't get infected. And she would put a warm compress on my ear to keep it from hurting so much. Fortunately, this was during the summer, so school was out and I could stay home and take care of my injuries."

"I didn't know you couldn't hear out of your left ear."

"Well, I can now because I've had surgery on it and I'm wearing a hearing aid. But for years, I was practically deaf in that ear."

"Did y'all ever find out who the white kid was?"

"No. But he must have lived around there somewhere. He just had the good sense not to come around our block any more. My mother made out a police report, but without a better description they didn't have much of chance of finding him, if they even wanted to. You know how things were back then."

"Yeah. But your scar doesn't look that bad now. Have you had surgery on that too?"

"Three times over the years. And each time it came out a little better."

"I'll bet you'd like to get your hands on that little white kid now."

"You know, I probably should thank him. Because when I was growing up after that I had a hard time making friends, being half deaf and having that ugly scar on my face, so I became my own best friend. I knew that I might be unpleasant to look at, but I was strong and I was smart. So I put everything I had into making myself stronger and smarter. When I wasn't studying, I was working out or running. And that perseverance and discipline are what eventually took me to where I am now. Whereas, if I had been just an average little poor black kid in my neighborhood, I might have just cruised along like most of them did and maybe wound up on the other side of the law. Who knows? So, I bear no grudge against the kid who whacked me across the head. He helped me get where I am."

"You're a better man than I am. I'd want to stomp a hole in him."

Foster laughs. "Yeah, I hear that you Mexicans can be mean as hell when you're provoked."

"Si, Senor."

A FEW DAYS LATER, Judge Jackson grants the joint motion and dismisses the charges against Butler. On his way home from the city impound lot where he has picked up his truck, Butler stops at Bubba's café, a small eatery in a rundown building on a back street in north Montgomery. As Butler walks in he sees that the lunch crowd has thinned out. Only two tables are occupied. Bubba Grant, the proprietor, is standing behind the linoleum-topped counter wiping his hands on a long white towel. He says "Hey, Billy Earl, I heard you was locked up. You out on bail?"

"Nah, Bubba, the charges were dropped on account of they found out that somebody else did it."

"That's great news, man. That means that lunch is on the house. How about pork chops and greens?"

"Sounds good, but I don't have time right now. I'm on my way home. I just came in to borrow your phone for a minute."

Bubba says "Sure" and hands Billy Earl a cordless phone from behind the counter.

Butler walks to the back of the café and takes a corner seat. He dials a number, and when he gets an answer, he says into the phone, "Mr. Smith, if you still want me to give you an estimate on that paint job, you can bring your car by this afternoon. I'll be at the shop in about forty-five minutes."

After listening to whoever was on the other end of the call Butler says, "Okay, I'll see you then."

He hands the phone back to Bubba and says, "Thanks for the phone. Can I get a rain check on lunch?

Bubba says, "Sure, anytime." Then they shake hands and Billy Earl walks out the door to get into his truck. When he gets to his body shop his wife Louise greets him with a big smile, a hug, and a fried baloney sandwich with Fritos on the side. Butler gobbles down the sandwich and the Fritos, finishes off his Pepsi, and says, "Thanks, babe. Can I meet you back at the house in a little while? I've got a customer coming in a few minutes. Shouldn't take too long."

Louise says, "Fine. Just don't be too long. I've missed you." Then she kisses him on the cheek, takes his plate, and walks back toward the house.

In about ten minutes, a silver 2014 BMW X1 sedan drives pulls into the body shop lot and parks in front of where Butler is standing with a clipboard. A chubby, balding middle-aged man in gray slacks and a light blue dress shirt gets out of the BMW and shakes Butler's hand. Then he grabs him by the shoulders and says, "Good to see you again, man. I was getting worried."

"Me, too. I thought they were gonna cook up some bogus evidence and do my ass in, but I had a good lawyer, a sharp black guy."

"Yeah, I know. I saw him on the news the other night walking into the courthouse. Couldn't believe you had a black lawyer. My wife and I both thought that was hilarious. But it turned out that he did right by you, and you have no idea how glad I am that the law didn't get to Lewis Duncan before our guys did. I know he's your cousin and all, but he screwed up big. I have no goddam idea why he shot Parlor. All he was supposed to do was collect a couple of thousand that Parlor owed us, nothing worth shooting anybody over. I think Lewis might have been getting to where he was believing that he was a drug kingpin like you see on TV. It probably wouldn't have been long before we would have had to drop him anyway.

"But I gotta say that scheme you came up with of having him impersonate you with your old customers and your middlemen was sheer genius. Nobody, and I mean nobody, ever suspected that it wasn't really you."

Butler says, "No. But you gotta remember that the plan was that Lewis would always operate late at night and never put on the hat and wig until just before he got to wherever he was going, and then take them off just as soon as he got back on the road. That way he could drive right by the cops and not even get their attention. Instead, he's driving around in that getup and getting himself videotaped at a gas station. I don't know what that dumb bastard was thinking. That almost got my ass sent back to the joint."

"Mr. Smith" says, "Yeah, he called me at about one o'clock the night that it happened from some Seven Eleven down the road from his house. I told him to ditch the gun and the disguise, and get the truck professionally cleaned the next day. Then to lay low until I got back to him. At that time I had no way of knowing about the gas station video or that he had been driving around with the wig and hat on. Until I heard about the video I thought that it was just the girlfriend who was the problem, because Anson would never have IDed you on his own. He knows better than that."

Smith shakes his head and asks, "Why in the world do you think Lewis was driving around like that, or, more important, why in the hell did he think that he needed to shoot Anson? That didn't accomplish a goddam thing."

Butler says, "Well, I've been kicking myself in the ass, because I taught him to dress like me, talk like me, walk like me, and stand like me, but I didn't teach how to think like me and not sample the merchandise."

Smith says, "I was hearing some rumors that he might be getting a little too fond of the bugger sugar. But, he was still getting the job done, so I didn't give it much thought." Then Smith hesitates a moment as though he's trying to remember something before he says, "You know what, I hadn't thought about it, but I don't think I've ever seen you take a hit of anything."

Butler says, "There's a reason they call it 'dope.' It's for losers." Then he laughs and says, "But I can't say too much because there's no telling how many brain cells of mine Mr. Jack Black and Mr. Bud Weiser have walked off with over the years. And now my liver's shot. So maybe I'm not so smart, either. My doctor says I may need a liver transplant in a couple of years. So, I've just about cut out drinking, too."

Butler looks up toward the sky and says, "Whatever it was that got into Lewis's head, it almost got my ass nailed. Think about that. Due to his stupidity I could've been locked up for God knows how long for something I didn't even do." Then he smiles and says, "Ain't that a bitch? After all the crap that I've done in my life and never got caught on, I could've been convicted of something that fool did… Say, what'd you mean when you said that our guys got to Lewis before the law did?"

"I mean they found him first, before the cops did. On the other side of Mississippi, near the Arkansas line. Lord knows where he was headed."

"What'd they do with him?"

"You don't want to know."

"What about the pickup?"

"Let's just say that neither of them will ever be seen again."

Butler stares down at pavement for a moment. Then he takes a deep breath and sighs before he says, "Well, I never cared that much for Lewis anyway, but this is gonna kill his mama. She loves that boy like you wouldn't believe. He was her only child, and her husband ran off with some honky-tonk whore a long time ago.

"But I understand. Business is business. And we both know that if the cops ever caught Lewis and put the squeeze on him, you and me, and a bunch of other people, would have had to hightail it to Mexico, because he would have blabbed his ass off."

Smith says, "Yeah." Then he reaches into his shirt pocket for his Marlboros.

Butler starts taking a slow walk around the car as if he's examining it for dents. When he gets to the other side of the car, he takes a pen from his shirt pocket and starts writing on a form that's attached to the clipboard he's holding. He signals for Smith to come around the car and join him. Butler points toward the back door of the car, then down to his clipboard. Mr. Smith looks at the form and sees that Butler has written in block letters COPS.

Butler looks at Smith as though he's asking him a question, but what he says in a very soft voice not much above a whisper is, "Don't look now, but there's a silver Toyota Corolla down the road, and I recognize one of the guys in it. Deputy Clark from the Sheriff's office."

Smith points at the clip board and says in a low voice, "They won't know who I am, but I should probably get on out of here. We can talk later."

Butler says, "They're probably gonna run your tag."

"That's all right. The car's clean. It's my mother-in-law's."

Butler taps the clipboard and says, "Don't go quite yet." He looks directly at Smith and says, "You know that this has to be it for you and me. There's gonna be just too much heat for me to stay in the business. Can you clear that for me with the Texas bunch?"

"They'll understand. But they're not gonna let you go that easy. You're too valuable to them."

"Well, tell Texas that I hate to walk away right now cause I need just a little more money for my liver transplant, when that time comes. But that's the way it goes. Sometimes you win, sometimes you lose, and…"

Mr. Smith says, "Sometimes you get rained out." Then he says, "I had a feeling you'd be telling me this, that's why I called Texas right after you called me today."

"And…"

"As I said, they understand the situation, and they're gonna shut down distribution in this immediate area till things cool down, but they've got another job for you that pretty much eliminates the risk you're worried about."

Butler stares at Smith for a moment then says, "Yeah, what's that?"

"Consultant."

"Exactly what does that mean?"

"That means that whenever they're looking at a new area or a new operation anywhere in this part of the state, someone will get in touch with you and pick your brain about how to set it up."

"Is there money in that?"

"Oh, yeah. Somebody with your smarts and expertise can save them a lot of time and a lot of grief, so you'll be well compensated. Just how much, of course, will depend on how lucrative the operation is that you help them on."

Butler walks around to the rear of the car, ostensibly looking at the truck lid. Then he walks back to where Smith is standing. He says, "Tell you what, partner. That sounds like something I could live with. Tell the boys I'm agreeable to doing that, but *only* that. I ain't doing nothing that could get my ass in a crack again. I'm getting too old for that, and the law in Elmore County and Montgomery has just got a little too eager to nail my ass. And I hate to say it, cause I hate cops, but they're pretty damn good at what they do." He snickers at the thought that he just complimented the police.

Down the road in the unmarked Toyota sedan Deputy Harris asks Deputy Carpenter, "Who's that with Butler?"

"Never seen him before. Could be just a customer, but we can run his tag when we get back to the office. We can probably get a good look at it when he leaves."

Butler takes a blank form from his clipboard and hands it to Mr. Smith. Smith looks at it then folds it twice and puts it in his shirt pocket. Butler follows Smith to his open car door, and Smith extends his right hand to Butler. Butler takes Smith's meaty hand in both of his and says, "I'm gonna miss working with you, man, but there's one thing that I gotta tell you before you go, cause I've got to tell somebody, and you're the only one who can keep it to himself."

"What's that?"

"You remember that story I told you one time about me taking a one by two and whacking a colored kid alongside his head and busting his cheek wide open?"

"Yeah. I remember that story. It was down on Columbus Street, right, when you were about ten years old. What about it?"

"I think I found that boy."

Smith looks surprised. "No way. How'd that happen?"

Butler starts laughing uncontrollably. Smith, who is still standing next to the BMW with his hand on the open door, stares at Butler and says, "What's so damn funny, Billy Earl?"

Butler, still giggling, chokes out, "He's my lawyer, or *was* my lawyer."

Smith takes that in, then says, "I'll be damned. Have you told him that?"

"Hell, no. Did you see the size of that sonofabitch. He'd stomp a hole in my ass. And you better not tell anybody either. I don't want that getting back to him, ever."

"No problem, Billy Earl. That'll be our little secret."

A WEEK LATER FOSTER is making his first visit to Kelly Construction where he is given a tour of the company headquarters by Jim Lord and Jake Kelly. In the main lobby of the central office is a wall of photos of members of the Kelly family, along with photos of some of their bigger construction projects. As he is taking in the photos, Foster asks Jake, "Did you ever know a guy named Erick Kelly?"

"I didn't know him, but I remember the name. He worked some for my father years ago, but moved off to Georgia if I remember correctly. I remember that my father and he used to call each another once in a while. Why do you ask?"

"He used to live in my old neighborhood. Was he a relative of your father?"

"No. We were Irish Kellys, and he was a German Kelly. But my father was really fond of him. Said he was a first rate guy as well as a master carpenter. As a matter of fact, he built the bookshelves in the library in the house where I grew up. Did a great job. Gosh, I hadn't heard that name in years. But, now that you mention it, I do recall my father telling me that Erick had once lived down on Columbus Street. My dad said that once in a while Erick and he would stop by after work at a little joint down the street from Erick's house called the Rendezvous and drink a few beers."

"Yeah, Erick Kelly's house was right across the street from where my mother and I lived. She knew him when she was a little girl. And I do remember the Rendezvous. It was real popular among the house painters in particular. Was in a little white concrete building. Had a loud jukebox that you could hear out on the sidewalk that always played that hillbilly music my mother couldn't stand."

Mr. Kelly looks at Foster and smiles. He says, "Small world, Foster. You just never know who's connected to whom, do you, son?"

"No sir. You never do."

Smokey Johnson's Guitar

Such sweet compulsion doth in music lie.

JOHN MILTON

PART I

It's a warm summer afternoon in Potts Camp, Mississippi, a small town about fifty-five miles southeast of Memphis. Dr. William Russell Harris, whom his friends call "W. R.", is standing in the open front door of his pawnshop on Church Street. He's smoking a cigarette and savoring the smell of burning hickory emanating from nearby Dean's Barbeque.

W. R. is a sixty-five-year-old bachelor. He has longish brown hair, and regular tennis playing keeps him tan and in pretty good shape. He's wearing gray corduroy slacks and a short-sleeve light blue work shirt with a torn left pocket. He's a native of Potts Camp and had been a professor of English at the University of Mississippi until two years ago, when he retired after 30 years of service.

Prior to his career in education, W. R. had spent eight years in the Marines as an infantry officer. It was while he was in the Marines that he attained his masters and doctorate degrees in English. His specialty is Southern Literature, and he has published three books on the works of Southern authors.

His interest in Southern Literature had ultimately led him to study Southern culture and Southern music, and he had used his skills as a country guitar player to learn to play Mississippi blues. Although he is not a master of either style, he can play both hill country blues and Delta blues.

While he was at Ole Miss, W. R. taught Southern culture courses as well as English and literature courses. However, during the final six years of his career, he taught only graduate courses in literature and writing.

Three years before he retired, W. R. inherited the Harris Pawn Shop from his father, who had inherited the shop from *his* father and operated it for over twenty-five years. As far as W. R. knew, the pawn shop was the only place that his father had ever worked, except for two years in the Army, because prior to inheriting the shop, his father had worked at the business for W. R.'s grandfather.

The shop looks like one from an old movie. It's in an aging one-story red brick building with two large front windows encased by black burglar bars. Inside, it has an oak floor, and the walls are paneled in walnut. There are four rectangular metal fluorescent light fixtures hanging from the ceiling by steel chains. In the ceiling is a large antique Hunter ceiling fan, slowly turning, circulating the air in the shop.

As far as W. R. can tell, the shelves on the wall and those that line the floor are the same as when he first set foot in the shop as a child.

Among the items on display in the shop are various types of weapons, TVs, radios, stereo systems, computers, musical instruments, jewelry, clothes, books, military flags and paraphernalia, small appliances, farm implements, and electric tools.

When W. R. first inherited the shop, he hired Buster Murphy, a childhood friend and retired postman, to manage it, with the understanding that W. R. would take over the management of the shop when he retired.

Both Buster and W. R. knew that it had been years since the business had made much of a profit, but they had spent so much time in there when they were growing up that they just couldn't let it die an inglorious death.

Buster still comes around three or four times a week, and will run the shop when W. R. needs to take a day or two off.

W. R. finishes smoking his cigarette, then goes inside and mashes the butt into the heavy glass ashtray that he keeps behind the counter.

When W. R. looks up from his ashtray, he sees a young man opening the front door that W. R. has just closed behind him. As the door opens, the shopkeeper's bell attached to the top of the door jingles.

The young man holds the door open for a young lady who walks in and begins to look around. The man joins her, and the two of them slowly walk around the shop before coming up to where W. R. is adjusting some items in the glass-front display case next to the checkout register.

Both of them are dressed in slim-cut blue jeans. She's wearing a tight pink t-shirt, and he's wearing a loose gray t-shirt on the front of which is a large red circle containing the letters "UC."

The girl is petite with long, straight blonde hair. The man is stocky and tan, with dark curly hair. W. R. immediately pegs them as college students. He smiles and asks, "What can I do for you?"

The young man says, "Hi. Are you Mister Harris?"

"Yes, I am."

"Well, I'm James, and this is my girlfriend Amy, and we were told by a guy down at Flick's gas station that you would know how we could get in touch with a blues musician named Smokey Johnson."

"Why do you need to get in touch with Smokey?"

"Well, we're graduate music students at the University of Chicago, and we're doing research on Southern blues. We were told that Mister Johnson lives in Potts Camp and decided that we would come here and try to interview him."

"Y'all came all the way from Chicago to interview Smokey?"

James says, "Well, actually, we've been to Beale Street in Memphis and also went down to the blues museums at Ole Miss and in Clarksdale. And we thought that since we were so close, we would try to meet up with Smokey Johnson. We tried to do some research on him at Ole Miss, but we couldn't find much information, so we thought that we might try to get it first hand from him."

W. R, says, "I see," then pauses a moment and says, "Well, if you know anything about Smokey, you know that he values his privacy and rarely does interviews. That's probably why you couldn't find much at Ole Miss."

Amy says, "Yes, sir. We've heard that, but we were also told that if anyone could get us an interview, it would be you."

"That's probably true, but it depends on what kind of mood Smokey's in. He can be real hard to get along with."

W. R turns his back to the couple and rubs the back of his neck. After a moment, he turns back around and says, "Look. You two seem like nice young people. I'll give Smokey a call and see if he's home, and, if he is, see what kind of mood he's in."

Amy says, "Oh, thank you so much, Mister Harris. We'd appreciate that very much."

W. R. says, "I'm not promising anything. Y'all can look around some more while I go in the office and give Smokey a call." Then he enters a door marked "OFFICE" and closes it behind him.

Amy turns to James and says, "It looks like he's going to try to help us."

James says, "Yeah, let's keep our fingers crossed."

As they browse through the store, they can hear W. R. talking, but can't make out what he's saying.

In about five minutes, W. R. comes out from his office and says, "Follow me." He leads James and Amy to a wall against which are hanging around a dozen guitars. He points at one of the guitars and says, "You see that Stella Harmony there."

In unison, James and Amy say, "Yes, sir."

"Well, that's Smokey's guitar."

James says, "Wow."

W. R. lets out a long sigh and says, "Well, look, here's the deal. Smokey said that he will give y'all thirty minutes of his time, and maybe play a song or two, if y'all will get his guitar out of hock and also bring him some whiskey."

James and Amy look at each other. James asks W. R., "What would it cost to get the guitar out of hock?"

"I'll check my book and see."

Amy asks, "What about the whiskey?"

"Well, I don't sell liquor, but I've got about half a bottle of Jim Beam that I could give you to take to Smokey, if that'll help y'all."

"We can't take your whiskey. Let us buy it from you."

"Well, let me check on the guitar, and then we'll talk about the whiskey."

W. R. looks at a tag hanging from the Stella, then walks over to a ledger lying beside the cash register. He flips some pages and settles on one. He says, "Smokey pawned the guitar for a hundred dollars, so with interest and fees, it'll cost a hundred eighteen to redeem it."

James asks, "Do you take Visa?"

"Sure do."

"Well, how about if you give us the guitar and the whiskey, and we give you a hundred forty dollars?"

W. R. contemplates James's offer for a moment, and then says, "I can do that. But, you understand that this is Smokey's guitar, and you've got to take it straight to him."

James says, "Yes sir," and hands W. R. his Visa card. W. R. processes the card and gives James a receipt for the charge. Then he gives James a second receipt and says, "Give this to Smokey. It's his receipt for redeeming the guitar."

W. R. walks over to the guitar display and takes down the Stella. He pulls the tag off the guitar and hands the tag to James, along with a ballpoint pen. He says to James, "If you will, put your name and address on the back of this tag so that I'll have a record of who redeemed the guitar."

James writes down the information, and hands the tag back to W. R. W. R. looks at what James has written and then hands the guitar to James. W. R. says, "I told Smokey that if y'all agreed to his terms, you'd be there by three o'clock."

James and Amy both look at their watches. It's two-forty. James asks, "How far is Smokey's house from here?"

W. R. walks over to the counter and writes something on a scrap of paper. He says, "This is Smokey's address. It's not too far. It's on this same street, Church Street, which is also Highway 178." He points to his right and says, "About a half-mile down the road, you'll see Potts Camp Church of Christ on the right. Smokey's house is on the same side as the church, just past there."

W. R. hands the scrap of paper to James and says, "I hope you get a good interview. I know how ornery Smokey can get. Just be patient with him."

Amy puts her hand around James's right arm and says to W. R., "Thank you so much for doing this. I'm sorry we took so much of your time."

"That's all right. But y'all better get going."

James and Amy quickly walk toward the door. As they exit, Amy turns and waves good bye to W. R. He smiles and waves back.

W. R. goes into his office to phone Smokey. When his phone rings, Smokey picks it up and says, "Hello."

"Hello, Smokey. This is W. R. They'll be there shortly with your guitar and whiskey. They'll be in a silver Volvo sedan. Don't be too tough on them."

Smokey laughs and says, "Who, me?" and hangs up the phone. Then he pulls his car keys from his pants pocket and hands them to his fourteen-year-old grandson, who's visiting for the summer. He says, "Pull my car into the garage for me, Jacob. Then close the garage door."

Jacob smiles and says, "Yes sir," then walks out the front door to the driveway, where Smokey's two-year-old black Mercedes GLE sedan is parked.

When Jacob comes back with the keys, James says, "Now, go get my wide brim hat out of the bedroom, and my shades, too."

Part II

A few minutes later, as James is driving down Church Street/Highway 178, Amy spots the Potts Camp Church of Christ and says to James, "There's the church. Smokey's house is supposed to be just past it."

James slows the Volvo down, and Amy looks for the address that W. R. wrote down for them. In a few moments, she points to their right and says, "There it is, the white house."

As they pull into the driveway of the white Craftsman-style bungalow with a gray roof, Amy comments, "This is a nice house. Not quite what I expected."

James says, "There he is on the front porch. I don't know why, but this is making me nervous."

Amy says, "Me, too. We've just got to remember not to get him upset."

James and Amy get out of their car and wave to a tall, muscular gray-haired Black man sitting on the porch in a metal chair. He's wearing a wide brim black hat and extra-dark sunglasses. He's dressed in faded bib overalls and a white t-shirt. He doesn't wave back. He just stares at James and Amy as they slowly walk toward the porch. When they get close enough, James says, "Excuse me, sir. Are you Mister Smokey Johnson?"

"Who wants to know?"

"I'm James and this is Amy. Mister Harris at the pawn shop said that he called and told you we were coming."

"Is that my guitar you're holdin'?"

"Yes, sir, and we also brought some Jim Beam for you that Mister Harris had on hand."

"Gimme the bottle."

James and Amy walk up the steps to the porch. James hands Smokey the bottle, along with the redemption receipt for the guitar. Smokey studies the receipt, then puts it into his front pants pocket.

Then he shakes the whiskey bottle and says, "Hell, this bottle's half empty."

"Sorry, sir. That's what Mister Harris gave us to bring to you."

Smokey sits the bottle down beside his chair and says, "Now hand me my guitar."

James passes him the guitar, and Smokey carefully looks it over, then starts tuning it. When he gets it tuned to his satisfaction, he strums a few chords and says, "Well, I told W. R. I'd give y'all thirty minutes, so you better get started. We already used up about five."

Amy takes a seat in a large metal porch chair that's about six feet from Smokey. James leans against a post at the entrance to the porch and asks, "Can we record this?"

Smokey says, "No. But you can take notes if you want."

Amy pulls a pen and a small writing pad from her purse and says, "Thank you. We'll do that."

Smokey looks at James and asks, "Well, what do you wanna know?"

James says, "First, can you tell us where you grew up and how you learned to play the blues."

Smokey strums an E chord and then leans the guitar against the porch railing. He adjusts his hat. He says, "Well, I growed up on tenant farms down in the Indianola area. I used to help my daddy with the farmin' till I was fifteen and had to leave 'cause the Klan got after me for flirtin' with a White gal."

James looks to see Amy furiously writing her notes and asks, "Where did you go?"

"Memphis. I stayed with my Aunt Bernice up there. That's where I learnt to play the blues." He paused a moment, then continued, "I was shinin' shoes on Beale Street. I used to sing while I was shinin', and one day this

Black man with fancy alligator shoes on came up and said he wanted a shine and he liked my singin'.

"Turns out he was a local bluesman named Arthur Rodell. He used to say he was Rodell from Slidell, but I don't know if that was really where he was from.

"Well, anyway, he took a likin' to me, and one day when I was shinin' his shoes, he tole me that I had some singin' talent and he thought I could be a bluesman, too, if I could learn to play the guitar. I tole him I'd shine his shoes for free if he would teach me to play the guitar, and so two or three days a week he would come by my aunt's house and show me somethin' on the guitar. He loaned me one of his ole guitars to practice on, and this went on for over a year till one night he got shot dead at the club where he was playin'."

Amy softly says, "My Lord," as she's writing down "Arthur Rodell from Slidell" and "shot dead."

James asks, "What did you do after Mister Rodell died?"

"Well, I kept on practicin', sometimes five or six hours a day. All I did was shine shoes, eat, sleep, and practice the blues. I'd listen to the blues station every night on the radio and try to sound like what I heard. I especially liked the ole blues songs. And finally I got good enough to play with some bands, and learnt all I could from every musician I played with."

He pauses again, then says, "Yeah, I played purty reg'lar for a long time, and got purty good, until I got in that trouble in Tennessee. Then, after that, I didn't play for prob'ly forty years or so, until I got a chance to do my Slicktalkin' album a coupla years ago."

James asks, "Would it be all right if I ask what kind of trouble you got into?"

"No. It's none a yo' business."

"Sorry."

Smokey looks at his watch. He asks, "How'd y'all hear about me, anyway. I ain't famous."

James says, "You're famous among the real blues lovers. You'd be surprised how well known you are since you got that review in Downhome Blues Magazine on your Slicktalkin' album. They put you right up there with the three Kings and Stevie Ray, and then, because of that review, everybody had to hear your album."

"That was a good album, but the label cheated me out of my share, on both the playin' and the songwritin.'"

James looks at Amy, then turns to Smokey and says, "I'm sorry. I didn't know that. Do you have a different label now?"

"No, not yet. I've been playin' the clubs around here, you know, like in Oxford and Memphis, and sometimes east Arkansas, and ever once in a while I'll do some studio work for some other player. I hafta do that studio work under another name, because I'm still under contract with those crooks who cheated me."

Smokey looks at his watch and says, "Y'all want me to play a coupla songs 'fore you go?" He reaches for his guitar.

James says, "Before you do, Mister Johnson, can I ask you one more question? Do you plan on making another album anytime soon?"

"Well, there is somethin', but I cain't talk about it yet."

James asks, "Is there anything you can tell us now?"

"Don't test me, son."

"Yes sir."

Smokey starts to strum a Delta blues progression and sing a song that neither James nor Amy has heard before. It's a funky blues song about drowning a woman in a catfish pond "because she wouldn't gimme none." Amy squirms a little as she is writing notes about the song.

Smokey finishes the song and says, "That might be on my next album." Then he looks at his watch again and, even though Amy and James have only been there about fifteen minutes, says, "I'll play a few bars of another new one, and then y'all are gonna hafta go."

As Smokey is playing the opening to another song, James says, "Well, thank you for your time, Mister Johnson, but I have one more question. Where'd you get that Stella guitar? It looks like a model from the 1950s."

Smokey strums an A minor, then says, "This is the guitar that Arthur Rodell loaned me to practice on."

James says "Wow" as he looks at Amy writing that down. Then he turns to Smokey and says, "Well, thank you for your time, sir. Can we take a photo?"

"No, and don't take a picture of my house, neither."

James and Amy look at each other, and then they stand up and say goodbye to Smokey. They walk down the porch steps and across the yard to their car.

As they drive off, Amy waves goodbye to Smokey. He ignores her and goes back to playing his guitar.

Part III

About an hour later, back at the pawn shop, W. R. is rearranging one of his display shelves when he hears the jingle of the shopkeeper's bell. He turns and sees that it's Dr. Ralph Thornton, one of his former colleagues at Ole Miss. Ralph has been an economics professor at the University for sixteen years. The last time that W. R. saw Ralph was at Square Books in Oxford about six months earlier.

As he's walking to the door to greet Dr. Thornton, W. R. says, "Hey, Ralph. What are you doing here on a school day? Did the University go out of business?"

"Not yet. Good to see you, W. R. No, I was at an economics conference over in Huntsville, and I thought I'd stop by here on the way home."

Ralph looks around and says, "Nice little shop you've got here. Very quaint."

"Thanks, Ralph . . . What was happening at the economics conference?"

"Well, the younger economists were conferring about how the government needed to exercise more control over large corporations, and the older economists were conferring about how the younger economists were a bunch of dumbasses.

"Actually, the only reason I went was to promote my new book on the collapse of the Venezuelan economy."

"Did you sell any?"

"I sold a few. And I gave a bunch away to the dumbass younger economists. You've gotta wonder sometimes what world they live in. How about you? How's retirement?"

"Great. I don't miss teaching. My retirement came at a good time.

Everything was getting too politically correct at Ole Miss. I mean my students didn't want to study Faulkner because they thought that he was a racist. They thought Erskine Caldwell was racist and sexist. And you remember that nonsense about trying to ban To Kill a Mockingbird. Good Lord."

Ralph nods and adds, "Yeah, I never thought I'd see the day when students at Ole Miss didn't want to read Faulkner. He was a literary god when you and I first started teaching there. And I remember the stink last year about Of Mice and Men when students objected to Steinbeck's portrayal of a retarded man. They also said the story was vulgar and sexist. I don't think they understood what it was about."

W. R. laughs and says, "Now, Ralph, you know you can't say 'retarded' anymore. You might get arrested by the thought police."

"Yeah, I know. I hear it's a felony now."

Just then the bell jingles again, and in walks Smokey Johnson holding his guitar in his right hand and the Jim Beam bottle in his left. Smokey is no longer wearing bib overalls. He's dressed in gray dress slacks and a button-down light blue oxford shirt.

Smokey says, "Hey, W. R. Who's your friend?"

W. R. says, "This is Ralph. He's an economics professor at Ole Miss. We've known each other for years. He's one of the good guys."

Smokey sets the whiskey bottle on the counter and leans the guitar against the display case. Then he walks over to where W. R. and Ralph are standing and extends his right hand to Ralph and says, "Glad to meet you, Ralph. I'm Raphael Johnson. Most folks around here call me Smokey."

After the two men shake hands, Smokey says, "I've only got a few minutes, W. R. I'm on my way to my broker's office in Memphis. I'll leave the guitar here for you to process, and I'll pick up my money later." Then he leaves the shop and gets into his Mercedes.

Ralph asks, "Is that Smokey Johnson, the bluesman? I saw him one time at Proud Larry's."

"That's him."

"He's really good. What did he mean by 'processing' his guitar?"

"Well, it's a long story."

"I've got nothing else to do. Give it to me."

W. R. says, "Okay. Let's go sit in my office. I'll get us a couple of beers, and I'll tell you the story of Smokey Johnson's guitar."

They walk to the office. W. R. retrieves two Millers from his refrigerator and hands one to Ralph. Then he takes a seat at his desk, and Ralph sits down on the couch against the wall.

"It goes like this, Ralph. Smokey grew up on a tenant farm in north Alabama, not too far from the Mississippi line. He dropped out of high school when he was sixteen to help his daddy with the farm work. When he was seventeen he joined the Army, with his father's blessing.

"The Army made him a mechanic, which suited Smokey because he had always been good working on cars, trucks, and tractors. While he was stationed at Fort Dix, New Jersey, Smokey got to be friends with another mechanic, a White guy named Ron Hardin, from Boston.

"It was Ron who first taught Smokey how to play guitar. Well, because of Smokey's natural talent, it wasn't long before Smokey was better than his friend, and that's when Ron got the idea of forming a blues band with Smokey as the lead singer and guitarist, because Smokey had this deep, raspy voice that was perfect for the blues.

"Now, you have to remember that at this time there was no Smokey Johnson. He was still Raphael, or 'Raph,' as some of the GIs called him. But, in order to get gigs, they created this fictitious 'Smokey Johnson' character, who was supposedly from the Mississippi Delta, and Raphael came up with the idea that Smokey would always wear a wide brim floppy hat and very dark sunglasses.

"Well, Smokey and Ron had so much fun playing together that Ron convinced Smokey to come to Boston College with him to study music after he got discharged. Ron helped Smokey study for his GED, and then, once he got that, helped him study for the ACT. And, get this, Ralph, Smokey scored 34 on the ACT."

Ralph says, "That's better than me. I scored 32."

W. R. says, "Same here" and goes on with his story, "Well, anyway, after Smokey gets out, he goes to Boston and joins Ron at B. C., and they room together in a dorm there.

"They both need money, because the G.I. Bill is not covering all of their expenses, so they decide to start looking for gigs as a blues duo, with Raphael once again performing as the Smokey Johnson character and Ron performing as 'White Boy Slim.'

"They wind up becoming very popular in the Boston area while they're still studying music at B.C., but at some point they quit performing as a blues duo and start playing with two different jazz quartets. Ron never got much better than he was when Smokey first met him, but Smokey kept getting better, both as a singer and a guitarist. After he graduated from B.C., Smokey enrolled at the Berklee School of Music in Boston and became a top-notch jazz guitarist."

Ralph interrupts W. R., "Wait a minute. Are you saying that the guy who was in here a few minutes ago is *that* Raphael Johnson, the one who played with the New England Jazzmasters?"

"Yep. That's him. Two-time Grammy winner and Playboy All-Star jazz guitarist."

"Interesting. What's he doing in Potts Camp?"

"He loves it here. He discovered it when he came down to one of Kenny Brown's Hill Country Blues Picnics to see a friend of his play. He told me that this area reminds him of where he grew up. Also, his wife is from Mississippi. She went to Jackson State. So, when Raphael retired from the Jazzmasters about four years ago, he bought a nice little three-bedroom house here, and he and his wife moved down from Boston.

"After he'd been here for about a year, he got the itch to start playing again. So, he decided to resurrect 'Smokey' and just have a little fun with it. He figured as long as nobody knew who he really was, he could keep everything low-key and just play when he felt like it.

"But, as you know, down here, Smokey got bigger than Raphael ever was, and then when Smoley came out with that Slicktalkin' album on his own label, and got that big write-up in *Downhome Blues* magazine, things started getting bigger than he ever wanted.

"In other words, what started out as a hobby was beginning to get completely out of hand. Smokey was even getting requests to perform in Japan and Scandinavia. Well, as much as that notoriety annoyed Raphael, he could still tolerate it until these yuppie blues lovers, most often college students, started coming around looking for him. First, there were just a few coming from Oxford, but now they're coming from all over.

"So, several months ago, Raphael decided that he needed to put his Smokey Johnson character out to pasture, but he wanted to have a little fun with it first. That's where my pawn shop comes in."

Ralph asks, "What do you mean?"

"Well, here's how it works. Whenever any of these annoying fans come around looking for Smokey Johnson, the local folks tell them that they need to come see me, because I'm the only one who can deal with Smokey.

"Then, when they show up at my shop, I give them this song-and-dance about how hard it is to get to see Smokey, but I'll do what I can to help. Then I go into my office and call Smokey to see if he's home and if he wants to see this person or those people. If he's not busy and is willing to see them, I tell them that Smokey will let them come and see him for thirty minutes if they will get his guitar out of hock and take him some whiskey.

"Then, when these fans get to Smokey's house with the guitar and the whiskey, he gives every one of them a different story. Told one of them that he was Robert Johnson's grand-nephew. He also likes to give them a hard time while he's feeding them a lot of bull.

"Anyway, after the visit's over, and the visitors are gone, Smokey brings the guitar and whiskey back to me, and we do it all again when the next nuisance fan shows up."

"Are you saying that you take their money under false pretenses? Can't you lose your license for that?"

"No. It's all legitimate. There're no false pretenses. Smokey pawns his guitar for a hundred dollars, and I do the proper paperwork and give him the hundred dollars. And when the guitar's redeemed, I do the proper paperwork for that transaction.

"When I tell the little yuppies that Smokey's guitar is in hock, I'm telling the truth. And when I tell them that Smokey will only talk to them if they redeem his guitar and bring it to him, that's also the truth."

"Well, what about the whiskey? Do they buy that from you?"

"I always first offer to give it to them. If they take my offer, I give the whiskey to them. If they decide to pay me for it, it's their idea, not mine.

And it's always my personal whiskey, not the shop's."

"But didn't Smokey just bring the whiskey back to you?"

W. R. laughs. "He doesn't drink. I always say that Smokey wants them to bring him some whiskey. I never say that he's going to drink it."

"But, apparently, neither of you needs the money. Why are y'all doing this?"

"Man, it ain't the money. It's just a couple of old farts jerking these spoiled little brats around a little bit."

"I can understand how you would like to toy with spoiled college students, but what about Smokey? What's his beef?"

"Well, he still has some unpleasant memories of going to school at Boston College. You have to remember that he was a poor Black Army veteran from Alabama going to college on the G.I. Bill in Massachusetts. He never fit in there. I mean, they tolerated him but, in his words, looked down on him."

Ralph nods his head and says, "I see what you mean. But, just out of curiosity, as an economist, I'd like to know the economics of these transactions."

"Well, Smokey pawns his guitar for a hundred dollars, and I give him a hundred dollars. Whoever redeems it pays my shop the hundred dollars plus interest and fees. The last couple paid eighteen dollars in interest and fees. Then when Smokey comes back with his guitar, he pawns it for another hundred, and the cycle starts again."

"What if someone redeems the guitar and then takes off with it?

"No big deal. I bought that guitar off a guy for three-fifty and sold it to Smokey for four hundred. He's already made over a thousand dollars off our little game. Besides that, I always get the name and address of whoever redeems it, so I'd call the Sheriff and report that Smokey's guitar was stolen."

"But, won't Smokey need his guitar?"

"Hell no. He's got a dozen guitars."

Ralph ponders the scheme for a few minutes, then says, "This sounds like something I heard about Furry Lewis doing some years back."

"Yeah, that's where Smokey got the idea."

Ralph says, "I see . . . But what if the fan looking for Smokey is not some annoying college student? Let's say it's a nice old lady from Pontotoc."

"Well, in that case, I'd call Smokey and, if he was available, either he'd drive up here to meet her, or I'd lock up the shop and drive her down to Smokey's house. No monkey business would take place."

"By the way, how is it that you know so much about Smokey?"

W. R. chuckles. "I'm writing his biography. It's a hell of a good story. From poor Alabama farm boy to Army mechanic to international jazz star, and then to mysterious Mississippi blues man."

"But, when your book comes out, all of your victims are gonna find out that they've been had, and some of them might raise Hell about it, maybe even go to the news media."

"Let them pitch a fit. That'll help sell my book, along with the album that Smokey's working on now over in Muscle Shoals. It's going to be on Smokey's own label, just like the Slicktalkin' album was, and it'll be the Smokey character's last hoorah. And I'd bet that most of the kids who got snookered will put it on social media. They'll want to let everyone know that they were bamboozled by the legendary Smokey Johnson."

Ralph says, "You may be right. The more noise they make, the better for you and Smokey."

"We plan on releasing the album and the book at the same time, and going on a promotional tour together for a couple of months. We'll probably start at Square Books, so I'll be sure to tell you when."

"Let me know. I'll be there for sure."

W. R. checks his watch. He says, "It's just about closing time. Let me buy you dinner at Flick's Restaurant after I take care of the paperwork on Smokey Johnson's guitar."

The Girl in the Photograph

It was a cold and windy evening on February 13, 2019 outside of Zack's Book Store & Coffee Bar in Huntsville, Alabama. The store is owned by Zack Milner, a Huntsville native who retired in 2010 from teaching English at Vanderbilt University. He opened the business to celebrate his two favorite pastimes: literature and coffee.

Zack's is located in a two-story cream-colored brick building that used to be a supermarket. Zack renovated the first floor of the building to have three sections. On the right side of the first floor is the book store, which also stocks music CDs and movie DVDs. On the left side is a coffee bar that has a dozen four-person tables. On one of the side walls of the coffee bar is a display of local art.

In the center of the store is a thirty-by-twenty-foot seating area where the store accommodates events such as book signings and acoustic music performances. On the second floor are the store's offices and storage rooms.

The event that was held at Zack's on that particular February night was a meeting of the Pageturners Book Club, a local women's-only reading and writing group, at which there would be a presentation and book signing by Travis Fuller. Travis had been invited by Mildred Atchison, President of the Pageturners, to discuss his recently-published book of photographs, as well as a poetry collection that he had published the year before.

At around six p.m. Mildred walked up to the podium at the front of the events room and loudly cleared her throat into the microphone on the podium. Mildred was a perky little seventy-year-old former high school history teacher. At the podium, she stood ramrod straight in her navy blue pantsuit and smiled to the audience of approximately forty middle-aged and senior women, among whom were scattered several husbands most of whom looked as though they wanted to be somewhere else.

In her best schoolteacher voice Mildred said, "Good evening members and guests of the Pageturners Book Club. Tonight we have a special treat. Mister Travis Fuller of Wetumpka, Alabama is here to discuss his new book of beautiful black and white photographs entitled *Images from the Road*. In addition to telling us about his new photography book, I've asked him to read from his poetry collection that was published last year and is entitled *Reflections*. Both of these books are available here at Zack's, and I can see that several of you have already purchased one or both of them. And, of course, Travis will stay around and sign your books for you.

"Before Travis begins his presentation, I'd like to ask Doctor Zack Milner, the owner and operator of this lovely store, to come up and say hello to everyone."

Zack, who knew many of the members of the audience, walked briskly from the back of the room and stood next to Mildred, who had come from behind the podium to greet him. Zack was in his late sixties. He had a gray goatee and long gray hair pulled back into a ponytail. He stood about five-foot-six and had a slight paunch. He was dressed in wrinkled khaki slacks and a black Vanderbilt sweatshirt. Zack looked around the audience and said, "Thank you, Mildred. I'm so glad that your book club has honored my store with their presence again this evening. This is a good turnout considering how cold it's been today. And, Travis, I appreciate your coming up here from Wetumpka in such uncomfortable weather." He looked at Travis, and Travis smiled and nodded to Zack.

Zack continued, "To show my appreciation, I'd like to invite each of you to have a cup of coffee of your choice on me at the coffee bar. But, of course, I also encourage you to pick up a copy or two or three of Travis's books while you're here. Especially if you're in the market for a Valentine's gift." He saluted the audience as he headed back toward the coffee bar and said, "Let me know if you need anything. Y'all have fun."

Mildred walked back over to the podium and said, "Thank you Zack. And we appreciate and will take advantage of your offer of free coffee." Then she smiled at Travis and said, "First, I'd like to echo Zack's appreciation of Travis's driving up from Wetumpka in this nasty weather.

"It is indeed our good fortune to have Travis here this evening. I have to admit that after reading about Travis in some newspaper and magazine articles that I found on the internet, I couldn't wait to meet him.

"Travis grew up in a poor family in a low-income neighborhood in

Montgomery. He started working when he was fifteen to help support his large family. When he was nineteen, he dropped out of college to join the Army at a time when the Viet Nam conflict was starting to heat up. While he was at the military processing center in Montgomery, he was recruited by the Army Security Agency, a military intelligence group. I did a little research on the ASA and found out that only soldiers who scored at the top of the Army IQ tests were recruited to join that outfit."

Mildred looked over at Travis and then continued, "Travis served seven years in the ASA. He was trained as an intelligence analyst at Fort Devens, Massachusetts and then, after being stationed for a year and a half in Okinawa, he returned to the United States to be trained as a Russian linguist at the Defense Language Institute in Monterey, California. After Travis served seven years in the ASA, he completed a degree in international relations at Georgetown University. Then he served three years with the CIA, which included two years in Europe."

Mildred turned her note page over and went on: "When he was thirty-two years old, Travis left the CIA and returned to Alabama where he earned a law degree at the University of Alabama. Soon after he passed the State bar exam, Travis was hired by the U.S. Attorney's Office in Montgomery, where he served for ten years before joining a small private law firm in Montgomery. He now has a solo practice in Wetumpka, which is just outside Montgomery.

"When Travis was an Assistant U.S. Attorney, Travis helped the FBI investigate and prosecute a Russian spy ring that was operating out of Miami. As a private attorney, he earned a reputation as a top-notch trial attorney. He was on the legal team that got a two billion dollar judgment against a Russian pharmaceutical company. You may have heard about that case. It involved claims made in several different countries.

"Travis lives now in Wetumpka with his wife Marie, who is an administrator with the Elmore County school system, and they have a son who is an English professor at Troy University.

"In addition to being a photographer and a poet, Travis is a songwriter who has had several songs recorded, the most well-known of which is "Every Shade of Blue," a song that was recorded about twelve years ago by Danny Angel, who I'm sure you've heard of."

Mildred motioned for Travis to come to the podium. As he rose from his chair the audience could see that he was about five-foot-ten and of medium build. He was wearing starched blue jeans and a maroon pullover sweater. Even though his wavy hair was white, he had a healthy complexion and moved with the grace of an athlete. His wife thought that he was handsome.

When he got to the podium, Travis lay down his two books and his laptop. Then he adjusted the microphone and said, "I also take in laundry."

As the laughter at his comment subsided, Travis turned to Mildred and said, "Thank you, Mildred, for the flattering introduction. I believe that you know more about me than my wife does. And thanks for leaving out all the bad parts." The audience laughed again.

"Before we go any further, I want to make it clear that the Russian pharmaceutical company against which we got the two billion dollar judgment didn't have anywhere near that amount of assets. But we were glad to take what they had and put them out of business. And I want to thank them for buying me a new house." More laughter.

"I have to confess that I didn't drive up from Wetumpka today. I had some business in Muscle Shoals yesterday and this morning, so I spent the night there and drove over this afternoon. It was a much easier trip than it would have been from Wetumpka."

Travis picked up his photography book and showed it to the audience. He said, "I see that several of you have already bought a copy of this book. Thank you very much for that. For those of you who don't have a copy to look at, Zack has been kind enough to set up the video screen behind me." Travis turned on his laptop, and a photo of the cover of *Images from the Road* appeared on the video screen.

"This book is composed of photos that I have taken during my various travels, as well as several that were taken here in Alabama. The book is divided into five sections: North America, South America, Europe, Asia, and Africa.

"For those of you who are interested in the technical aspects of the photos, the book contains info on each picture such as the camera and film used, camera settings, lighting, and so on. I'm not going to talk much tonight about that stuff, because I don't want to put you to sleep. What I'll do is show and discuss a representative group of photos from each section of the book and answer whatever questions you might have."

For the next thirty minutes, Travis followed that plan, showing photos from Canada, Massachusetts, Virginia, and Alabama followed by photos from France, England, Scotland, Russia, Okinawa, Japan, Egypt, and Morocco. The photos included pictures of people, buildings, mountains, rivers, valleys, deserts, statues, and monuments.

Once he finished his presentation, Travis invited additional questions.

A gray-haired woman in the second row raised her hand and asked, "Why are all your pictures in black and white?

Travis answered, "The main reason is that all of my earliest photos were in black and white. I learned to shoot and process black and white photos from an Army buddy of mine when I was at Fort Devens. Back then, color photography was expensive, but most Army posts had a black and white photo darkroom that soldiers could use. For those reasons, all of my early overseas photos were black and white.

"Once color photography became affordable, I began shooting in both color and black and white, but I have always preferred the character of black and white pictures. That's not to say that I don't like good color photography. I have a nice digital camera now, and I take mostly color photos because it's so simple, and the pictures are so easy to manipulate and duplicate.

"However, I have a darkroom at my house, and I still like the experience of processing black and white negatives."

Another woman asked, "Will you ever do a book of color pictures?"

"I don't know. I haven't ruled it out. I don't travel internationally like I used to, but I've thought about traveling throughout Alabama and taking, I don't know, maybe a thousand digital color photos and picking out the best ones. Alabama is not only a beautiful state, it has a lot of history, and there are lots of places that need to be photographed before they're torn down or modified. I particularly want to photograph some of the old honkytonks before they disappear. I have a special place in my heart for old-time honkytonks."

A woman on the front row said, "Mildred said that you spent three years in the CIA. You don't look like a spy."

Travis looked to his right and then to his left. He leaned over the podium into the mike and whispered, "This is a disguise. In real life, I look like a young Sean Connery." Once again, the audience laughed, and Travis was feeling a real connection with them. Even the men seemed to be paying attention.

Travis then asked, "Do any of you have a favorite photo in the book?"

A woman sitting in the rear of the room stood up and asked, "I loved the photo of the sun coming up behind the pyramids."

Travis brought that photo up on the video screen and said, "Thank you. I've always liked that one myself. I took it after I'd been up all night drinking with a bunch of Egyptian soldiers, so I was shocked at how well it turned out."

One of the younger women in the group raised her hand and asked, "Who's the ballerina in the picture on page 23, the one called 'White Swan'?"

Travis brought up on the screen a photo of a dark haired ballerina in a white tutu standing behind a curtain on the right wing of a large stage on which other dancers were performing. The ballerina was stretching her arms upward, apparently loosening up before going on stage herself. The photo was taken from directly behind the dancer and showed none of her face.

"Thanks for asking that. That photo was taken in 1967. It's the oldest photo in the book. It was taken with a camera that I borrowed from my Army buddy at Fort Devens who taught me how to take pictures.

"But, to answer your question, the ballerina was a girl that I met in Boston who was studying dance at the Boston Conservatory. That's where the picture was taken. She helped me sneak backstage, and I took the photo from just off the right wing of the stage."

When one of the men in the audience asked, "Was she your girlfriend?" many of the women leaned forward to hear the answer.

Travis smiled, "Yes. We were very close. But shortly after that photo was taken, I was transferred to Okinawa. She and I wrote each other for a few months, but then I lost all contact with her and never saw or heard from her again. I'm sure that she found someone else and forgot all about me."

In unison, the women said, "A-a-h," and Travis chuckled.

"Well, since you're so interested in my old girlfriend, I have to tell you that there's a poem in my other book that's about her. It's called 'Near the Charles.'"

Mildred asked, "Will you read that one to us?"

Travis said, "Sure" and opened his copy of *Reflections*. He read:

It was Valentine's Day 1967
I was a poor soldier
from Alabama.
She was a rich girl
from Pittsburgh
studying ballet
at the Conservatory.
Somehow
our paths had crossed
and here we were
in Boston
leaving the theatre
where we'd seen
Blow-Up.
She understood it.
I didn't
but acted like I did.
I started to hail a cab
but she said
Don't.
Let's walk.
It's not that far.
I said
Girl, it's twenty degrees
and snowing
and my Southern blood
is thin.
She said

I'll keep you warm
and hugged me
to her side
and kissed my cheek.
Her lips were cold
but soft.
Let's go see
if the river's iced over
she said
pulling me, shivering,
toward the Charles.
As we neared the water's edge
the snow increased,
reminding me
of one of those
paperweights
with the plastic snowflakes inside
falling
on a tiny Santa sleigh.
Look here
she said
falling backwards
into a pile of freshly fallen snow
flapping her arms
to make angel wings
and then beckoning me
to join her.
Leaving my senses
for a spell
I fell beside her
and made my own angel wings.
And then she rolled over on me
and licked the snowflakes
from my chin

and kissed my frozen mouth
with hers.

When he finished reading the poem, Travis said, "Tomorrow will be fifty-two years since that day," and once again there was a chorus of "A-a-h."

Travis smiled and shook his head at their reaction to his poem. Then he went on to read several more poems from *Reflections* before he said, "Thank you very much for your time and attention." He pointed to a small table to his right and said, "Zack has set up a table for those of you good people who want me to sign a book for you. But, first, I'm going to get my free cup of coffee. Then I'll come back and sit at the table for as long as you need for me to."

On his way to the coffee bar, Travis spoke to a few members of the audience. Then he made a stop at the restroom before meeting Zack in the coffee bar. Zack handed him his coffee and said, "That was entertaining. You did a good job. And I see that several of them are headed to the bookstore to buy books."

Travis thanked Zack for the coffee and the compliment, then went back to the meeting room where he took his seat at the table in front of which a line had already formed. The line even included a few of the men who had initially looked so disinterested.

As he sat down, Travis placed his cup on the table and said, "Thanks for waiting. I needed this coffee."

The woman at the head of the line said, "Thank you so much for coming" as she handed him her copy of *Images on the Road*. She said, "Could you make my book out to Sally?"

Travis said, "Of course," and as he signed her book he said, "I hope you enjoy it."

The next woman had a copy of *Reflections*, and the one after her had two copies of *Images* and one copy of *Reflections*.

After about twenty minutes of signing books and engaging in small talk, Travis got to the last person in line. She had two copies of each book.

Travis asked, "Would you like these personalized?"

"Yes, please. Sign one of each to Miriam and one of each to Danielle."

"Danielle. One of favorite names. Are you Miriam or Danielle?"

"I'm Danielle."

"What a coincidence. That was the name of the girl in the ballerina photo."

The woman smiled. "I know."

Travis said, "How do you . . . " and then he leaned back in his chair and looked at her. She was very attractive and appeared to be in perhaps her mid-sixties. She had shoulder-length auburn hair and was dressed in what was an obviously expensive dark green dress.

Travis smiled and asked, "Is that really you?"

She smiled back at him and said, "It's me."

Mildred overheard their conversation and asked, "Are you the girl in the photograph?"

Danielle nodded. Mildred said, "Well, how about that?"

Two nearby women stopped talking to one another, and one of them asked, "Did you say that you're the ballerina in the picture and the poem?"

The word quickly spread and before she knew what was happening, Danielle was being asked by several of the women to sign the "White Swan" photo in their books.

After autographing Danielle's books, Travis rose from his chair and said, "Danielle, why don't you sit here in the chair and sign their books. Once you finish let's go over to the coffee bar and catch up on the last fifty-two years."

Travis gave Danielle a quick hug as she walked around the table. He noticed a hint of expensive perfume. Then he went to the front row of seats and sat down in one of the folding chairs. As he loaded his laptop and books into his briefcase, he watched the excitement surrounding Danielle. He wondered to himself: How in the world did this happen? Then, for some reason, *Casablanca* came to mind, and he thought: *Of all the book joints in all the towns in all the world, she walks into mine.*

It was hard for him to sit there and wait to talk to Danielle, but he was enjoying the attention that she was getting.

After Danielle had finally satisfied all her new fans, Travis escorted her to the coffee bar. He led her to a table in a corner away from the door and pulled out a chair for her, then, after she was seated, he sat down in the chair opposite her. He set his briefcase on the floor next to his chair, then smiled at Danielle and said, "That was very nice of you to sign their books. Now, tell me, how the hell did you wind up here tonight?"

Danielle lay her purse and the bag containing her four books in the empty chair next to her. Then she smiled and said, "It's a long story. How about ordering us some coffee. I'll take a mocha latte."

Travis got Zack's attention, and when Zack got to their table, Travis introduced Danielle to Zack and placed their order. As Zack walked away, Travis said, "Before you begin to tell me how you happened to be here, may I say that you shore are purty for a woman of your..."

"Watch it."

"Let's just say that you're very striking."

"Thanks. You're not so bad yourself."

"Did the white hair shock you?"

"No. Your photo is on your book jackets. Did my red hair fool you?

Travis said, "I guess it did. The last time I saw you, your hair was dark brown and shorter. But I like the auburn."

"What color is your wife's hair?"

"Marie's a blonde."

"Is that her natural color?"

Travis smiled. "It was thirty years ago. She just turned sixty-four."

"I'll bet she's pretty. Do you have a picture?"

Travis said, "I've got one on my phone" as he opened his briefcase and pulled out his iphone. He showed the photo to Danielle. It was of a blonde with classic features and hazel eyes.

"She is pretty. Very pretty. How'd you meet her?"

"She was in graduate school at Alabama when I was in law school there. We dated off and on for about six years before we got married."

"Why so long?"

"Probably because I didn't fully mature until I was forty. I was a very slow developer."

"I can believe that. Is she the secret to your success?"

Travis answered, "Absolutely. Sometimes I call her my 'little mama' because she keeps me in line. I really don't know what I'd do without her."

Just then, Zack arrived with Travis's black coffee and Danielle's mocha latte. Zack asked, "Can I get you anything else?" and both Travis and Danielle said, "No thank you."

As Zack was walking away, Travis leaned over the table and looked into Danielle's dark brown eyes. He smiled and said, "Okay, enough of this chit-chat. Tell me your story. You already know mine."

Danielle sighed, and started, "Well, after I graduated from the Conservatory, I went to New York and worked for a small dance company. I loved what I was doing, but after I'd been there about two and a half years, I had a serious accident and had to quit dancing."

"What happened?"

"One really cold night in January, I was running to hail a cab and I slipped on the icy sidewalk and fell onto the concrete curb. I tore up my left knee, cracked two ribs, and broke my left wrist. I had to have two surgeries on my knee and one on my wrist."

Travis grimaced and said, "Good Lord. That's terrible."

"It was. It was over six months before I could get around very well."

"Did you go back home to Pennsylvania after you injured yourself?"

"No. I stayed in New York, because I liked it there and that's where my friends were. And I'd been away from home for about seven years by then.

"My company couldn't afford to keep me on the payroll, but the two dancers with whom I shared an apartment let me stay there rent free while I was recuperating. And my parents sent me money every month and came to visit when they could."

"But I imagine that you were still miserable as hell."

"It wasn't as horrible as it could have been. My roommates were really sweet, and my other friends would come by sometimes and cheer me up. And there was this one guy who was a patron of our ballet company and a big fan of mine who would come by and bring me gifts and fancy meals."

"Was he an old guy drooling over your hot young body?"

Danielle chuckled softly and said, "No. I'll have you know that he was a handsome man in his mid-thirties. His name was Saul Ginsberg. He owned a successful accounting firm and was very smart and charming."

"Umm. I think that I can see where this story's going."

"Don't be a smart aleck. Well, anyway, even after I was able to get around again, I realized that it would be a long time, if ever, until I could dance again. That's when Saul offered me a job as a file clerk at his accounting firm at what I later found out was about twice the going rate for file clerks."

Travis smiled. "Of course he did."

"You're a very suspicious man. Well, anyway, I took him up on the job offer, and after I had learned my way around the firm, he had one of his senior accountants start training me to do basic accounting tasks. That's when I found out that I had a real talent for accounting, and I liked the work. That eventually led to my working at the firm in the mornings and taking accounting courses in the afternoons and evenings at a local college, at the expense of the firm."

Then Danielle smiled and said, "And, as much as I hate to accommodate your suspicion, I have to admit that you're right about Saul's motives. After I had been at the firm for maybe eighteen months, Saul and I started having an affair. About six months later, his wife found out about it, and they went through a nasty divorce."

"What happened after that?"

"Two things: I got my accounting degree and . . . Saul and I got married."

"So he made an honest woman of you."

"So to speak. But then, after we'd been married about three years, I caught him having an affair with another young dancer. To make it even worse, she was a friend of mine."

Travis groaned and said, "I don't think I like this guy."

"Well, anyhow, Saul and I wound up getting divorced, but I kept working with the firm while we were going through that process."

"Surely you left the firm after the divorce."

"I did. I was offered a good job by one of my accounting clients. The job was as an in-house accountant for a media company in the City."

"Where does your story go from there?"

"To a much better place. I was at the media company for about five years when I was promoted to chief financial officer, and then, sometime later, the company owner and I fell in love, and we eventually got married."

"You didn't break up *his* marriage, did you?"

"No, I did not. He was a widower at the time."

"Are y'all still married?"

"Yes. I've been married to Ben Grissom for almost thirty-four years."

"That's about the same as Marie and me. Do y'all still live in New York?"

"No. We moved to North Carolina, just outside of Asheville, about ten years ago because we wanted to open a branch operation in the South. Once we opened that branch, Ben's sons took over the New York headquarters."

"How old is this Ben?"

"He just turned seventy-seven. He was forty-three when we got married. He'd lost his wife to breast cancer about four years before that. Her name was Marcia. I knew her well. She was really nice."

Travis thought for a moment, then said, "Let's see. You're seventy-one now. So that's not a big age difference. It's less than the difference between my age and Marie's."

"No, and he's a young seventy-seven."

"But you're an extra-young seventy-one. Like I said, you look great."

Danielle blushed slightly and said, "Thank you. I have a good team who keep me looking presentable."

Travis thought for a moment, then said, "A team. You mean like the Kardashians?"

"Yes, something like the Kardashians. I have a make-up artist, a hair dresser, a personal trainer, a manicurist, a masseuse, and a fashion adviser. And, of course, a cosmetic surgeon."

Travis smiled and said, "The media business must be treating you well."

"Yes, we've been very successful. Ben and I could have retired already, but we both still enjoy the business. It's very stimulating. It's not really like work to us."

"What's your position in the company? Are you still the chief financial officer?"

"No. One of Ben's sons holds that position now. I'm the Executive Vice President."

Travis said, "Well, that's impressive. I'm proud for you. Do you and Ben have any children of your own?"

"One daughter, Miriam. That's who you signed the books for. She lives here in Huntsville."

"So that's how you wound up here. But how'd you know about the book signing?"

"This part of the story will be slightly discomforting for me to tell you, but let me first lay the foundation. Do you remember the record label that recorded Danny Angel on your song Every Shade of Blue?"

"Yeah, it was Roundhouse Records."

"Do you know what company pays you royalties on that recording?"

"Yeah, it's Grissom Productions . . . Wait a minute. Is that your company?"

"Yes. Roundhouse Records is one of our company's divisions."

"Okay. Now you've got my attention."

"Well, when Roundhouse Records recorded the album that song was on, I was still the company CFO, so I saw the contract with your name and publishing company address on it and starting doing some detective work on what you'd been doing and where you were living and so on. And it's a little embarrassing to admit, but ever since then, I've been keeping tabs on you . . . By the way, do you remember the signature on your first royalty checks?"

"No. What was it?"

"D. K. Grissom. That was me."

"D. K. for Danielle Kovak? Why didn't you give me a call, D. K.?"

"I don't know . . . I guess I wasn't comfortable with the idea of contacting you out of the blue, because I figured that you had probably forgotten all about me by then. But when *Reflections* came out last year with that poem about me, I knew that you hadn't forgotten."

"Of course I hadn't forgotten about you. You're one of my favorite people ever."

Danielle smiled and said, "And you're one of my favorite people."

Travis hesitated a moment and then said, "You know, I have a theory. I believe that in each person's life there are a handful of people who're significant in shaping who that person ultimately becomes. In my case, I think that you were one of those people."

"What did I do?"

"Well, when I met you I was about as redneck as a person could be, and you were about as sophisticated as a young girl could be. Do you remember that?"

"No. I thought that you were charming and interesting, and smart, and I didn't feel particularly sophisticated."

Travis said, "Well, anyway, when we were together for those seven months in Boston, you not only took me to the ballet, you took me to a Metropolitan Opera tryout, and two plays, and two or three art galleries, and you talked to me about books that you were reading. And I didn't realize it at the time, but I think that those kinds of things helped scrape off a lot of my redneckedness. If I hadn't met you, I might have wound up pumping gas instead of practicing law."

"Nobody pumps gas for a living anymore. Besides that, when I met you, you were in the Army intelligence, so I'm pretty sure that you weren't as big a rube as you're making yourself out to have been. You would have done just fine with or without me."

"Hey, don't ruin a good story. I'm trying to compliment you."

"Well, thank you. I'd like to think that I was important in your life, because you were important in my life, as well. Why do think I was keeping track of you? It was you who encouraged me to reach out and grab a hold of life and not just sit back and wait for things to come to me."

"Well, you certainly seem to have done your share of life-grabbing. You've had a very interesting life."

Danielle said, "Well, nothing like yours, but it has had its moments." She took a sip from her latte, then said, "I'm curious. In that poem about us, how in the world did you remember all those details of that day after fifty-something years? I didn't remember any of that until I read the poem and it came back to me."

"Actually, I wrote that poem in 1969 when I was in Monterey at language school. It was published in a West Coast poetry magazine in 1970. I put it in *Reflections* because it went so well with the theme of the book . . . Now I'm glad I did." Travis stared at his coffee mug for a moment, then said, "By the way, you still haven't explained exactly how you happened to be here tonight."

"I saw this event on your publisher's website, so I scheduled a trip to come and visit my daughter."

"Well, I'm glad you came. This may be the most pleasant surprise I've ever had. I just assumed that I'd never see you again."

Danielle said, "This has been great for me, too." She looked at her watch. She said, "There's one more thing. I'd like to make a business proposal. It may be egotistical of me, but I really like that White Swan photo, and I'd like to get your permission to make prints of it and sell them through our fine arts division. That division manufactures and sells art reproductions and high quality prints. I believe that I could market prints of your photo to ballet schools and dance companies in particular. I still have a lot of contacts in the dance biz."

Travis thought for a moment, then said, "Sure, why not. I'll make a copy of the negative and send it to you. You can email me a contract, and I'll sign off on whatever terms you want. After all, it's your picture, and I never would have shot it if you hadn't sneaked me backstage. And if you want me to sign some of the prints, just send them to me once they're done."

Danielle said, "Thanks. That would be great," then reached into her purse and pulled out a business card. She handed it to Travis and said, "This has all my contact info on it."

Travis reached into his briefcase and found one of his business cards. He handed it to Danielle. She looked the card and said "Travis C. Fuller. When I saw your contract with our company, I remembered that you told me that your middle name is Clyde. Is that true or were you were pulling my leg?"

"It's absolutely true. That's my middle name. I was named after my father's brother, Clyde Earl Fuller, who died just before I was born. He was killed in a moonshine accident. His still blew up."

"You're making that up."

Travis raised his right hand. "God's honest truth. He died in North Elmore, not too far from where I live now. Back then, Elmore County was still dry and there was still a demand for shine."

Danielle said, "Your uncle got killed in a moonshine still explosion. Maybe you weren't kidding about being a redneck when I first met you." Then she shook her head and smiled.

Travis said, "Well, at least you thought I was interesting."

Danielle smiled again and said, "I still do" as she looked at her watch again. She said, "I really hate to leave now, but I have to go. My daughter has plans for us tonight, and I have her car. Will you walk me to the car? It's about a block away. The store's parking lot was full when I got here."

Travis stood up and put on his corduroy sport coat, then he helped Danielle with her long woolen coat. He snapped his briefcase shut after taking out his iphone and putting it into an inside coat pocket. He then motioned to Zack and asked what he owed for the coffees.

Zack replied, "Nothing. They're on me. Just come back again sometime."

"Thanks. I'll do that. I really like your store."

As Travis walked Danielle to her car in the cold night air, he put his right arm around her shoulders, and she put her left arm around his waist. She scrunched up her shoulders and said, "This winter wind reminds me of us walking the streets of Boston together all those years ago."

Travis said, "Funny, I was just thinking the same thing."

Neither spoke again until they got to Danielle's car. When they reached the car, a white Audi sedan, Danielle unlocked the door, and Travis opened it for her. She dropped the bag containing her books onto the back seat and then turned and kissed him on the cheek and said, "It was so good to see you again, Travis Clyde Fuller. I'll be calling you about the prints."

Travis said, "I'm so glad you came, D. K. Looking forward to doing business with you."

Travis waved to Danielle as he watched her drive away. Then he turned and started walking to his car. On the way to his car, he called Marie and told her that he was about to leave Huntsville. She told him to be careful, because the highways had iced over in places. He assured her that he'd be careful, then told her that he loved her and not to wait up for him.

Marie was right. The highway was treacherous that night, so Travis drove his Lexus SUV slower than usual. Just north of Birmingham, he had to stop for about fifteen minutes while a jackknifed tractor-trailer was being moved to the side of the highway so that vehicles could pass by.

It was almost one a.m. when Travis got home. He parked his car in the driveway instead of the garage to avoid waking Marie. He picked up his suitcase and briefcase from the back seat, then quietly walked onto the porch and slowly opened the front door. As he entered the living room he saw that Marie was asleep in the leather recliner in front of the fireplace. He turned off the gas logs and got a blanket from the hall closet. He gently placed the blanket over her, kissed her forehead, and lightly patted her arm.

He went to the bedroom and set his alarm clock for nine-thirty a.m. so that he could make the eleven o'clock meeting that he had scheduled for the next day in Montgomery.

After the alarm woke him the next morning, Travis went into the kitchen to make coffee. Marie had left a note next to the coffee maker: "Happy Valentine's Day. Glad you made it home safely. Please pick up a pepperoni pizza on your way home this afternoon. Love you."

As Travis read the note, he remembered that Marie wanted to celebrate Valentine's Day on Friday the fifteenth, rather than Thursday the fourteenth. She'd made a reservation for them at her favorite restaurant. The note caused Travis to remember the diamond earrings that he'd put into his briefcase after he'd bought them at Grogan Jewelers by Lon in Florence while he was in the Muscle Shoals area. He'd give them to Marie on Friday.

It was about five-thirty when Travis got back home from work. As he opened the door, Marie pulled him to her and kissed him on the mouth. Then she hugged him tight and said, "I've missed you. Where's my pizza? I'm starving. By the way, how'd the book signing go?"

Travis handed her the pizza that he had almost dropped when she hugged him and said, "It was great. Everything went well, and I saw an old friend from Boston. I'll tell you all about it after we see this movie that I brought home to watch while we eat."

On her way to the kitchen to get plates and drinks, Marie asked, "What's the movie?"

"Blow-Up. I want to see if I understand it this time."

NOTE: The poem "Near the Charles" is from Dark Roast, *a collection by the author, published in 2016 by NewSouth Books. Although "Near the Charles" is based on an actual event, this story and its events, characters, and dialogue are purely fictional.*

Tales from Elmore County

It was two o'clock on a warm, clear Sunday afternoon in early April. Steve was driving the new black Buick Regal GS that he had picked up the day before at Brewbaker Buick, and he was headed for Windsor Terrace nursing home to meet his grandmother Pearl. Pearl had always had an affinity for Buicks, and Steve had promised her that she would be the first one to ride in his once it came in.

Steve was just shy of fifty years old and had been divorced for slightly over a year. He had moved into a loft apartment in downtown Montgomery that was within walking distance of the large accounting firm where he worked as a CPA. The Chevy SUV that he traded in on the Buick had been the last reminder of his rocky twelve-year marriage to Tammy.

Tammy and Steve had no children, and Steve had made the last payment on their divorce settlement, so he was ready to get on with his life. The Buick was a symbol of that new beginning.

Pearl had recently celebrated her ninety-fifth birthday at the home of Steve's parents, and it was then that she found out about the Buick and told Steve she had always wanted a new Buick, because that's what the rich people drove when she was growing up. Steve laughed when she told him that and assured her that he certainly wasn't rich, but he also said he would make sure that once his car came in, she would be his first passenger.

Windsor Terrace was on the outskirts of East Montgomery, just off I-85. When Steve got there at a few minutes after two, he parked his car in front of the main office and went inside to tell them that he was there to pick up his grandmother. Before he got to the reception desk, he spotted Pearl talking to the nurse who was in charge that day. They were both laughing about something that Steve couldn't quite hear.

The nurse pointed to Steve, and Pearl turned around. She had on her Sunday-best light blue summer dress and was holding a large dark blue handbag. Pearl wasn't very tall, about five-foot-three, but she stood straight up with her shoulders pulled back and gave the impression of being taller.

Pearl's white hair was recently permed in what Steve's mother called her "helmet head," and she was wearing dark red lipstick. She had a touch of rouge high on each cheek.

Steve said, "Grandma Pearl, you sure look pretty this afternoon."

Pearl smiled and replied, "It's nothing. It's what I wore to the church service this morning."

"Well, I'll be proud to show you off."

The nurse asked what time they expected to be back, and Steve said they'd be back before dinner.

When Steve turned around, Pearl was already at the front door, trying to get a look at the new Buick. Steve walked to the door and opened it for his grandmother, who walked through the door and said, "Lord, what a beautiful day." Then she spotted the Buick and asked, "Is this your new car?" Steve told her that it was, and she said, "Mighty fancy."

Steve walked over to the car and opened the passenger-side door. Then he reached out and said, "Let me put your purse in the back seat." After he placed the handbag in the back seat, Steve gently held his grandmother's arm and helped her into the front seat.

Once they both had settled into their seats and Steve had started the engine, he asked, "Where do you want to go? I'm at your service."

Pearl said, "I've been thinking about that, and I'd like to go back to Elmore County where I was raised. I haven't been there in over forty years."

"That's a long time. What kept you away?"

"Sad memories. You have to remember that when we grew up, my sisters and my brother and me, it was during the Depression, and times were just hard back then. You might say the Depression was depressin'."

"Yes, ma'am. I've heard those were hard times. Where did y'all live?"

"You know where the town of Elmore is?"

"Yes, ma'am. Is that where you want to go?"

Pearl sighed, "Yeah. I'd like to see it one more time."

Steve tuned his satellite radio to a soft jazz station and began the drive to Elmore. Pearl sat quietly, watching East Montgomery pass by.

About a half-hour later, they were on highway 143 entering the town limit of Elmore. Steve asked, "Is there any particular place you want to go?"

Pearl answered, "Just stay on this road. Goodness, nothing looks the same as I remembered." She pointed to her right and said, "There used to be a church right there. That's where my friend Judith went to church. No sign of it now. We went to Mt. Hebron Church. It's up the road a piece. That's where my folks are buried."

Steve asked, "Do you want to stop there?"

"Yeah. Let's stop by there on the way back."

Pearl pointed to their left and said, "There was a grocery store right over there that we used to shop at."

Steve asked, "Any memories coming back?"

"Oh, yeah. A lot of 'em. They're kinda floodin' my brain right now. Matter of fact, I just remembered somethin' that happened to my brother Will and me one time when we went shoppin' at the grocery store that was back there where I showed you.

"We lived quite a ways up the road from here, but me and Will used to walk down to the store for any groceries that we needed. One day Mama sent us to the store for a loaf of bread, and back then the bread wasn't sliced. On the way back, me and Will sat down on one of the gravestones in the old cemetery between the store and our house, and we ate some of the inside of the bread. We didn't mean to eat but a little bit, but when we got back home, about all that was left of half of the loaf was the crust.

"I thought Mama was gonna whip our butts, but she didn't. Instead, she wouldn't let Will or me eat any of what was left of that loaf. That meant that we didn't have any bread to make sandwiches to take to school. So all we had for lunch every day that week was a half an apple apiece.

"Believe me, we didn't do that again."

Steve laughed and said, "Y'all must have been something."

"Oh, yeah. We didn't have much money, but we had a lot of fun.

"Will was a mess. We used to walk to school together, and Will hated to wear shoes, so every day about halfway to school, he would take off his shoes and hide 'em in the bushes. One day in October, we had a few cold mornins, but Will still took off his shoes and went to school barefoot anyway.

"On the way home, we went to where he had hid his shoes, and they were gone. We looked all around and couldn't find 'em. Somebody must have took 'em. And back then, Daddy couldn't afford to buy us but one pair of shoes a year. So Mama and Daddy raised Cain when they found out what Will had done. He had to go to school barefooted for three weeks until one of our neighbors felt sorry for him and gave him an old pair of shoes that her son had outgrown."

Steve said, "So y'all only got one pair of shoes a year."

"Well, one new pair apiece. Sometimes one of us could still wear a pair of our old shoes, but most of the time, we only had one pair, so we had to take care of 'em."

Pearl was still looking around, taking in the scenery, when she said, "That reminds me of another funny story. My sister Erlene was real funny about her shoes. She would polish her new shoes every time she wore 'em, and even though three of us could wear the same size, she wouldn't let my sister Lorrie or me ever borrow her shoes. She used to say that our fat feet would stretch her new shoes and she just couldn't have that.

"Well, anyway, she usually wore her old shoes and only wore her new shoes to church or some other special occasion. So, she would hide 'em from us whenever she left the house. Lorrie and me would look through the whole house for those shoes, but we never could find 'em.

"Well, it turns out she had a special hidin' place. She was hidin' 'em on a little ledge up inside the chimney. And one time when she was spendin' the night with a cousin up the road from us, it got so cold that Mama decided to build a fire in the fireplace. Now, it had been warm that day and there was no reason to think that it was gonna get so cold that night, so Erlene had hid her shoes up the chimney like she always did.

"Not too long after Mama started the fire, we heard my uncle's old Model A come drivin' up into the yard, and Erlene jumped out of the car and yelled, 'Did y'all start a fire in the fireplace?' She ran through the door and went straight to the fireplace. We all thought that she had gone crazy, especially when she tried to reach up the chimney and burned her hand.

"She yelled, 'My new shoes are in there,' and then she started bawlin'.

"Mama put out the fire with some water, but it was too late. The shoes had burned to a crisp.

"After she calmed down, Erlene told us that she had looked out the window at my cousin's house and saw smoke comin' out of our chimney, and that's when she woke up our uncle from his nap and made him give her a ride back home.

"Me and Lorrie had no sympathy whatsoever for her. We told her that's what she got for not sharing. Lord, that was mean of us."

Steve said, "Sounds like shoes were a big deal back then."

"You got no idea. That particular year, Daddy had to sell a hog to get us money for shoes. And that was a hog that we would've slaughtered to eat if he hadn't sold it. And that was the same month that Will lost his shoes. I thought that Daddy was gonna have a fit when he found out about Erlene's shoes on top of Will's shoes, but he just shook his head and went out on the porch to smoke a cigarette."

Pearl chuckled softly to herself, then said, "That reminds of another funny thing that Erlene did. It was back when she was around twelve or thirteen. She had three dresses to her name, which is about what the rest of us had, but she got to where she would wear all three of her dresses, one on top of the other, to keep Lorrie and me from wearin' 'em."

Steve laughed and said, "That's got to be one of the craziest things I've ever heard."

"Yeah. Lorrie and me just thought that Erlene was just getting fatter. We had no idea of what she was doin' until we caught her one mornin' tryin' to pull one dress down on top of another. She had got in a hurry, and the second dress got tangled up, and we had to help her get it loose. That's how we found out. We told Mama, and she made Erlene quit doin' that."

Pearl paused a moment, obviously reflecting on that day. Then she started back, "Oh yeah, and, speakin' of hogs, Daddy used to send me and Will out to pull hog weeds for our hogs. Both of us had a sharp knife, and one time Will said, 'Bet you won't cut my finger,' so, naturally, I took a whack at his finger and it started bleeding like crazy.

"It was bleedin' so much that we walked over a mile and a half to Dr. Huddleston, and he sewed it up. We asked how much we owed him, and he said three cents. So we walked all the way home to get three pennies from Daddy, then walked all the way back to pay Dr. Huddleston. The next time Dr. Huddleston saw Daddy, he said you've got some honest children.

"Will never dared me to cut his finger again."

Pearl turned to Steve and said, "Turn left at the dirt road coming up on your left."

When the traffic cleared, Steve turned up the bumpy gravel road and drove slowly, trying not to stir up the rocks too much. "Where are we going?"

"I think that we used to live on this road, about a quarter mile from here."

"Let me know when we get there."

In a few moments, Pearl said, "There it is. See those two chimneys. That's where the house was."

Steve pulled off the road and parked the car in the yard of where a house had been. All that was left was a chimney on each side of the remnants of a rotted wood floor, and some random bricks and boards strewn throughout the yard. In front of where the house had been was what appeared to be a well. It was round and made of stacked gray stones. It was about forty inches high and about four feet wide.

Pearl got out and went over to the well. She peered into the hole in the center of the concrete cover, and then she walked over and stood in front of the remains of the house.

When Steve walked up and stood next to her, she softly said, "Yeah, this is definitely it. This is where we lived."

Pearl pointed to the middle of where the house had been and asked, "You know what a dogtrot house is?"

Steve said, "Yes, ma'am."

"Well, this was kinda like that. It had been a dogtrot house once, but the man we rented it from had closed in each end of the breezeway so that it was turned into a long hallway.

"Lord, that reminds me. Daddy was a mechanic but also was a tenant farmer, and he kept his fertilizer in that long hallway, next to the back door.

"You're not gonna believe this, but one day when Mama and Daddy were gone somewhere, me and Will decided to open the fertilizer bag and make it snow all over the hallway, and, of course, the fertilizer floated all over the house. Good Lord, that was a dumb thing to do.

"Needless to say, when Mama and Daddy got home, we got the whippin' of our lives, and then we had to sweep up all the fertilizer and put it back in the sack." Pearl shook her head and said, "It must have took us two hours to clean that mess up."

Steve looked at his grandmother and said, "I didn't realize you were a juvenile delinquent when you were growing up."

"Oh, yeah. We were awful. But that wasn't the worst thing that me and Will did. Like I said, my Daddy was a mechanic, and sometimes he worked on cars in the back yard. This one time, Will decided that the car needed some gas, and we filled up the tank with sand from out of the front yard.

"Thank God, Daddy didn't know it was us who put the dirt in the car, so he just took the tank off and cleaned it out and cussed the whole time about the fool who put the sand in the tank. Except he didn't say 'fool,' he said 'sonofabitch.'"

Pearl pointed again and said, "There was a porch that went all the way across the front of the house, and one time our Uncle Victor brought over a Victrola, the first one that I had ever seen, and him and Daddy set it up on the front porch and played a record. It was the first record that I ever heard. I can't remember who sang on it, but the song was called Rattlesnake Daddy."

Steve asked, "How long did y'all live here?"

"Oh, it was several years. But we did move a good bit back then. Most of the time when Daddy lost his job, we'd have to move in with his mother in Tallassee. We called her 'Big Mama,' but sometimes we would stay with Granny and Grandpa, my mother's parents, until he could find work again. Even though it was the Depression, Daddy was good about findin' work. Daddy had this old Ford coupe, and when we went to Tallassee to Big Mama's, right before we got into town, we would have to get out of the car and push it up this hill. It wouldn't get up the hill with all of us in it, so three of us would get out and push while Daddy steered the car. You know, we didn't think anything of it. That's just the way it was."

Steve asked, "Where did your Granny and Grandpa live?"

"In North Elmore, not too far from here. They had a good-size house. It's a nursing home now. I'll show it to you if you want.

"Lord, Grandpa was funny. He was from Coosa County, and every time he got mad with Granny, he'd say he was goin' back to Coosa County. One time he told her that, and we all thought he was gone 'cause he was nowhere to be found for two days.

"But Granny kept missin' food out of the warmer on the stove, and then one day when she opened the closet door in the kitchen, there was Grandpa. He had been stayin' in the closet and slippin' out at night to eat.

"When Granny saw him she almost hit him with the fryin' pan she was holdin' till she realized it was him. And then she got mad at him and still almost hit him with the fryin' pan. Lord that was funny."

Pearl walked around the yard for a few minutes looking around, and then she sat down on a tree stump that was between the house and the well. She smiled at Steve and started another story.

"Down the hill from Grandpa's house was a spring where we used to have to go get water for Granny. Grandpa had some geese who used to like to drink at that spring, and if they saw us, they would try to peck us on the behind. If they got you, they would pinch a plug out of your butt.

"There was one time in the summer when it was real hot, and Mama sent Erlene and me down to the spring for a bucket of water. We didn't have any summer shoes, so we had to walk up and down that red hot hill barefooted. Our feet got so hot comin' back that we would stop and pour a little water on our feet to cool 'em off. We did that two or three times, and when we got back to the house, we didn't have hardly any water left. So, Mama made us go back down to the spring again."

Steve laughed and shook his head. It was amazing to him how much his grandmother, whom he had always known to be almost solemn in her demeanor, was opening up to him about her childhood.

Pearl was silent for a while, as though she was remembering something else from her past. Then she said, "Mama told me that when I was a little baby, she used to take me with her when she went down to that same spring to wash clothes. She said that she would put me on a quilt behind her while she was doin' the wash, and one day she heard me cryin' behind her, and she turned around to see why I was cryin', and there on the quilt next to me was a small snake.

"She said that when she saw the snake, she yelled and then picked up a big stick and beat the snake to death. She said she picked up the wet clothes and put 'em on the quilt with me and went back to the house without finishin' the wash. Told me that she was really shook up by that experience.

"For some reason that spring had more than its share of snakes. One time, when I was about four, one of 'em crawled up the hill and laid next to me when I was sittin' on the front steps. I was too scared to move, but Grandpa came along and knocked it off the steps and squashed its head with his boot."

Pearl got up from the tree stump and walked to the left side of the house. She pointed toward the woods behind the house and said, "I remember one time when I was twelve or so, Will and me went into those woods and cut down a holly tree for Christmas. The tree had real pretty red berries on it.

"We brought it back to the house, and Will took some scrap wood pieces and made a stand to hold it up. When he was doin' that us girls were makin' a paper chain, and when we put the paper chain on the tree, we thought that it looked real good with those red berries.

"I remember that Christmas I got a handkerchief, an apple, and an orange for Christmas, and I thought that I was a lucky girl.

"Back in those days, almost everybody was poor. There were a lot of tramps that would travel up and down the roads back then. Sometimes one would come by our house lookin' for somethin' to eat, and my Mama never turned anybody away without somethin' to eat, even if it meant she might have to do without.

"I hate to think about it now, but I had an uncle and aunt back then who would drive up and down the road and, if they saw an empty house, they would move in until the owner found out, and then they would be back on the road again.

"The Depression was somethin' to remember, but I hope we never have those days again."

Pearl went back to the tree stump and sat down again. She pointed away from the house toward a clearing about a quarter mile away. "There's an old cemetery down there. One time there was a little girl buried there, and her family had put a tea set that she used to play with on her grave, along with a set of little china dishes.

"Erlene and me were walkin' through the cemetery and saw those little dishes, so we helped ourselves to those dishes—we thought they were real pretty. But as soon as Mama saw us with those dishes, she sent us right back to the cemetery with 'em."

Steve said, "I'm liking what I'm hearing about your mother. I wish I'd met her."

"Yeah, she was a good woman. Real quiet and humble, but strong.

"She also liked her church. She would make us go almost every Sunday. Daddy wasn't a church goer, but he would make us go, too.

"I used to love it when the preacher would come eat with us, 'cause I knew that meant we would be havin' bologna sausage for Sunday dinner, which was a treat back then. I remember that when the preacher came to eat, me and Erlene would stand at each end of the table with one of those old-fashioned paper fans, and we would fan the flies away. We didn't have any screens in our windows."

Pearl stood up and stretched her back and then gingerly sat back down on the tree stump. She waved her hand in front of her and said, "You see this front yard, how it's all dirt and no grass?"

Steve looked down at the ground and said, "Yes, ma'am."

"Well, there was this one time after a spring shower that we thought we saw the end of a rainbow in this yard, and Erlene said that meant that there was a pot of gold buried here. So, naturally, we went and got Daddy's two shovels and started digging. Me and Earline and Lorrie would take turns digging until we had spent the whole afternoon diggin' and had dug up the whole front yard.

"By the time we finished the yard was one big wet mess full of holes, and we were all wore out and filthy and had blisters on our hands and, of course, we didn't find any gold. When Daddy got home and saw it, he made us fill in all the holes that we had dug before we could have supper. Will was with Daddy when he got back and he laughed and laughed, but he felt sorry for us and helped us fill the holes back up.

Steve said, "What would you have done if you had found the gold?"

Pearl laughed and said, "That's what we were talking about while we were digging. We came up with all kinds of crazy stuff. That's probably what kept us goin.' But, you know what, one of my things was to buy a brand new shiny Buick. How about that?"

Steve said, "Well, I guess that you and I think alike."

"Well, thank goodness you got to do it."

Pearl was quiet for a few minutes before she continued, "One of the best memories I have of those days was when we used to visit Grandpa at his grist mill. Grandpa would let us scoop up hot meal with our hands, and we would eat it like candy. To us it was as good as candy."

She paused a moment and then said, "Grandpa would drain the pond that powered the grist mill once a year, and the men would catch the catfish that were in the pond, and they'd cook 'em in big pots and we'd have the best time eatin' that catfish. People would come from all around, and the men would pitch horseshoes, and the women would catch up on all the gossip."

Steve commented, "So things weren't always bad."

"Lord, no. I don't guess there were any children that had more fun than we did. Our favorite thing, once we got a little older, was to go out in the woods and find a small pine tree, then we'd bend it down until one of us could grab onto the top part of it and then we'd let it go, except for whoever was holdin' onto top part of the tree, and that one would go flyin' into the air for a ride."

Steve grimaced as he tried to picture that in his mind. Then he asked, "Did y'all always live in Elmore?"

"No, we lived in Deatsville, just north of here, for some time when I was a teenager, and then later we moved to Montgomery."

"Did y'all have the same kind of fun in Deatsville?"

"No. We were too old for that kind of foolishness by then. The most fond memories I have of those days was when Hank Williams would come and play at Holtville High School. He was just startin' out then, and the band was called 'Hank and Hezzie.' Hezzie was Hezzie Adair.

"Well, anyway, sometimes when they would play here, Hank would walk me home after they finished, and Hezzie would walk Erlene, and the rest of the band would drive along side of us in the car.

"The first time they walked us home, when we got to our front porch,

Hank tried to kiss me, and I said if you do I'll call my Daddy. He didn't try that again.

"Hank's band would play on WSFA radio back then on Saturday mornins, and me and Erlene would sometimes ride the train down to Montgomery and watch the show. The show didn't last but fifteen minutes, but after the show we'd speak for a few minutes with Hank and Hezzie and then we'd walk back down to the train station and catch a train back home."

"How much did it cost to ride the train then?"

"I can't remember, but it couldn't have been much, 'cause we didn't have much money then. We just had a lot of fun."

Pearl thought a moment and said, "One time when we were livin' in Deatsville a few years earlier, Daddy was runnin' a good-size farm, and he bought our first radio. We ran the radio and what lights we had with some big batteries in a little house out in the yard.

"That reminds me. That farm had a big barn; and when we first moved in, we got the brilliant idea of climbin' up in the hayloft and jumpin' out holdin' a big towel over our head. We were sure that we could fly that way. But when I jumped, I came down across the fence in front of the barn and almost killed myself. We didn't do that again."

Pearl looked at Steve, who had a pained look on his face, and said, "Lord, I've done wore myself out with all this storytellin'"

Steve looked at his watch and said, "We need to be going anyway. Do you still want to stop by the Mt. Hebron Cemetery."

"Yeah, for just a few minutes, if you don't mind."

"I don't mind at all."

Steve helped Pearl back into his car, and she settled into the front seat with a long sigh. As they were driving away, she looked at where the house had been, knowing it would probably be her last time. It brought tears to her eyes, and she dabbed at the tears with a tissue that she had pulled from her purse when they first stopped.

After a short drive, Steve pulled into the driveway of Mt. Hebron Church. He noticed that it was a large, modern brick building and said, "I'm assuming this is not the same building that was here when you grew up."

"Goodness, no. It was an old-fashioned frame church. It's been gone for years. It burned to the ground."

As they got closer to the church, Steve asked, "Is that the cemetery behind the church?"

"That's it."

Steve drove behind the church and parked in one of the several parking spaces next to the church. Then he got out and walked around the front of the car to help his grandmother get out. After Steve closed the door behind her, Pearl stood tall and surveyed the cemetery. She noticed that their family section looked about the same as when she last saw it many years before, but there appeared to be several new headstones in some other sections of the cemetery.

Pearl started walking to the left corner of the grounds and said, "That's our family over there." When she and Steve got to the "Vance" section, Pearl pointed to two long marble slabs and said, "That's my Mama and Daddy." Then she said, "My sister Erlene is buried somewhere around here. I'm not exactly sure where. I had to miss her funeral. I was in the hospital the day that she was buried, and they wouldn't let me out to come to her funeral. I cried all that night."

Steve walked around, reading the names on the stone markers. He said, "Here it is. This is Erlene" and pointed to a marble slab with her name above an engraved bird. On the slab was a pot of faded silk poinsettias probably left there from the Christmas before.

Pearl walked over and stood next to Steve. She held out her arm and said, "Help me kneel down."

Steve held her right arm while Pearl slowly sank to her knees and reached over to touch her sister's name. She said, "We had fun, didn't we, little sister." Then she took her tissue and wiped the tears from her cheeks.

After Steve helped her back up, Pearl pointed out a small headstone about thirty feet from where they were and said, "That's my little brother Raymond. He died when he was three."

Steve said, "I didn't know you had a little brother named Raymond."

"Yeah, it broke my heart when he died. He used to sleep with me every night. When he got cold, he would cuddle up against my side. I missed him so much I'd cry every night till Mama would come in there and comfort me and tell me he was with Jesus."

Steve almost cried over that.

Pearl continued, "I used to have a picture of little Raymond with a group of five midgets that spent the night with us one night."

Steve raised his eyebrows and said, "I've got to hear that story."

"Yeah, the midgets were with a circus that was ridin' a train through town. For some reason, the train stopped in Elmore and the midgets got off, but didn't get back on the train on time. And then somehow they wound up at our house. The railroad tracks ran right behind our house. And, naturally, my mother fed 'em and let 'em spend the night with us.

"The next mornin' they got up and caught another train to wherever it was they were goin'. But little Raymond had a ball with those midgets that night. A couple of weeks later we got a postcard from 'em thankin' us for our hospitality."

Once again, Steve shook his head in wonder. Then he checked his watch and said, "I'm afraid we're gonna have to start back now."

Pearl said, "You don't know how much this meant to me today. I didn't realize how many good memories I hadn't thought of in years. I was expectin' that this might be a real sad trip, but it wasn't that at all. This was good for me."

Steve said, "It was good for me, too. Because not only did I get to know you so much better, you also made me realize that sometimes you just have to stop dwelling on bad memories, and think about the good times."

"Well, just don't tell anybody how much I cried today. It'll ruin my reputation."

"That'll stay between you and me."

For the first fifteen minutes of their trip back, Pearl said nothing. She just sat and stared straight ahead, and every once in a while she'd dab at her eyes with her tissue. Then, after sitting quietly for so long, she brightened up and said, "There is one more story. Mt. Hebron Church reminded me of it.

"Back when we were livin' in Elmore, there was a little Black church across the road from the garage where Daddy worked, and one time when they were holdin' a revival, me and Will and Erlene would sneak across the road and over the railroad tracks and peep in the windows and watch them sing and shout. We were still little then and had never seen anything like that.

"Well, one night when we were doin' that, the preacher saw us peepin' in the window, and he came outside and took us into the church and sat us down in a pew on the front row, right in front of the pulpit. We were so embarrassed at gettin' caught peepin' we never did that again. But the preacher was nice about it. He was just tryin' to teach us a lesson. He walked us across the road to the garage. He told my Daddy what had happened, and Daddy laughed about it. I didn't know it at the time, but the preacher knew my Daddy."

"And you're still going to church?"

"Every Sunday. Me and the Lord got a deal. If I behave myself and go to church every Sunday, he'll let me live as long as I've still got my faculties."

As promised, Steve had Pearl back to the nursing home just in time for dinner. He helped her out of the car and retrieved her purse from the back seat. After Pearl took her purse from him, Steve put his right arm around her waist and walked her to the front door of the nursing home. He hated to have to leave her, but he had a dinner date that night.

When they got to the door, he opened it for her and said, "Let's do this again sometime."

Pearl said, "I'd love to. Next time we'll go to Deatsville."

NOTE: All of the "tales" within this story are based on stories told to me by my mother, Evelyn George, and my aunt, Pauline Oswalt, about their days growing up in Elmore County during the Great Depression.

The Ram

ONE SATURDAY NIGHT IN BIRMINGHAM, ALABAMA

It's a pleasant evening in May around nine o'clock. Two thirty-five-year-old men are standing in front of a small nightclub in the Five Points district. The sidewalk is wet from an earlier shower. The club is in a red brick building that looks as though it may have been built in the nineteen forties. On either side of the tall wooden front door there is a large picture window that has been darkened to the point that very little light shines through.

One of the men is White, of medium build, and about five-foot-ten. He's wearing khaki slacks and a starched light blue button-down oxford shirt. The other is a Black man, slightly heavier and taller. He's wearing gray summer weight wool-blend slacks and a blue-and-white striped button-down oxford shirt. Both men are smoking cigarettes and periodically looking down the street as though expecting someone or something to appear.

The Black man, Edmond "Ed" Tyler, says, "Think he'll show up?"

The White man, Raymond "Duke" Ellison, answers, "Who knows. You never know with the Ram."

Ed nods and says, "That's true."

They finish their cigarettes and drop the butts onto the damp concrete sidewalk, where they mash them out under their identical black loafers.

Duke says, "Let's go on in. The band's about to start."

When they walk into the club it takes a while for their eyes to adjust to the dim lighting. Once they can see well enough to negotiate the room, they see that the room is approximately two-thirds full. Bud, the club owner, greets them on their way to a table in the second row from the bandstand. The table has a white tablecloth and four straight-back wooden chairs.

Ed takes a seat facing the bandstand and motions to Carol, the waitress, whom both he and Duke know well. They both had a crush on her when they were eighth-graders and she was a high school cheerleader. She's still attractive, but now a little fleshier. And three divorces have hardened her face and put streaks of gray in her brown hair.

Duke and Ed represented Carol, at no cost, in her last divorce. So she always goes out of her way to accommodate them when they show up at the club.

Carol asks, "The usual?" Ed nods yes.

Duke pats Carol's arm and says, "How about bringing me a Miller High Life."

Carol smiles at them and says, "Be right back."

Duke turns and peers through the dim light of the club toward the front door.

Ed, whose back is to the door, asks, "See anything?"

"I don't see the Ram, but I think I see Marcia."

Duke stands up to get a better look. "Yeah, that's her. She must have finished early." He waves his right hand and gets Marcia's attention, and she walks to their table. She is a slender, attractive redhead in a gray business suit. She gives him a quick hug and a peck on the cheek.

Duke pulls out the chair next to his and says, "Have a seat, babe. You finish early?"

Marcia sits down, places her small black handbag on the table and says, "Lord, no. This could last all night. We decided to take an hour break to unwind."

Ed asks, "What are you working on?"

"A consolidation of two publishing companies who can't stand each other."

Ed looks puzzled. "Then why do they want to merge?"

"If they don't merge and combine their staffs and resources, they'll both go under. And they both know it, so everybody feels trapped. And that's making them ornery as hell. Both companies are run by grumpy old men who don't want to admit that they need each other."

Ed says, "Been there. Duke and I are working on a Federal court settlement that has the same sort of personality clash."

Marcia says, "Well, I hope that y'all have better luck than we're having."

Just then Carol arrives with Ed's and Duke's drinks.

Duke thanks Carol and says to Marcia, "I've got faith in you, babe. You'll get it done. Want a drink?"

"Oh, yeah. Jack and ginger, Carol."

Carol says, "You got it, Marcia," and walks away.

Marcia asks, "Seen the Ram and Michelle yet?"

"Nope," says Ed.

"Too bad. I got the impression from what you told me that y'all were really looking forward to seeing him again. I know I am."

Duke adds, "I sure hope he shows up. We need to talk to him before someone else does."

"About what?"

"Remember that album he put out about ten years ago that got nominated for a Grammy?"

"Absolutely. Southern Winds. Love that album. What about it?"

Duke says, "The original recording deal is about to expire, and the Ram will get all the mechanical rights to the album, and we'd like to re-release it under the label that we just set up. We think that we could make a good bit of money on it using the electronic music platforms that have cropped up over the last several years."

"What's to stop him from renewing his contract with the original label?"

Ed says, "Nothing. That's why we want to get to him tonight."

Marcia says, "I see," then makes a face as though she's slightly perturbed.

They've been there about ten more minutes when Ed turns and looks over the rim of his glass toward the front door. Then he puts his glass down and stands up. He smiles and holds his right hand up to get the Ram's attention.

When Duke sees Ed waving toward the front, he rises from his chair and turns to see the Ram approaching. The Ram is the same age as Ed and Duke, but looks much fitter. He's a little over six feet tall and has a healthy tan. He has short brown hair with a few spots of sun-bleaching. He's dressed in faded blue Wranglers and a black corduroy shirt. He's holding hands with a tall, beautiful young woman with long chestnut hair. She's dressed in black stretch jeans and a turquoise blouse.

As the Ram arrives at the table, Duke reaches out his open right hand and says, "Man, it's good to see you, Ram. It's been quite a while." Then, after the Ram and Duke shake hands, Duke looks at the young lady and says, "You must be Michelle. Marcia told me that you used to be a model. I can believe that. You're very pretty."

Michelle smiles and says, "Thank you. You must be Duke."

"I am, and this other character is Ed."

Ed says, "Glad to meet you, Michelle. Let me get another chair so that we can all sit together."

Ed walks over to a nearby table and politely asks the middle-aged couple sitting there if he can take one of their empty chairs. The man says, "Sure," and Ed takes the chair and sets it next to Marcia's.

As the Ram is saying hello to Marcia and taking a seat in the chair on the other side of Michelle, Carol walks up with Marcia's drink. She places the drink in front of Marcia, and says, "Well, Ramsey Cantrell, it's been a long time. Where have you been?"

The Ram says, "Around. Good to see you, Carol. Meet my friend Michelle."

Carol says, "Glad to meet you, Michelle. Would you two like something to drink?"

Michelle answers, "I'd like white wine, please."

The Ram says, "Black coffee."

Carol says, "Got it" and walks off.

Duke looks to Michelle and says, "I couldn't believe it when Marcia told me that you and the Ram would be here tonight."

Michelle says, "Well, Marcia made it sound like it would be fun. She talks very favorably about Ed and you. But it did take some effort to get Ramsey out of the house. He's become a real homebody."

Ed looks to the Ram and says, "Man, you're really looking good. How do you do it? You're the same age as Duke and me."

"I work for a living. You two wouldn't know anything about that."

Marcia chuckles and punches Duke in the shoulder.

Ed asks Michelle, "How'd you two meet? You're way out of his league."

Michelle looks at the Ram and says, "Oh, I don't know about that. But we met when he did some work on my townhouse about a year ago. He was renovating another townhouse on my block, and I kept seeing his truck parked on our street. So, one day I went out and asked him to look at some water damage that had been done to my living room floor.

"So, right after he finished with the renovation down the street, he fixed my floor; and I haven't been able to get rid of him since."

The Ram looks at Michelle and says, "Hey, I'm no fool. I know a good thing when I see it."

Ed nods and says to the Ram, "Did you know that three of your former bandmates are playing here tonight?"

"Really, who?"

"Roger, Mark, and Wayne."

"Well, how 'bout that. When do they start?"

Ed looks at his watch and says, "Supposed to have been thirteen minutes ago."

The Ram smiles and says, "I can believe that. They're probably out back partaking of some illicit substance."

About five minutes later, a short dark-haired man comes onto the stage carrying a white Fender Stratocaster guitar. He puts out his cigarette in an ashtray on the floor next to his mike stand and plugs his guitar into a Marshall amp. Then three more musicians take the stage, one after the other. One is a tall skinny blond carrying a black Fender Precision bass guitar, one is a long-haired chubby guy who takes a seat behind the drum set, and the third one is a somber-looking, gray-haired Black man who sits down at the piano. Each of the musicians is dressed in black pants and a long-sleeve gray polyester shirt.

The Ram asks Duke, "Who's the old guy?"

"Tom Raymond."

"Really. I've heard him on records. He's really good."

Ed says, "Not as good as you were."

"That nice of you to say, but he's much better than I ever was."

They hear a tapping on the microphone in the center of the stage. Wayne, the bass player and lead vocalist, leans into the mike and says, "Good evening everybody. Glad to see y'all. I see a lot of familiar faces, and I even see one of our old bandmates, the legendary Ramsey Cantrell, sitting right over there." He points toward the Ram's table.

"Ram gave us out first big break when he hired us to play on his Southern Winds album. Then he hired us to go on a six-month tour with him to promote the album. We owe him a lot. Y'all give him a hand."

The audience of about seventy people applaud perfunctorily and a few of them try to get a glance at the Ram as he waves to Wayne.

Wayne turns to the drummer and gives a countdown with his right forefinger, and the band starts their first set with Willie Nelson's "Crazy." They play several more familiar songs before Marcia, in the middle of "Green Onions," downs the last of her drink and announces that she has to leave. She kisses Duke on the cheek and says, "See you later tonight, I hope." Then she looks to Michelle and says, "I'll see you Saturday." As she walks away, she lays her hand on the Ram's shoulder and says, "Good to see you again, Ramsey." Then she points at Duke and Ed and says, "You two behave yourselves."

When the band takes a break after the first set, the Ram's three former bandmates all come over to say hello and shake his hand. Wayne says, "Man, we miss you. Still doing construction?"

"Hey, I miss y'all, too. We had some good times. I'm glad y'all are still playing. You sound better than ever. And, yeah, I've still got my construction company."

Mark asks, "You still writing songs?"

"I'm still knocking out a song now and then."

Mark says, "Reason I'm asking is we're almost through with the album we've been working on with this band, and we need a couple of more new songs. Got anything that would fit our style?"

The Ram turns to Michelle and asks, "Michelle, you still got that demo on you that we listened to the other day?"

Michelle reaches into her purse and pulls out a CD. It has a plain white label with handwriting on it. "Here it is."

The Ram takes the CD and hands it to Wayne. The Ram says, "This CD has four new songs on it that I just put together. Take it with you and let me know if you're interested in any of them."

Wayne looks at the CD and says, "Thanks, man. This is great. What kind of royalties do you want if we use any of them?"

"Oh, I don't know. How 'bout seventy percent of standard?"

"That'll work. We'll draw up a contract if we can use any."

"That's fine."

Roger clears his throat and says, "Guys, we need to have a short band meeting out back before the next set," and Wayne says, "Oh, yeah." Then he turns to the Ram and says, "Good to see you, man. I'll let you know about the songs."

After the musicians leave their table, Duke says to the Ram, "What Wayne said while ago about the Southern Winds album reminded me of something I've been meaning to ask you. What's the status of that album?"

"What do you mean?"

"Is it still out?"

"Yeah, but my contract with the label expires in about . . . three weeks, and I haven't decided whether to renew the contract or shop the album to another label. Y'all wrote the contract for me. Remember that it was for ten years and then I could walk away with all the mechanical rights."

Ed says, "Oh, yeah. Has it been ten years already?"

Duke says, "Time flies," then asks, "Got any prospects to pick up the album?"

"A couple of folks seem to be interested. Why?"

Duke and Ed look at each other with mild consternation, then Ed asks, "Before you make your final decision, can you give Duke and me a chance at it? We just started this little music production company and we're looking for products. We might be interested in reissuing that album using some of those modern electronic formats, as well making CDs under our label. What do you think?"

"I don't know. Depends on the deal. Y'all are my old buddies, but I should probably look at what all the offers are. Besides that, y'all don't have any experience in the music business."

"That's true, but we've got Dolph Emerson as a managing partner for the record label. He just moved back here from Nashville. You know him. He's one of the best producers in the business."

The Ram nods and says, "He's good, for sure."

Duke says, "Now that you know that Dolph would be in charge of the project, what kind of offer would you consider?"

"Don't know. Haven't thought a lot about it. But working with Dolph might be interesting. What kind of offer would y'all make?"

Duke turns to Ed and says, "Ed, do you think that we could offer maybe twenty-five percent of the net?"

Ed says, "That sounds high to me. What about twenty?" Then he turns to the Ram and asks, "What do you think, Ram? Would twenty work?"

The Ram says, "I don't know. You wouldn't have any recording costs, because the album is already done." He hesitates as moment and asks, "Have y'all thought about the songwriter royalties? Cause all the songs are mine. And I would be due artist royalties on top of that."

Ed says, "We were including songwriter and artist royalties as part of the twenty percent net. Don't you think that would be fair?"

The Ram asks Michelle for a pen and a piece of paper. Michelle pulls a ballpoint pen from her purse and looks for a scrap of paper. She finds a receipt from her lunch that day at Cracker Barrel and hands it the Ram.

The Ram starts writing some numbers on the back of the receipt. He looks up and says, "I could agree to songwriter royalties at the standard rate and then thirty percent of the net, no separate artist royalties."

Duke says, "Whoa, Ram. That's way too steep."

The Ram leans back in his chair. He looks up toward the ceiling, then looks at Duke and asks, "Do y'all have any empty office space in your building?"

Ed says, "We've got a couple of empty offices on the third floor and one on the second floor and one on the first floor, why?"

"Are those two on the third floor adjoining offices?"

"Yeah."

The Ram looks at Michelle then back to Ed. He says, "Tell you what. Michelle is looking for space for a new modeling agency that she's starting up. Right now, she's working for an agency in Atlanta four days a week. She does their training and also helps with recruiting and advertising. When she's in Atlanta, they let her stay in a four-plex apartment building they own. It's where their models stay when they're in town.

"Michelle told them that she's getting tired of traveling back and forth, and having to stay in Atlanta overnight, and that she wants to start a small agency in Birmingham. They told her that they'd be willing to contract with her to keep doing training for them and that they might also want to use some of her models once she gets her agency going.

"So, I'm thinking that your building, being right off I-20, would be a good location for what she wants to do, if she could get those two adjoining offices."

Duke furrows his brow and asks, "What are you getting at?"

"How about you lease those two offices to Michelle's new agency for a year, rent-free, beginning the first day of July, then give her a discount of, say, twenty-five percent on the rent after that for, say, four additional years? By that time, she should be well established, and y'all can re-negotiate the rent."

Ed audibly lets out a breath and says, "Okay, let's get down to brass tacks. What's your final offer to us if we agree to the office lease arrangement you're proposing?"

"If y'all will work with me on the office space for Michelle, I'd be willing to waive the songwriter and artist royalties and take twenty-six percent of the net."

Ed says, "What do you think, Duke? Could we live with that?"

Duke says, "Let's take a walk" and motions Ed toward the men's room.

Michelle turns to the Ram and asks, "What do you think they'll do?"

The Ram replies, "Don't you worry, they're back there calculating dollars. They'll come around."

When Duke and Ed return, they take their seats and Duke says, "Well, we're not making any money on those offices right now, and it might be nice to have young models coming in and out of our building. That might add a little glamour. So, if you'll help us promote the album, we could live with the twenty-six percent."

Ram pauses a moment, then says, "I'll help with promotion if it's only on weekends, and if you pay my travel expenses and also Michelle's, if she wants to go with me."

Duke drums the fingers of his right hand on the table. He asks, "Do you have any videos for that album?"

"I've got maybe fifteen or twenty from the album tour. If we make the deal, I'll show them to you, and y'all can make copies of the ones you might want to use."

Ed and Duke look at each other for about twenty seconds without giving any indication of which way they will go. The Ram takes a sip from his coffee mug.

Then Ed and Duke slowly rise to shake the Ram's hand.

Duke says, "Write down the name that Michelle's agency will be using, and we'll work up a contract for you and a lease for Michelle. I'll have our courier bring them by your office. Is it still next to the Seven-Eleven in that strip mall?"

The Ram asks Michelle to write down the name of her agency for them, then says, "Yep. Still there."

Ed says, "When I drove by there the other day there was some renovation going on. What was that?"

"A State liquor store is moving into the last unit on the left, so there's another thousand square feet being added to the back of that unit for storage space."

Duke nods and says, "A State store. Man, that's a good tenant to have. That's long-term stuff. Who's your landlord? He must have some clout."

"Me."

Ed asks, "You own that strip mall?"

"Yeah. I bought it two years ago."

"How'd you pull off a State liquor store as a tenant?"

"I do good work; and I did some of that good work for some of the right people."

Ed looks at Duke, and Duke says, "Well, okay then."

The Ram says, "By the way, when you write up the contract, I want it to say that you'll pay me twenty percent of the net and that the other six percent will go to Roger, Wayne, and Mark, two percent each. Speaking of them, have y'all talked to them about putting out their album on your label?"

Ed says, "No. Do you think we should?"

"I would if I were y'all."

As Duke and Ed look at one another, the Ram gets up from his chair, drinks the last of his coffee, places the mug and a ten dollar bill on the table, and says, "I hate to leave such good company, but I'm used to going to bed early, so we're gonna have to take off."

Michelle stands up and says, "I'm so grateful for the chance to have my office in your building. You just don't know how much that means to me."

Ed says, "You'll be a welcome addition."

The band members are slowly walking onto the bandstand, taking their positions. The Ram waves to them as he and Michelle begin walking toward the front door. After they're out of earshot, Duke turns to Ed and asks, "What just happened?"

"Well, partner, I believe that two high-priced lawyers just got outmaneuvered by a junior college dropout. I believe that we got Rammed."

Duke nods twice and says, "I believe you're right." He lifts his beer stein and says, "To the Ram."

Ed clinks his cocktail glass against Duke's stein and says, "To the Ram."

The Thursday before that Saturday

It's a little after nine p.m. and Michelle is just getting home from Atlanta. The Ram is sitting in a brown leather recliner watching the Braves game on TV. Michelle walks over to him and kisses him on the forehead. She asks, "Who's winning?"

"The Phillies."

"The fillies. There's a team called the fillies?"

"Yeah. They from Philadelphia, so they're called the Phillies."

"Oh. I see. They're not named for horses; they're named for the city."

The Ram chuckles and says, "You really don't know much about sports, do you?"

"Nope. By the way, I got an interesting call from Marcia Jackson on the way home."

"Duke Ellison's girlfriend. How do you know her?"

"She's in my Saturday yoga class."

"What'd she have to say?"

"She wants us to join Duke and her, and Duke's partner Ed Tyler, at Bud's Place on Saturday night."

"Did she say why?"

"What do you mean 'why'? I thought that y'all were friends."

"We are, but those two guys only contact me when they need something. It's been that way since we played high school basketball together. They're really good guys, but they're conniving as hell. Always have been."

"They seem to be doing really well in their law practice."

"That's 'cause they're a perfect team. Duke's the creative one, always coming up with good ideas; and Ed's the analytical one who can figure out how to get things done. But I wonder what they're up to now. Why this get-together?"

Michelle says, "Oh, and Marcia said that some of your old musician friends will be playing at Bud's on Saturday. I think she said Wayne and Mark and one other that I can't remember."

"Was it Roger?"

"Yeah, it was Roger."

The Ram thinks for a moment, then asks, "How long has Marcia been in your Saturday yoga class?"

"About three weeks, I guess."

"Did she single you out to make friends?"

"I don't know. Why are you so suspicious of her joining my class?"

"She lives in Mountain Brook. There's probably a half-dozen yoga studios between where she lives and downtown Birmingham, so there's no reason for her to drive that far."

The Ram leans back in the recliner and says, "I'm gonna get online and do some research on your computer."

"Suit yourself. But I'm glad that Marcia joined my class. She's told me all sorts of stuff about you that I didn't know."

The Ram turns to Marcia and says, "Such as?"

"That you were a college basketball player, and that you used to be in a rock band and had an album that was nominated for a Grammy."

"I played one year of basketball at Lawson State Community College. They were the only school that offered me a scholarship. And I was in some bands that were pretty popular around here, but I gave up performing about ten years ago."

As the Ram was talking, Michelle was changing into gray sweatpants and the Ram's faded red Alabama t-shirt. She sat down on the loveseat next to the recliner and asked, "Why'd you only play basketball one year if you had a scholarship? Marcia said that you were really good."

"I was a good high school player, but I knew I would never be a very good college player, because I had reached my peak in high school like most athletes do. And I was playing music at the same time two or three nights a weeks, so I dropped out of college and focused on my music for the next five or six years. It was during that time that we put out the Southern Winds album that was so popular.

"Funny thing is I actually only intended for that album to be a showcase for songs that I had written, because I was hoping that some big-time artists would pick up some of them. But for some reason, it did way better than I ever expected. Got good reviews, even from *Billboard.*

"Anyway, when I was about twenty-five or so, I realized that I wasn't getting any better as a musician. I was an okay singer and a so-so piano player, and it got frustrating to keep doing it and not making any progress, especially when most of the people I played with had more talent than I did. I felt like I was holding them back, or at least not contributing much. The only real musical talent that I had was as a songwriter. So, I left the band I was with at the time and went to work with the same construction company that my father worked for."

Michelle looks at the Ram. He has an expression on his face that she has never seen before. He says, "My dad started teaching me woodworking and carpentry when I was still a kid, and I had a real knack for it. So I had no trouble doing construction work, and I kept learning from him and the other older guys, and getting better and better at it. And I really liked the idea of building something. It's not like music where you play a song and then it's gone. You actually have something to show for your effort."

Michelle thinks for a moment about what the Ram has said. She asks, "When did you start your own construction company?"

"After my dad passed away from lung cancer about five years ago. When he died, he left me his work truck, all of his equipment, and twenty thousand dollars. He left my mom the house, his bank accounts, and his car, and she also got a quarter of a million dollars from a life insurance policy that he took out when they got married. So, I didn't feel bad about taking the truck and the equipment and the twenty thousand and starting my own company, like he always wanted me to."

"Is that when you bought that little house next door to your mom's? After your dad died?"

"Yeah. She was only fifty, but I still wanted to be nearby if she needed me. And she wanted me to have dad's workshop that he had built behind their house. So it worked out pretty good for both of us. We look out for each other but still have our privacy."

Michelle says, "Yeah, that does make sense." Then she says "You said that you didn't like the music business, but you're still writing songs. I see you working on them all the time."

"Well, it really wasn't music that I got tired of; it was performing. I still love music. And songwriting is like construction. There's always something to show for your effort." The Ram gets up from the recliner and walks over to Michelle's computer desk.

After he sits down and turns on the computer, he smiles at Michelle and says, "Besides that, I keep getting royalties long after the work is done. There's nothing like that surprise check coming in the mail."

Michelle contemplates what the Ram has told her. She says, "Actually, I kind of understand what you're saying. I never liked runway modeling as much as photo modeling. With runway modeling, once it's over, unless it's being filmed, there's nothing to show for all the work that you put into it. But with photography, that picture will be around for as long as somebody wants to look at it."

She stands up and says, "And I'm proud to say that some photos of me have hung in art galleries. Maybe some still are."

"I didn't know that. I hope they weren't nudes."

"Only a few are. Does that make you feel better?"

"Well, no."

Michelle says, "Too bad" and walks to the kitchen to make herself a sandwich.

Meanwhile, the Ram is on Michelle's computer trying to figure out what Ed and Duke are up to. That's when he sees a short article about their law firm in which Duke told the interviewer that Ed and he are "humble and grateful for their good fortune and will be investing in the future of Birmingham through other ventures such as buying and renovating downtown commercial buildings and establishing a music company and studio in the downtown area."

"A music company and studio," the Ram whispers to himself. "So that's it. They want my Southern Winds album."

He sits back and thinks for a few minutes, then calls out, "Michelle, I know what they're up to now. I'm going to do a little more research to see if we can figure out a way to take advantage of it."

"Okay, honey, knock yourself out. Want some hot chocolate?"

"No, thanks," says the Ram as he types "Tyler-Ellison Building."

Trapped

It's 10:40 on a fall evening. Sylvia Stanton, the 62-year-old wife of millionaire real estate developer Arthur Stanton, is sitting at her desk at the head of a classroom on the eighth floor of the Library Tower at Montgomery University. She's dressed in a well-tailored burgundy business suit. She's wearing an antique ruby and diamond ring next to her wedding band. She's also wearing tasteful diamond earrings. Sylvia is reviewing charts handed in by students in her graduate class on Southern genealogy. She's been teaching the class for about a month, and these are the first genealogy charts that the students have been assigned to construct on their own.

Before she married Arthur twenty-one years ago, Sylvia had been a career high school English teacher. After the marriage, she left her teaching position and helped her husband with his business ventures. During that period she was also writing what would become a very successful book on the history of famous Southern families. It was due to that book that the University had asked Sylvia to teach a class two nights a week to their graduate history students. Sylvia is in the third week of teaching that class.

She hears a soft knock on the open classroom door and looks up to see a stocky, middle-aged Black man in a University maintenance uniform. The uniform is navy blue, the school color. The man is holding a red metal lunch box and a large ring of keys.

In a deep, raspy voice he says, "Excuse me, ma'am. I got to lock up the buildin'. Are you gonna be much longer?"

Sylvia looks at her watch and begins gathering papers and putting them into her black leather briefcase. She says, "I'm almost finished. I just need to organize these last few papers. I didn't realize the building needed to be evacuated."

"Yes, ma'am. The liberry closes at ten, and we sposed to lock up at ten-thirty to clean up the buildin', and it's a little bit after that now."

Sylvia says, "Oh, I'm so sorry. I didn't know that. I'm just a part-time instructor, and this is my first semester."

"Yes, ma'am, I understand."

Sylvia puts the last of the charts into her briefcase and snaps it shut. She says, "There. Everything's packed. I'm ready to go."

"I'll hafta ride down on the elevator with you. The doors're already locked, and I'll hafta let you out."

Sylvia rises from her chair, picks up her briefcase, straightens her skirt, and says, "All right. Let's go."

She walks to the door and asks, "Should I lock this door, or will you need to get back in here?"

"You can leave it unlocked. I need to sweep the flo' and empty the trash cans, and then I'll lock it up. You can leave the lights on, too."

"All right, then. I'm ready to go. By the way, I'm Sylvia. What's your name?"

"I'm James. I'm the night custodian for this buildin' and the admin buildin'."

Sylvia holds out her right hand and stiffly says, "Glad to meet you James. From what I can tell, you do a good job."

James reaches out and gently shakes her delicate hand as though he is afraid that he might injure it. He says, "Yes, ma'am. Thank you, ma'am. I do my best."

They walk together down the hall to where there are four elevators, two on each side. James pushes the down button on the wall between the two elevators on their right.

They hear an elevator coming from a lower floor and then coming to a stop. When the heavy brass door opens, Sylvia enters, followed by James. James reaches over and presses the button for the lobby. As Sylvia passes James, he noticed that she smells like some kind of flower, maybe a gardenia.

Sylvia walks to the rear of the elevator car where she stands stiffly, clutching her briefcase and her matching black alligator handbag.

The door closes, and the elevator begins to move. In just a few seconds, the lights flicker and the elevator jolts to a stop.

James and Sylvia look at each other, then James reaches over and pushes the LOBBY button again. There is a faint whirring sound, and the elevator car shakes but doesn't move. James begins pushing buttons at random, but the elevator remains still.

Sylvia says, "Let me try."

James moves aside and lets Sylvia press all the buttons on both panels in the elevator. There is no sound or movement.

Sylvia points to a phone in the car and asks, "What about this phone? Can we reach someone with it?"

"No, ma'am. That phone rings at the liberry desk. It won't do no good. They're all gone home."

"What does this mean? Are we going to be stuck in the elevator all night?"

"If we can't get it movin', I guess so."

"I can't have that."

"Yes, ma'am."

"Don't you have a college cell phone?"

"Yes, ma'am, but it's in the front pocket of my jacket that's hangin' in the maintenance closet. I'm sorry."

Sylvia laughs and says, "I can't get upset at you for that. I left my cell phone on my kitchen counter."

James nervously laughs with her, and says, "Well, that makes three phones that we got that we cain't use. Lord help us."

James opens his large lunch box and fumbles around inside. He pulls out two good-sized oatmeal cookies. "Wanna oatmeal cookie? They're good. My wife made 'em."

Sylvia smiles and says, "No, thank you."

Sylvia is standing with her back pressed hard against the back wall of the elevator car, looking very uncomfortable. She is still clutching her briefcase and handbag.

James begins to eat one of his cookies.

Sylvia puts her handbag and briefcase on the floor of the elevator and then kneels and opens the briefcase. She pulls out a handful of papers and says, "I'm teaching a course on Southern genealogy. I may as well use this time to look at some of the charts my students have turned in."

"Yes, ma'am."

Sylvia reviews each of the charts. Having found none of them particularly well-done, she sighs and puts them away. She closes her briefcase, then looks at her watch.

She says, "It's only eleven-twenty. It seems that we've been here all night already."

"Yes, ma'am."

"Well, if we're going to be stuck here, we may as well get to know each other. I'm Sylvia Stanton, Arthur Stanton's wife."

"I'm James Waters, Lillian Waters's husband."

"How long have you been working here, Mister Waters?"

"About . . . six and a half years."

"What did you do before working here?

"Well, ma'am, when I was real young, I worked on chicken farm for about three years, more or less. And then I worked for about ten years for Proudfoot Construction, and then . . . well . . . I had to do a little time."

Sylvia furrows her brow, "What do you mean by 'a little time'?"

"Well, it's not somethin' I'm proud of, but I spent a little over twelve years in State incarceration, first at Fountain, then at Draper, then I spent my last year in a work release facility. When I was on work release, I was assigned to work on the outdoor maintenance crew here at the college on weekends, and that's how I come to work here."

Sylvia pauses for a moment. She says, "I see."

She pauses again and says, "I know that it's none of my business, and you don't have to tell me, but what were you convicted of?"

"Well, they say I murdered my first wife, Pauline, but I didn't"

Sylvia visibly tenses up, then asks, "Who do you think really killed her?"

"Oh, I kilt her all right, but it weren't murder. It was self-defense. She was comin' at me with a butcher knife, and I pult out my twenty-five pistol and shot her in the head."

Sylvia recoils at hearing that.

James continues, "The police said I shoulda run out the house instead of shootin' her, and that's why they charged me with murder. But they let me plead to manslaughter."

James pauses, and then goes on, "I got sentenced to twenty years, but I got out on parole. I'm still on parole, but I'm on what's called unsupervised parole. I just have to call Mister Lord, my parole officer, once a month to tell him that I'm still workin' and hadn't been arrested for anything. And every once in a while, he calls my boss, Mister Jacobs, and checks up on me."

Sylvia looks more uncomfortable than ever, but attempts a strained smile. Then she says, "Well, I suppose you've gotten your life together now."

James nods and says, "Oh, yes ma'am, I'm doin' my best."

Five minutes pass.

As hard as she tries, Sylvia can't contain her curiosity. She asks, "Why did your wife try to kill you?"

"Don't rightly know. But we never did git along real good. And I had come in a few times drunk and beat her up a little . . . And she thought that I had a woman on the side, but I didn't . . . least not the one she thought."

"I see."

More time passes. Sylvia looks at her watch. It was ten after one.

James sees Sylvia begin to tear up. He squirms a bit and then says, "I'm sorry you got locked in here."

Sylvia says, "Thank you, Mister Waters, but that's not why I'm stressing out right now. This is so embarrassing, but I need to go to the bathroom."

James looks perplexed. He has no idea how to respond to that statement, but he asks, "Is there anything I can do, ma'am?"

Sylvia chuckles. "Not unless you can build me a restroom real fast." James smiles in spite of himself. "No ma'am. Cain't do that." He hesitates a moment and then awkwardly says, "But I got this empty thermos bottle here, if you can use that. It's got a big mouth on it."

"I can't ruin your thermos bottle."

James pulls a large silver thermos from his lunch box and holds it out to Sylvia. He says, "Then, here, I'm givin' it to you. Now it's your thermos bottle. You can ruin it if you want to."

Sylvia looks at the bottle and says, "I'll take it, but I'll have to pay you for it. What would a new thermos cost?"

"Prob'ly about twenty dollars."

Sylvia reaches into her purse and pulls out two ten dollar bills and a five dollar bill.

"I'll give you twenty-five and not a penny less."

James takes the money and thanks Sylvia.

Sylvia removes the top from the thermos bottle and then looks around for a place to have some privacy. Obviously, there is none.

"Mister Waters, I don't know if I can do this."

"I'll turn around and cover my eyes till you tell me to turn back around."

"But, you'll still hear everything."

James says, "Yes, ma'am," then thinks a moment and says, "Okay . . . I'll go to the corner over there and turn around and close my eyes and hum real, real loud until you tap me on the shoulder."

Sylvia contemplates what James just said and, realizing that she has no other option, she sighs and says, "All right. Let's go for it."

James walks over to the corner that he pointed to, and Sylvia goes to the corner catty-cornered from that one.

James closes his eyes and covers his ears with his hands. He begins to hum "What a Friend We Have in Jesus" as loudly as he can.

Sylvia opens the bottle and places the top on the floor. Then she turns her back to James and, laughing to herself, looks skyward, takes a deep breath and lowers her panties to her ankles. She pulls the panties off her left ankle, leaving them on only the right ankle. She looks over her right shoulder at James, then shakes her head again, softly says, "Oh, my Lord," and places the open bottle between her thighs.

For a few seconds, nothing happens, but then Sylvia relaxes and slowly begins to relieve herself.

Once she finishes, Sylvia gingerly screws the top back onto the thermos bottle. Then she pulls her panties back on, straightens her skirt, and turns around.

She walks over to James and taps him on his left shoulder. James hesitates, then very slowly turns around.

"Mister Waters, you are a life-saver. If you hadn't thought of my using your thermos, I don't know what I would have done." Sylvia laughs. "I guess that I would have either urinated in my pants or exploded."

James smiles slightly. He's not sure how to respond. He says, "I'm sure you woulda thought of somethin'."

"You know, I've been married thirty-six years including both my marriages, and I've never gone to the bathroom in front of my husband. Not even when he was in the shower."

"Yes, ma'am."

"Now, what about you? What if you have to go?"

"Don't worry 'bout me, ma'am. I went just before I saw you. Beside that, one thang I learnt in prison was how to hold thangs back."

More time passes. It seems that they've been in that elevator forever.

James and Sylvia are sitting in opposite corners of the elevator car, both with their heads down, obviously weary of their situation.

James looks at his watch. It's 3:20 a.m.

Just then, he hears noises outside the elevator. It sounds like another elevator coming to a stop.

He asks, "Miz Stanton, did you hear that?"

"Yes, I did. I hope that's someone looking for us."

Sylvia stands up and begins to beat on the elevator door with the thermos bottle. She shouts, "IS ANYBODY OUT THERE. WE'RE TRAPPED IN HERE."

James bangs on the door with his lunch box. He shouts, "SOMEBODY LET US OUT OF HERE."

They look at each other and then they each put an ear to the door to see what they can hear. They hear the muffled sound of people talking.

A few more minutes pass. Then, below them, there are clanging sounds of someone apparently attempting to get their elevator to move.

James says, "Sounds like they know we're in here."

"Thank goodness."

Suddenly, the elevator car groans and inches upward. Then it stops.

Again, they can hear people talking outside the elevator, but can't understand what they're saying.

They hear a male voice shouting, "MISSUS STANTON, ARE YOU IN THERE?"

Sylvia answers, "YES. MISTER WATERS AND I ARE IN HERE."

"ARE YOU ALL RIGHT?"

"YES, WE'RE FINE."

"WE'LL HAVE YOU OUT IN A FEW MINUTES."

"WE'LL WAIT RIGHT HERE."

James laughs. Sylvia offers him a high five, and he gently taps her hand.

In about ten minutes, the elevator door opens. Outside are the Chief of Campus Police, two City Policemen, the Director of Campus Maintenance, and a very stressed-looking Arthur Stanton.

One of the City Police officers points at James and says, "Waters, come out of there with your hands up."

James immediately raises both hands high above his head and slowly walks out of the elevator into the tiled hallway.

As soon as James is out of the car, the officer pats him down and then reaches for his handcuffs.

James looks resigned to the situation, but, as Arthur is walking up to embrace Sylvia, she says in her sternest voice, "What's this all about? He hasn't done anything wrong."

Ted Rawlings, Campus Police Chief, says, "Missus Stanton, this man is a convicted murderer, and he's on parole."

Sylvia says, "Yes, I know."

Looking surprised, Chief Rawlings asks, "How do you know that?"

"He told me all about it. Now you all quit treating him as if he's done something wrong. He got trapped in the elevator just like I did. And I'll have you know he saved my life."

Chief Rawlings looks at James and then at Sylvia. He asks, "What do you mean, he saved your life?"

"Never you mind. You just leave Mister Waters alone."

Joe Jacobs, Director of Campus Maintenance, asks, "James, how come you didn't answer your cell phone?"

"Sorry, boss, it's upstairs in my jacket pocket."

Chief Rawlings puts his hand on James's shoulder and says, "Well, you can see how this looks, James, with Missus Stanton missing, and you not answering your phone."

"Yessir, Chief. I think I understand, with my record and all."

Chief Rawlings smiles at the two City officers and says, "Thanks, guys. Y'all can go now. I'll put this thing to bed and send Sergeant Clark a copy of my incident report tomorrow."

One of the policemen says, "Well, let us know if you need anything else from us," and then they turn and walk toward the stairs. One of the officers, who apparently knows James, turns toward him and says, "Sorry about this, James."

James says, "That's okay."

Arthur Stanton moves toward the officers to stop them and shake each policeman's hand and thank them again.

As Arthur is walking over to the City officers, Sylvia reaches over to James and puts her arm around his shoulders. She says, "Mister Waters, if I can ever repay you for saving my life, you just let me know. I'll be here teaching every Tuesday and Thursday evening."

James sheepishly lowers his head and softly says, "Yes, ma'am."

Arthur thanks Chief Rawlings and Mr. Jacobs for getting out of bed to take care of the situation, and then he reaches over to take Sylvia's hand in his.

Sylvia and Arthur walk over to the elevators on the other side of the hall. As Arthur presses the down button, he asks Chief Rawlings if he wants to ride down with them.

Chief Rawlings says, "No, thank you. James and Joe and I are gonna go into the faculty lounge and make some coffee. I've got to apologize some more to James, and get a written statement from him on the elevator breakdown so that I can do an incident report."

Once Sylvia and Arthur are out of the building, Sylvia stops at a trash can just outside the front door and disposes of the thermos bottle.

Arthur asks, "Did I see you just throw away a perfectly good thermos jug? And what's this talk about that man saving your life?"

"Well, it's a little embarrassing to talk about right now, but suffice it to say that Mister Waters and I did something that you and I have never done."

Arthur is taken aback. He says, "What the hell are you talking about? Do I need to go back in there and shoot him myself?"

Sylvia laughs and kisses Arthur on the cheek, then says, "Heavens no. There's no need for violence. Let's just go get some breakfast, and I'll tell you all about it."

As they enter the parking lot, Sylvia points to her left and says, "My car's parked right over there. I'll meet you at the Waffle House."

The Dead Pecker Gang

Frank's Feed & Seed is at 42 Main Street near the corner of Main and Poplar in the small south Alabama town of Mosby. The store is directly across from the Mosby town hall square in a two-story red brick building built in the 1930s. The building has two large picture windows with a wide dark green door situated between the windows. Above each window is a faded green canvas awning stretching out over the cracked concrete sidewalk.

Before Frank's Feed & Seed moved into the building in 1987, it housed Al Jackson's hardware store.

On one warm April afternoon, Frank was standing behind the store's ancient wooden counter writing out an order for fertilizers when he heard the tinkle of the merchant's bell at the top of the front door. He turned to see Walter Burch, one of his regular customers, walking in.

Frank removed his reading glasses and said, "Walter, you tall drink of water, what are you doing here on a Saturday. You always come on Wednesdays."

Walter pulled off his sweat-stained blue Auburn baseball cap, showing his blond crew cut and the tan line across his forehead. He wiped his brow with the back of his left hand and answered, "Couldn't come on Wednesday. Had an injured calf to take care of."

"What kind of injury did it have?"

"Had a bad cut on his left hind leg 'bout a half inch deep and three inches long. Looked like a barb wire cut, but I can't say for sure."

"Is the calf okay now?"

"Yeah. I brought him to the barn and cleaned the wound out on Monday right after I first saw it, and then I called Doc Williams. Then Doc came by on Tuesday and sewed up the cut and put medicine on it and gave him a shot. Then he wrapped the leg up and told us to keep him in the barn for a few more days and keep an eye on him. Me and Betsy, and our daughter Jolie, took turns tending to him and feeding him." Walter chuckled and said, "That worked out good except that now Jolie thinks he's a pet. She named him Elmo."

Frank smiled and said, "Figures. How old is Jolie now?"

"Nine."

"Wow, she was just a baby last time I saw her. Nine's a good age for kids. One of my grandsons is that age. Always asking questions."

"Same with Jolie."

"Well, what can I do for you today, Walter?"

"I need some chicken feed. Six forty-pound bags."

"Usual brand?"

"Yeah. But I don't see any on the shelf."

"That's all right. Got some in the back. Won't take but a minute."

When Frank returned from a back room with a flat cart holding six bags of Purina chicken feed, Walter asked him, "Who's the four old guys sitting on the bench out front?"

Frank smiled and said, "That's the Dead Pecker Gang."

Walter squinted and said, "That's not a nice thing to say. Do they know you call them that?"

"Oh yeah. That's the name they gave themselves. You oughta hear what else they call each other."

Walter nodded and said, "I see," then turned and looked out the window at the four men. "I recognize Mister Barlow. He was my banker before he retired. But I don't know any of the other three."

Frank reached behind the counter and pulled out a wooden ladder-back chair. He said, "If you've got a little while, have a seat and I'll tell you the story behind the Dead Pecker Gang."

Walter took the chair and set it so that it faced the front window. He sat down in it and said, "I got some time."

Frank slid another wooden chair next to Walter's and took a seat. Then he reached into the left hand pocket of his gray work shirt and pulled out a pack of Pall Mall Reds after which he reached into the right front pocket of his faded blue jeans and located his old Zippo lighter. He lit a cigarette, took a long draw, and began, "The one on our right is Slick Simmons. His real name is Pierre—his mother was a Cajun—but his friends always call him Slick. Somebody told me that they started calling him that when he was a kid and slicked his hair back with Wildroot Creme Oil. Anyhow, the name stuck."

Walter looked at the back of the head of a large man with curly white hair showing from under a red baseball cap.

Frank continued, "Slick owns two GM dealerships. One in Mobile and one in Fairhope. Sells Cadillacs, Chevys, and GMCs. He only works a couple of days a week now. His sons run the dealerships."

Then Frank pointed toward the bench and said, "Next to Slick is Ben Barlow, who you know."

Walter remembered that the dignified man with the neatly combed light brown hair almost always wore a starched dress shirt and a cardigan. Today the shirt was light blue and the cardigan was tan.

Frank went on, "The one directly to the left of Ben is Ralph James. He's retired from the hotel business. He started with Hilton and then bought a couple of Marriotts. About five years ago he sold his hotel interests and moved back to Baldwin County from Montgomery."

Walter noticed that Mr. James was a man of average build whose dark hair was balding in the rear. He was wearing a white polo shirt under a lightweight sky blue jacket.

"The one on the far left is Sol Thomas. He retired some time back from being a dean over at the Community College in Bay Minette. Since he retired he's been writing history books, mostly about the South and the Civil War."

Walter saw that Sol Thomas was a tall thin man wearing a dark blue sweatshirt. A rather worn out gray fedora sat atop his longish gray hair. Walter asked Frank, "How often do they get together?"

"Almost every Saturday afternoon since Ralph moved back. They'll sit and gab for a couple of hours. Remember that domino table that I used to have in the back corner?"

"Yeah."

"Well, they used to come by and play dominoes every Saturday, but they cussed so much and got so loud—none of them can hear worth a damn— that they were disturbing my customers. So I had Jim Tremble, you know Jim, build me that extra-long oak bench to put out in front of the store.

"I told them that I had to remove the domino table to make room for more merchandise, but that they were welcome to sit out front on the bench and use my restroom whenever they needed to, and keep stuff in my refrigerator. I kinda think that they knew what I was up to, but now I believe that they like the bench better, because they can see what's going on in town and also talk to their friends passing by."

Again Walter nodded, taking in what Frank was telling him. He asked, "Do they do that all year round?"

"Usually they take off November and December because of the holidays, but almost every other weekend."

"What about when it's too cold to sit out there, or raining?"

"Most of the time they'll go over to Dan's diner and worry the crap out of him, or sometimes they'll go sit in the coffee shop at the Half Moon Motel."

Walter thought about that for a moment, then asked, "How do they know each other?"

"They all grew up together. Ralph, Ben, and Sol all lived in that old trailer park that used to be on Highway 59, and Slick's family lived in a little frame house not too far from there. They were all the same age and poor as dirt, so they spent just about every day together when they were little. Then they went all the way through school together and played ball together and all joined the Army on the same day not long after they graduated from Mosby High. That was back during the Vietnam War."

"Did they all go to Vietnam?"

"Three of them did. Slick probably would have, but when he went to mechanics school at Fort Lee, he did so well that they kept him there and put him on the training staff. His daddy was a mechanic all his life and he had Slick helping him work on cars after school even when Slick was still in elementary school. So, by the time he joined the Army he was already an ace mechanic.

"Anyhow, Ben, Sol, and Ralph all went. Sol and Ralph were in the infantry and Ben was in finance in Saigon. Sol wound up getting a Bronze Star and a Purple Heart when he pulled a couple of wounded soldiers to safety during a mortar attack and then knocked out the mortar with a rocket grenade. That's the way Sol was when he was young, never dodged a fight. But he got hit in his left thigh with some shrapnel during the attack.

"Ralph was in some serious scraps, too, but he never got wounded."

Walter stared at the men who were now laughing and slapping each other on the shoulder and said, "That's something. Do they all live here now? Well, I know Mister Barlow does, but what about the other three?"

"Well, Ben's the only one who lives right in Mosby. Sol and Ralph live next door to each other about ten miles out of town in the Burlington community with the rich folks, and Slick's got a beach house on the Gulf."

"Sounds like they've done all right. Are they all married?"

"Well, you know Miz Barlow. And Sol's still married, but Ralph's wife died some years ago, and Slick's divorced. Been married three times. Divorced the last one a couple of years ago."

Walter stared out the window for a few more moments before he stood up from his chair and said, "Thanks for your time, Frank. That was interesting." He placed the chair back behind the counter and said, "Don't forget to charge that chicken feed to my account."

Then he walked over to the cart and asked Frank if he could use it to take the feed to where he'd parked his truck across the street.

Frank stood up and said, "Sure. I'll walk over there with you and help you load it." He called out to another customer who had walked in while Walter and he were talking and told her that he'd be right back.

While Frank and Walter were loading the bags onto Walter's truck, they saw a striking young redhead get out from a white BMW sedan parked a few spaces down from them and stretch her back as though she'd been driving for a while. She was wearing dark sunglasses, a white tee shirt, and cutoff Levi shorts. She was tall and fit with long, well-tanned legs.

After the feed was loaded and the tailgate shut, Frank said good-bye to Walter and turned the cart toward his store. That's when he saw all four of the Dead Pecker Gang intently watching the redhead cross the street in their direction. Once she got to the sidewalk in front of Frank's, she waved at the Gang then turned away from them and started walking toward Poplar Street.

Frank smiled at the four old codgers staring at the young lady's tight cutoffs as she rhythmically sashayed down the sidewalk.

As she began to disappear around the corner, Slick turned to his friends and said, "You know, I'd give fifty dollars just to run my hands over that."

Ralph and Ben nodded in agreement.

Sol stared toward the sky above the town hall, took a deep breath, and said, "I'd give a hundred dollars just to want to."

NOTE: This story was inspired by Girl Watchers, *an oil painting by Donna Pate of Deatsville, Alabama.*

Searching for the Gwork

Hank had no clue on that day in March of 2014 that his life was about to change forever.

It was a pleasant spring evening around eight-thirty when Hank went out for his daily walk through the woods that bordered the subdivision where he lived.

Sullivan Plantation was an upper-middle class neighborhood in a suburb of Montgomery. It had been built on what once had been a two thousand-acre cotton plantation that was in the Sullivan family for over a hundred years.

The houses in Sullivan Plantation were large and comfortable homes of traditional styles, and they were occupied primarily by successful professionals and well-off retirees. It was a good place to live.

Until that fateful spring evening, the most unsettling thing that Hank had witnessed in Sullivan Plantation was a tablecloth catching on fire at a fourth of July cookout.

He was sixty-seven and planning to retire soon from his position as an administrator with the State Banking Department. He was married to Helen, who was two years younger and worked as a broker in a small real estate firm in Montgomery. They had an adult son and daughter who were both married and living out of state.

Hank was healthy and fit for his age, and part of his exercise routine was his daily three-mile walk on an old gravel road, formerly a farm road, that ran through a wooded area in the part of the old Sullivan Plantation that had not yet been developed for houses.

Even though it was sometimes after sundown when Hank got home from work and took his walks that time of the year, he knew the road well enough that he could easily navigate it by moonlight. That particular spring night, however, was cloudy and moonless, and unusually dark.

About fifteen minutes into his walk, Hank rounded a bend in the road and was startled to find what in the darkness appeared to be a group of men in front of him. His first instinct was to take off running in the direction from which he had come, but he was afraid that if they were night hunters, they might think that he was an animal and shoot at him. So, instead, Hank froze in his tracks and waited for his eyes to focus on whoever they were.

It turned out that they were five men in what appeared to be blue police uniforms. Hank called out, "Officers, can I help you?"

One of the men stepped toward Hank, and Hank heard him say, in a strangely artificial voice, "We are looking for someone."

As the men came into better focus, Hank noticed that they appeared to be flickering, like an old-time silent movie. And they seemed to fade and blur and then come back into focus. Hank was a combat veteran, and had been in a number of dangerous situations, but this one was quickly becoming as spooky as anything that he had ever experienced.

He continued to stare at the men. His mind began to race as he tried to sort out what was going on, and what his options were.

Then, all at once, the policemen disappeared, and in their places were a group of what matched a description that Hank had once heard from people who claimed to have been abducted by aliens. They looked a good bit like humans, but had larger heads. They were tall, maybe six-foot-three. They were completely bald, had no eyebrows, and had pale gray, metallic-looking skin. They were wearing plain, light gray clothes that also had a metallic sheen to them.

Hank was overcome by a feeling that he remembered from combat—a feeling of extreme calm, and acceptance of possible death. He softly asked, "Who are you?"

The one who appeared to be the leader stared at him with large dark eyes and said, or rather communicated without speaking, "We are visitors who mean you no . . . harm." Hank quickly realized that the leader was communicating telepathically because he had a feeling that his mind was being stimulated by something from outside himself.

Hank had an uncomfortable sense of pending doom, but he told himself that if they were going to kill him, or abduct him, he might as well try to find out who they are and where they came from.

Before he could ask any questions, the leader said, "We have no intention of harming or . . . abducting you," and Hank immediately knew that they could read his thoughts. That confirmed to him that escape was impossible, so he relaxed and continued his questions.

"Why are you here?" Hank asked.

Hank heard the leader communicate to him that the visitors were there to "recover" what Hank heard as a "gwork." As the leader was communicating with Hank, the other four visitors took off into the woods as though they had heard or seen something.

Hank asked, "What's a gwork?"

The leader communicated, "Someone who has . . . escaped . . . from what you would call . . . confinement."

"Do you mean a criminal?"

"No . . . we have no crime . . . The confinement from which the gwork . . . escaped was to separate him from our . . . general society . . . because he was no longer . . . compatible with our . . . ways. He had become . . . socially defective."

"Is he dangerous?"

"Not to you."

"What does he look like?"

"Like me . . . only . . . shorter and with darker . . . clothes. However, he can . . . cloak his appearance . . . in the manner that we attempted when you first saw us . . .

"He is much better than we are at the cloaking because he is of a . . . different segment and learned the technique from those who . . . created it. My . . . colleagues and I are still learning the cloaking technique. That is why we had difficulty . . . maintaining it just now."

"Why do you need a cloaking technique?"

"It has been used by other . . . segments of our . . . society in their visits to other . . . societies. They used the technique to . . . replicate the . . . members of the society being visited so as not to be . . . discovered. The gwork has been here on other occasions and . . . successfully used the technique. That is why he chose your . . . world as a place of refuge."

"Do you mean he has been on Earth before, but disguised as a human?"

"Yes."

"So, I may have seen him in his disguise."

"Yes."

"Wow," said Hank, wondering how many other disguised aliens he may have come across and not known it.

Hank realized that the one whom he assumed was the leader was staying with him to keep him from running off, so he asked, "What are you going to do with me?"

The leader said, "We only want you to remain here until we complete our . . . mission. Then you can go."

"Where do you come from?" Hank inquired.

"You would not . . . understand. We are not . . . from a . . . place as you understand . . . place."

"Are you from this universe?"

"No."

"Are you familiar with this universe?"

"Yes. We are . . . very . . . knowledgeable about what you call your universe."

As they communicated, Hank was sensing that the hesitation between words from the leader was caused by his searching Hank's mind for the proper word or image. Once Hank was convinced that he was not going to be killed or abducted, he became intrigued by what was going on.

The leader looked into the woods as if he heard something, and then turned his attention back to Hank, who asked "Will you answer some questions for me about our universe?"

"Yes."

"How long has our universe been here?"

"In terms of your concept of . . . time, it has existed . . . forever. It has existed for as long as time has existed."

"Are you saying that before the beginning of the universe, there was no time?"

"Not as you know it."

"What about space?"

"There was no space as you know it . . . before your universe."

"Is there time where you come from?"

"Not as you know time."

"Is there space?"

"Yes, but . . . somewhat different from your space."

"How can that be?

"It is."

"Are there other universes like ours?"

"No. But there are other . . . systems."

"Do they have time and space?"

"Not as you know it."

"Where did our universe come from?"

"It was . . . created."

"By whom, or what?"

"By the . . . creator."

"Do you mean God?"

"I mean the creator."

"Do you understand the term 'God' as we use it?"

"Yes."

"Did the creator of our universe create the other universes, I mean the other systems?"

"Some of them."

"Do you understand that many of us worship the creator?"

"Yes."

"Does God, or the creator, hear our prayers?"

"Yes."

"Does he answer our prayers?"

"Sometimes . . . when it . . . complies with . . . his plan."

"You're saying his plan. Is the creator male?

"No. But I sense that you are more . . . comfortable with the creator as him rather than . . . it. The creator is neither 'him' nor 'it'."

"Does that mean that the creator is female?"

"No . . . The creator is in a form that is not . . . describable or understandable in . . . human terms."

"Does the creator need our worship?"

"No . . . but humans need to worship . . . the creator . . . It is part of the plan."

"Do you know the plan?"

"Only some . . . very few parts. The plan is known only by the creator."

"Does the Holy Bible give us the plan?"

"No . . . But it . . . appears to be . . . somewhat . . . compatible . . . with the plan . . . in that it helps some humans in their . . . relationship to the creator . . ."

"What about atheists?"

The leader hesitated a moment, as if to figure out what Hank meant by "What about." Then he answered, "If by atheists you mean those who . . . claim that there can be . . . creation without a creator . . . and that your universe is without . . . intelligent design . . . they are also part of the plan; and they also have their . . . purpose."

Hank began to feel that he was not going to have much more time to pick the leader's brain, so he decided that he had asked enough religious questions and needed to ask some more science questions.

"How many dimensions does our universe have? Some scientists say as many as eleven or more."

"Five."

"I'm familiar with four. What's the fifth?"

"The one not bound by . . . time or space. The one in which we are . . . communicating now."

"Do you mean that our minds are in the fifth dimension?"

"In a sense. You could say that . . . thoughts exist in the fifth dimension, as do human . . . dreams."

"What about black holes. Can you explain them?"

"Yes . . . but they are not . . . exactly as your . . . scientists believe. What your . . . scientists believe would be contrary to the . . . design of your universe. But the scientists should soon . . . learn where they are . . . wrong."

"What about the effect of gravity on a collapsing star?"

"Your . . . scientists do not yet fully understand gravity. Once they do, which should have already . . . taken place, they will . . . recognize why the . . . black holes are not . . . precisely . . . as they . . . describe them. Once they fully . . . comprehend gravity, they will . . . better understand what they call black holes."

Just as Hank was going to ask the leader about the theory of evolution, the leader once again turned and looked into the woods.

Right after the leader turned, Hank heard a commotion and saw two of the other four visitors holding on to what Hank assumed was the gwork. As the leader had said, the gwork looked like the others, but was noticeably shorter and wearing clothes of a darker gray. From the difficulty that he was causing his captors, he also seemed to be incredibly strong.

When the gwork sensed that Hank was present, he immediately transformed into what looked like an elderly woman in a cotton dress, and began to wail, in a frail human voice, "Help me, mister. These monsters have grabbed me, and Lord knows what they're going to do to me."

If Hank had not gotten a glance of the gwork in his true form, he would have no doubt been completely fooled by the guise, and may have done his best to rescue the "old woman."

But as it was, he was merely impressed by how quickly and completely the gwork had assumed such a convincing human form and voice.

The leader turned to Hank and communicated, "We have completed our mission and must . . . depart now." Two of the captors began pulling the "old woman" into the thick woods to Hank's left. Hank did not see any flying saucer or other alien craft in the area toward which they were heading, so he called to the leader, "How do you travel?"

The leader turned and communicated, "In a . . . vessel similar to what your society calls a spaceship. We call it what in your language would be a 'transport craft.' It does not actually . . . travel through space . . . in the way that you are familiar. It . . . manipulates space and time so that we may . . . directly transport ourselves from your universe into our system."

That explanation was incomprehensible to Hank.

He asked, "Where is your transport craft?"

"About . . . fifty of your feet away from where you stand."

Hank peered into the woods where the visitors had taken the gwork, but it was too dark there to make out any type of craft. He turned to the leader and asked, "Can I watch you take off?"

"Yes. But do not move from where you are until we are in the . . . sky. Otherwise, you might be harmed by the . . . energy from the craft. "

Hank anxiously waited to experience his first UFO sighting, and in no more than a minute, he heard what sounded like hissing, and then he heard leaves rustling and saw the outline of something slowly rising through the trees. As best he could tell in what little light there was, the craft was flat black, about fifty feet long, and shaped somewhat like a football, except that it was flat on its top and bottom. It was not silver like flying saucers in the movies, nor did it have any windows or blinking lights like movie UFO's. Hank thought to himself: *Of course it has no lights. Why would they need lights?*

Once the craft cleared the trees, it completely vanished in about a second. All Hank could say was, "Good Lord, that was quick."

Hank began to mentally list what he had learned in the short conversation that he'd had with the leader: First of all, he found out that there are extraterrestrials; and there is a God, or at least a creator who sounds a lot like what people call God; that there is a plan for mankind, and the Bible is part of the plan; that atheists are also part of the plan; that the universe has five dimensions; that there may be black holes, but they're different from what we assume; and that we have much more to learn about what gravity is.

About two minutes after the vehicle vanished, Hank decided to forget about his walk and return to his house to tell Helen what he had learned.

But just as he was thinking about how he would tell Helen what had happened, he heard the leader's voice saying, "Thank you for not interfering with our . . . mission. Be careful what you say about it and to whom you speak about it, because, as happened with our gwork, your society may find you . . . defective, and place you in . . . confinement."

To this day, Hank has told no one what he saw.

But, sometimes on his evening walks, as he approaches that fateful bend in the road, he wonders if everything that the leader told him is true, or were they just things that the leader made up to keep Hank occupied while the gwork was being rounded up . . .

www.ingramcontent.com/pod-product-compliance
Lightning Source LLC
Chambersburg PA
CBHW021140190726
48288CB00008B/2757